THE MORETTI MEN
DEATH'S Favor

JILL RAMSOWER

Death's Favor is a work of fiction. Names, characters, places, and incidents are the products of the author's imagination or are used fictitiously. Any resemblance to actual events, locales, or persons, living or dead, is entirely coincidental.

Copyright © 2025 Jill Ramsower

All rights reserved. In accordance with the U.S. Copyright Act of 1976, the scanning, uploading, and electronic sharing of any part of this book without the permission of the publisher is unlawful piracy and theft of the author's intellectual property. Thank you for your support of the author's rights.

NO AI TRAINING: Without in any way limiting the author's exclusive rights under copyright, any use of this publication to "train" generative artificial intelligence (AI) technologies to generate text is expressly prohibited.

Author's reassurance to readers: No artificial intelligence (AI) was used in the development/writing/editing/proofing/formatting/publication of this novel.

Edits by: Editing4Indies
Cover photographer: Daniel James
Cover Model: Josh

 Created with Vellum

Books by Jill Ramsower

The Moretti Men Series
Devil's Thirst
Death's Favor

The Byrne Brothers Series
Silent Vows
Secret Sin (Novella)
Corrupted Union
Ruthless Salvation
Vicious Seduction
Craving Chaos

The Five Families Series
Forever Lies
Never Truth
Blood Always
Where Loyalties Lie
Impossible Odds
Absolute Silence
Perfect Enemies

The Savage Pride Duet
Savage Pride
Silent Prejudice

DEATH'S FAVOR

JILL RAMSOWER

1
Danika

I've never had cancer, but I suspect this is how a patient might feel as they walk back to their doctor's office to learn their diagnosis. Stomach wedged high in my throat. Heart jackhammering inside my chest. Uncertainty sending my panicking nervous system into chaos. I am terrified.

Memories of the last time I came to this place provide an endless supply of ammunition to the fear assaulting my body and mind. I swore I'd never come back here, but I had no choice. When Biba Mikhailov, boss of the Russian bratva, summons you, you come, especially when he's your father. Not that I think of him as my father—I've never even met the man. But in this part of the city, you don't have to be on a first-name basis with Biba to know you don't refuse him.

I can't fathom what I've done to earn this summons. That's the worst part. I have no clue what this is about, and the less-than-courteous man who came to deliver Biba's message was about as informative as a brick wall. Which brings me here—to a run-down auto repair shop deep in the heart of Brooklyn. I'm walking down a dimly lit hallway so saturated with tobacco that the substance is literally dripping from the yellow walls. The sickly sweet odor does nothing for my already rioting stomach, but I do my best to hold myself together.

You avoided him the last time you were here. Maybe you'll manage to avoid him again.

Right, and if he kills me, I'll be too dead to care.

Hate to break it to you, but that's not how optimism works.

Debatable. But not right now.

I've come to the last door in the hallway. A door guarded by a bald man with a gruesome scar on his cheek and eyes bleached of any possible empathy. This is where Biba is hiding. Word is he's rarely ever seen anymore. I'm taking that as a good sign—that perhaps the guy is terminally ill or hopelessly agoraphobic. Though, it appears he doesn't have to leave his hidey-hole to be a menace. It's a lesson I won't soon forget, should I be lucky enough to leave this place alive.

The guard utters a few guttural words in what I assume is Russian as I approach. I'm about to tell him I don't understand when a single syllable resonates from inside the office.

"Da."

The guard presses the door open enough for me to enter, eyes trained on me the entire time as though ready to take me down should I make the slightest wrong move. He isn't taking a single inch of my five-foot-two, hundred-and-ten-pound frame for granted. As if I'd try something. I wouldn't know where to begin. Instead, I nod and take the final steps on wobbly legs to discover my fate.

"Danika, so good of you to join me." Biba sits at a large intricately carved desk, papers spread across it with a bottle of vodka and several crystal glasses atop them. His skin is noticeably more leathery in person than photos had conveyed, and his voice grates like a hacksaw thanks to a lifetime of smoking. He's tried to overcome a receding hairline with a classic combover. It looks somewhat incongruous with the rudimentary tattoos etched on the backs of his hands. Everything about this man is designed to intimidate, and it's working. I have to clear my throat twice before I can coerce my voice to function.

"Mr. Mikhailov." I nod, unsure what else to say or do.

"You know who I am, yes?"

"Yes, sir." I wish I didn't.

He flashes a wide, yellowing grin. "Good, and you should call me Biba. We're family, no?" He motions to a chair. "Sit and talk."

The slur of his Russian accent rings in my ears as I hear the word *family* echo repeatedly in my mind. Technically true but irrelevant until now. Why? What could he possibly want from me? I can't think of a single answer that ends well for me.

I sit and wait for him to pull the rug out from beneath my feet.

"Your mother, she's good?"

"Yes, thank you."

"She's done well with you. Such a beautiful young woman."

"Thank you," I repeat, feeling increasingly awkward and desperate for him to tell me what I'm doing here.

"And my men here tell me you're quite an artist. Isn't that right?" He looks at the guard and my escort and waits until they each murmur their agreement while I mentally unravel.

Why is he talking about my art? Has he seen my paintings? What else does he know about me?

Pleased by his men's affirmation, he looks back at me. "Yes, very talented," he continues. "And I'm sure you are also very curious why I've brought you here."

I offer a thin smile, my heartbeat thudding against the inside of my skull.

"I have wonderful news for you. As part of my family, you have the honor of uniting us in a very important alliance." His eyes glint as he grins at me as if eagerly anticipating my excited reaction. As if this man genuinely believes I will feel honored by his proclamation rather than the gut-wrenching horror now coursing through my veins.

"Alliance?" I ask shakily. Between the blood draining from my head and the utter disbelief, I'm having trouble thinking coherently. I'm pretty sure he's hinting at an arranged marriage, but that can't be right. I never even considered that as I racked my brain on the way over here about what he could want since I'm nothing more than a distant afterthought to this man. Hell, I've never even met him until today. Why now? Why me? I know I'm not the only female family member he has. Why not one of his two sons if the alliance is so important? This can't be happening.

"There is a man—a very powerful man—known as The Reaper." Biba waves his hand dismissively. "Ignore the silly nickname. He has displayed an impressive ability for leadership, and I've decided to bring him into the fold. Together, we are stronger. Once we are all family, we own this city. And you ... you get to be the one who makes it all happen."

I can't even balk at his audacity because my brain snags on the name Reaper.

Holy *hell*.

What kind of monster earns a name like The Reaper? And Biba wants to marry me off to this man for his own selfish reasons? This is so grossly unexpected that I can hardly comprehend it. I thought ... I don't know exactly what I thought, but it wasn't this. Never this.

My head begins to shake in small, jerky movements. I know I can't outright refuse, but rising panic overrides my logic with the need to escape.

"Now, Danika." His tone lowers with an edge of warning. "You need to understand how important this is. It will be a huge honor, and he is a very wealthy man. This will set you and your mother up to live like queens. I know you'd like that. No more living in that shithole apartment of yours."

For a man who's been clever enough to control a small army of Russians in the middle of New York City, he sure is clueless. Instead of reassuring me, every word he utters incites my anger. As if I want to marry a stranger for money. Our apartment may be small, but it's no shithole. That's my *home*. A place my mother worked hard to provide and where so many happy memories have been made.

I collect myself and make my very best attempt to respond without offense. "I appreciate your effort to provide for me, but I don't think I'm the right person for this responsibility."

His features take on a frightening savagery as he stands and slowly stalks around the desk toward me. He doesn't speak until he's close enough to look down his nose at me. Close enough that his menthol-laden breath constricts my lungs to a painful degree. "You misunderstand. I am not asking your permission. You *will* marry The Reaper, or I will take everything you love in this world and burn it to the ground. Your mother included." His slowly enunciated words drip with malice.

The temperature in the room plummets to arctic lows. I have to fight back a shiver.

My head spins, and tears burn the backs of my eyes.

This can't be happening. What do I do? I can't let him hurt my mom and gran. They're all I have in this world. All that matters, that is. And if the threat came from anyone else, I'd call it a bluff, but not coming from Biba. The man has no humanity left. Where does that leave me?

I slowly nod, my eyes unable to meet his.

"I am glad we understand one another, Danika, because disobedience is messy, and I have too much riding on this marriage for childish games. My hope is that in one week, you will be married, and life will be much more peaceful."

"A week?" I squeak, unable to stop myself.

"Da. I suggest you spend the time wisely. Learn to see this as the opportunity it is. We will get you all new clothes, and you will never have to work again. It will be good, you will see, so long as you don't do anything stupid. Giving me a reason to punish you will only make you miserable. I promise."

He returns to his chair opposite the desk, fingers twining together with finality.

With the issuance of one final threat, I've been dismissed.

I stand on unsteady legs and walk robotically down the hallway, feeling as though I am not in control of my own body, but rather a puppeteer is pulling my strings. That's exactly what's happening in a figurative sense, and I have no idea how to free myself.

God, please tell me this is a nightmare.

This can't be real. I can't spend the rest of my life—however short that may now be—bound to a psychopath.

What choice do you have? You can't risk Mom and Gran.

He won't just kill them. He'll torture them to get back at me.

I only make it two steps outside before my stomach seizes beyond my control and forces me to retch against the crumbling brick exterior of the building. Biba's thug mutters what can only be a string of Russian curses, judging by his disgusted tone. As I wipe my mouth with my hand, I hear the door slam shut behind me before the lock clicks shut. Why am I not surprised? Of course, it would be too much to ask for a napkin or a sip of water. And on top of everything, it looks like I have to find my own way home from this shady Brooklyn neighborhood.

I want to bang my fists on the glass door, screaming and raging until Biba comes out and realizes his mistake, but that won't happen. For starters, my arms are too shaky to pound on anything. Then there's Biba. He's a spineless, malicious virus of a man who infects everyone around him with toxic cruelty. He won't relent until he gets what he wants.

I hate him, and that hate is utterly meaningless because he holds all the cards.

Does he?

My mind goes silent as the suggestion sinks in. I do have at least one other option: the police. This is modern-day America. People don't get to *own* other people. Law enforcement is here to protect us from men like Biba, but they can't do their job if we don't report a problem.

My feet intuitively take me in the direction of the nearest subway stop while I try to convince myself that the authorities can help. They'll keep us safe if I can summon the courage to do what's right.

With a renewed flare of hope energizing my pace, I take myself to the nearest police station. I hardly notice anyone or anything around me until I see a flash of my reflection in the mirrored glass of the entry. I do a double take of my splotchy cheeks, wispy tangles of strawberry-blond hair—heavy on the strawberry—flying in every direction, and a pair of wide eyes with way too much crazy staring back at me.

They're going to think I'm a lunatic.

They'll think you're upset, and that's okay. You have a right to be flustered when the head of the Russian freaking Mafia is after you.

I nod to my inner voice—a cherry on top of my cray-cray Sunday.

"Excuse me," I say to a man at the reception desk. "I need to speak with someone to report a crime."

He spares a glance my way, totally unimpressed with my appearance. "Take a number. You can wait over there with the others."

I look behind me at a packed seating area. A number? This is a police station, not a butcher's shop. I tear off a paper number and retreat to wait with the others for my turn. I try not to overthink what I'm doing when I catch sight of a series of portraits of officers in uniform. Above them is a sign saying Wall of Honor. These are the men and women who have died in the line of duty.

A fist plows deep into my gut when I see a face with wide blue eyes. Eyes that will never see again. The man was a cop, and now he's dead because of men like Biba who aren't burdened by the constraints of laws or morals.

How can I expect the law to protect me when they can't even protect themselves?

This is a mistake. A *huge* mistake. I have to get out of here. *Now.*

The numbered paper in my hand drifts to the floor as I shoot to my feet and rush to the exit. I don't even care that I look schizophrenic running from the building. My urgency to disappear overrules all other thoughts, which is how I end up shoulder checking a man as I flee out the front entrance onto the sidewalk. I may have run into him, but I'm so much smaller that I take the brunt of the collision. I whirl nearly all the way around, and my tote bag flies off my shoulder, scattering half its contents onto the filthy concrete sidewalk.

"Oh my God. I'm so sorry," I say without even looking at the poor man I've assaulted. I'm too flustered and horribly embarrassed. Instead, I lunge forward to collect all my crap off the ground at the same moment he bends to do the same, causing our heads to knock against one another in the process.

"Fucking *Christ*," he snaps the surly curse as I blurt *ouch*, finally bringing my gaze to the man in front of me. With my hand on my now throbbing head, I take in the Roman God of a man and am suddenly so overwhelmed with the absurdity of my life that a peal of hysterical laughter forces its way past my lips. Not an infectious sort of joyful laughter. This is a half-crazed, might-actually-be-crying sort of laughter because the man opposite me is the most stunningly beautiful person I've ever seen. The angular lines of his face are carved in perfect symmetry, something the artist in me is quick to notice and recognize for its rarity. He's dressed in work attire—a crisp button-down shirt and slacks that fit his athletic frame as though made to his precise measurements. His aristocratic brow and sharp jawline look right out of Hollywood. And those lips—such perfectly full lips even when pursed as he glares disapprovingly at me.

My eyes rise to his dark glare as I confirm that he definitely is not seeing the humor in the situation. His scrutiny sobers me faster than dumping an icy bucket of water over my head. "I'm so sorry. Are you okay?"

"I'm fine. You, on the other hand, seem to be far from it." His scathing jab sends a pink flush to my cheeks.

"I can't help it," I say in my defense. "Sometimes life is so absurd you just have to laugh." I squat and pick up my makeup bag and two tampons. Of course, the tampons managed to escape.

My disgruntled victim collects my ChapStick, phone, and a few other random items before standing and studying them in his hands. "If by absurd you mean unfortunate, failing to take your problems seriously won't improve the situation."

Heavy drops of rain begin to splat down on my proverbial parade. I don't like it. Not one bit. This day—no, this *week*—has been hard enough, and I don't need this man's judgment making it worse.

I take my things from his open palms with a tad more aggression than I should. "Actually, it does make things better. It lifts my mood. And sometimes perspective and outlook are the only things we *can* control. It's better than wallowing."

The words are forceful in a way that I'm proud of. I stood up for myself, which I'm not always great about doing.

He stares at me, our eyes locked in an inscrutable battle of wills. "You're not wrong," he finally concedes, "but you'd feel a lot better if you changed more than just your attitude."

Okay, it's time to get out of here before I punch this guy.

Where does he get off giving me advice when he knows nothing about me?

"Some problems have no solution," I say, desolation creeping into my voice as the weight of my troubles crashes down upon my shoulders.

"No solution, or just no *easy* solution?"

Why on God's green earth am I engaging this man? This eerily gorgeous, maddeningly blunt man who somehow holds me captive in his fathomless brown stare?

Come on, Dani, let's go home. Forget him.

I clutch my bag tighter and lift my chin before marching past him, checking his shoulder again, but this time, the attack is 100 percent intentional, and I hold his stare to make sure he knows it. I'm not sure I've ever done anything so brazen in my life. I'm feeling rather proud of myself until the man's voice brings me to a lurching halt.

"Danika Dobrev."

My name. How the hell does he know my name?

I look over my shoulder to see him holding my ID card. My freaking ID with my name, birthdate, and home address.

Will the delights of this day never end?

His inscrutable gaze lifts to mine as he holds out the card between two fingers in offering. When I return and try to take the card from him, he retracts his fingers, denying me.

"Is it a man?" he asks with an edge.

"Is what a man?" I have no idea what he's talking about, so the question throws me for a loop.

"The problem with no easy answer." His eyes take a swift glance at the 13th Precinct sign beside us. "Were you here to report someone?" This time, his calculating stare looks me over as if trying to glean an answer from my outfit.

"No," I snap before grabbing the card from his hand, but I don't get far when his other hand clamps around my wrist. I gasp in disbelief that this wild confrontation is happening, and in front of the police station, no less.

My wide eyes collide with his, then follow his gaze to my hand, where I notice red paint stains on my fingers and under my nails. I'm always covered in paint, so I don't even notice it anymore. But this man noticed, and he thought it might be blood. My blood. He thinks I'm here to report an assault or abuse, and I get the sense he's livid on my behalf.

All my indignant irritation evaporates, leaving me physically and emotionally drained.

"It's paint," I say softly. "My problem *is* a man, but not like that." I gently tug my wrist away from him, and he lets me go. "Look, I'm sorry for everything. It's been a rough day."

I flash a weak smile and give him one last look before walking away for good. I'd wonder what he must be thinking, except Biba's horrific ultimatum looms with such catastrophic potential that nothing else even registers.

An arranged marriage to a violent criminal or refuse and risk the lives of the people I love.

It's an impossible choice. Even the mere thought breaks my heart until I can feel pieces crumbling away and trailing behind me like breadcrumbs to a past where life was worth living.

Tommy 2

"You're not Sante."

I sit in the visitor's chair opposite the cop and audibly sigh. "With such keen observational skills, it's no wonder they made you a detective. Did you have something to say or not?"

The pig pen isn't my favorite place to be, and I certainly have no interest in sticking around if this clown is going to question my ability to handle business. Sante swears that Officer Malone has half a brain, unlike so many of his colleagues. I haven't spent much time around him. So far, I'm unimpressed.

He rounds the desk to close his office door, waiting to speak until he can't be overheard. "A week ago, three men were murdered."

"Sounds like a pretty normal week in the city."

Malone sits at his desk, ignoring my attempt to goad him. "All three were Russian and appear to have been killed by the same weapon—likely the same person. The blade that was used was small with minimal damage inflicted. This guy struck fast enough that it looks like the three had no chance to fight back, each receiving a single stab to a critical artery with surgical precision. We've seen seven other kills over the last year with the same signature methods, though never three at once. This guy is so good at what he does that we don't have a single scrap of evidence giving us a lead. We've heard rumors of the name Reaper, but nothing more."

"And you want our help."

"I was hoping for information—anything is better than nothing, and that's all we've got right now."

Sante chose the wrong man to come in his place if he thought I'd give this guy anything. I have no allegiance to other organizations, but that doesn't mean I'll share anything with our common enemy. The cops would lock me away just as quickly as they would The Reaper. However, Sante was adamant that I play nice when he sent me on his behalf.

That fucker is going to owe me.

"We don't have much information to give. There have been rumors of a new organization building in power, but they've been feeding off the weak. We haven't had any issues, and without reason to step in, we've not actively pursued information." It's mostly true. We've garnered a few tidbits, but Malone's right in his assertion that The Reaper stays off the radar. The man earned his moniker for a reason.

"So he's not just a random vigilante," Malone says through a grimace.

"You didn't honestly believe that, did you?"

His gaze shifts irritably to the wall. "No, but it would have been nice."

"It doesn't change anything. A killer is a killer whether he works alone or heads an outfit."

Malone scrutinizes me astutely. He's wondering if I'm speaking from experience. I stare right back at him and, for once, project what I'm thinking.

You better fucking believe it.

"You and Sante may have found some common ground," I tell him quietly, "but don't forget who you're dealing with."

"Wouldn't dream of it," he says back without hesitation.

"Excellent. Then I'd say we're done here." I let myself out of the office and leave the station. It's time to end this day, though I still need to make a few calls once I'm home. My brother will want to hear about my visit with Detective Malone, and while I'm not crazy about reporting to him, he's my boss. My oath to him and the family will always outweigh my personal preferences.

As soon as I get back to my new apartment, I call Sante. He and I are on equal footing as far as the Moretti family goes, so I wouldn't normally report to him, but he's also my closest friend and first cousin. We spent four years in Sicily together, including a hellish month-long stay in a pig barn. That was the worst of it by far, but the experience bonded us. He's more a brother to me than my own.

To be fair, Renzo isn't a bad person. The six-year age difference between us didn't help our relationship, but more than anything, we think nothing alike. And because he doesn't understand me, he thinks something's wrong with me—that I'm untrustworthy. That's how it was when I left for Sicily, and nothing seems to have changed since my return.

I take a long, deep breath and make the call.

"Yeah?" he answers curtly.

"I talked to Sante's cop buddy Malone today—he wanted to talk to Sante, but Sante was busy. Malone's working the murder investigation of those Russians. Thinks it's The Reaper and wanted to know if we had any info on the guy."

"You tell him anything?" His question reeks of accusation.

I angle my head to stretch my tensing neck as I respond. "Not really. He was hoping the guy was a random serial killer. I corrected his misapprehension."

"We don't know enough about this Reaper character to share what we *do* know, especially with the cops. We don't need to be sharing shit with them."

"I wouldn't have shared anything at all had it not been for Sante." My words have bite, and while I meant to hit back on his mini lecture—as if I don't know how to keep my mouth shut—I realize too late that I've inadvertently thrown Sante under the bus in the process. "Look," I continue with a sigh. "I just thought you'd want to know it looks like that job was linked to The Reaper, if you hadn't already confirmed it with your own sources."

Silence lingers across the line. I start to suspect the call dropped when he speaks again.

"You don't always have to be so defensive with everything I say, you know."

"I wouldn't have to be defensive if you didn't constantly doubt me."

"I don't doubt you. I just can't predict your thoughts, so I prefer to clarify." He's sounding more exasperated. I'm not great at interpreting emotions without the aid of facial expressions, but I know his tone. I've heard him use it on me more times than I can count.

"You know what they called me back in Sicily? They called me Moret Silenziosa because my targets were six feet under before they ever knew death was coming, and you think I don't know how to keep my mouth shut where the cops are involved?"

"I think you've been gone for years, and I hardly know you anymore."

"Let's not pretend you ever did," I counter with finality. "I didn't call to argue, Renzo. Malone is working the triple murder. You want to keep tabs on it, get with Sante." I end the call without waiting for a reply. I try to treat Renzo like the don that he is, but sometimes old habits die hard. In some respect, he'll always be my too-perfect older brother.

I pour myself a glass of wine to help me relax and sit on the sofa where I can enjoy the panoramic view of the skyline. The view overlooking the East River was the main reason I bought the place. Now that my designer has almost wrapped up renovations, it's starting to feel like home. Having a sanctuary to retreat to at the end of the day is essential for me. I need an escape from all the sights and sounds of the city. Just knowing this oasis of calm is here helps me stay focused on my day.

In Sicily, things were more serene. I didn't have to ground myself the way I do here in the city. I could have stayed there forever, but I'm not upset we returned to New York. It's good to see my mother, and I know that being here has made Sante happy, though the process of getting to this point was a mystery to me. He was so fucking fixated on Amelie the whole time we were in Sicily.

As someone who has battled the pull of compulsions and hyperfixation, I know what it's like to need things a certain way, but what I couldn't understand was how he knew he needed her when he'd never known life with her before. How was he supposed to know she was what he wanted? I need the silverware in my drawer to be neatly stacked and the shades on my windows to be at precisely the same level. I need to keep a detailed schedule to know what my day will entail. In the morning, I eat six scrambled eggs, one lightly ripened banana, and a slice of sourdough toast with real butter because that gives my body the fuel it needs for me to operate at optimal energy levels. These things give my life order, and when they're lacking, I feel unbalanced. Craving certainty and control makes sense to me. Fixating on the concept of a woman you hardly know like Sante did is so foreign to me that I can't comprehend it.

I slide my hand into my pants pocket and retrieve a small bundle of pink satin fabric. I glare at it as if I expect it to explain what the fuck it's doing in my pocket.

It's hers. The woman from the police station.

I picked it up after she stormed away, and I still don't understand why, except the second the silky fabric touched my skin, I couldn't let it go. It's one of those hair ties girls wear with bunched fabric surrounding the elastic band. I can't remember what they call the damn things. It's a vibrant shade of pale pink, if that is such a thing. It suits her—delicate yet bold.

The woman was completely mystifying. I've never seen someone so uniquely beautiful and such a mess. Everything I said upset her. I'm used to that. I often rub people the wrong way. Usually, it works out because I'm not much of a fan of people outside of a select few.

So why am I still thinking about her?

I can't stop wondering what had her so frazzled. I don't normally concern myself with the people around me. I've asked myself repeatedly why I even stopped to help her collect her things. Why I snagged her ID from her phone case when I handed the phone to her. I was oddly intrigued, and I don't understand it.

Then I do something completely unfathomable on impulse and sniff the pink satin fluff. The light, feminine scent of beauty products fills my lungs and shoots a bolt of lust straight to my balls. They pull so damn tight with need I have to shift in my seat to relieve the ache.

My fingers reflexively clench tight around the scrap of fabric. Wild lions couldn't tear the damn thing from my grasp. It's like my hand has grown a mind of its own and claimed ownership. I don't think I could force myself to throw the damn thing away if I wanted to. And I don't. Quite the opposite. I feel an overwhelming need to keep this ridiculous memento.

Compulsion—it's a sensation I've grown to accept. It rarely frustrates me like it used to when I was growing up. This instance doesn't just frustrate me, it makes me furious because I don't understand it at all. This need doesn't align with any of my usual strictures. A compulsion like this would bring chaos rather than order. It's completely illogical.

Is that how Sante felt all those years in Sicily?

My entire body shudders.

I can only hope it's a passing fixation that time will erode into nothing. I won't be seeing her again, and knowing me, I'm bound to hyperfixate on something new eventually.

The first thing I need to do is toss the damn hair tie.

I force my fingers to relax and stare at the pink fabric bearing her scent, then I return it to my pocket.

I'll throw it away tomorrow. Maybe by then I'll feel less attached.

The same way I might feel less attached to my own fingers—it's not going to happen.

Fuck.

3
Danika

Mom, Gran, and I live in the same apartment I grew up in nestled in a neighborhood known for the predominant presence of Eastern European immigrants. Gran's parents came over from Slovakia and settled nearby. They never left the area, and now, it's the only home I've ever known.

The location isn't ideal from an investment standpoint, considering the area is unofficially run by the Russian mob, but I still love the community. Gran believes corruption is a natural part of life. In her opinion, it doesn't matter where we live—someone of power will always lord over everyone else. At least here, we have extended family and a community that supports one another. I can't really say since I've never lived anywhere else, and I never wanted to because leaving would mean being alone.

As I open our apartment door, I have to face the fact that my time here may be at an end.

Dread fills my body like wet sand, weighing down my every movement. Things could still change, but for now, it's not looking good for me. I'm either shackled to a psycho killer, or I live on the run and pray my family doesn't end up hurt as a result. Both options suck, yet at the moment, I don't see any other alternative.

"Where have you been? I thought you were just going to the park for an hour. I was ready to send out a search party." Mom has always been a worrier. Normally, I'd laugh off her concern and tell her not to exaggerate, but today, I can hardly summon a sliver of a smile to reassure her.

"Something else came up," I offer vaguely, unsure if I should tell her what happened. I debated about it the whole way home and am still no closer to knowing what would be best.

Silly me, I should have known I'd have no say in the matter.

Mom's eyes narrow as she stalks closer. "What's happened? Something's wrong."

Gran does her best to twist in her seat on the couch to look back at us. "What are you talking about, Petra? What's happened?"

"I don't know, Ma. Dani hasn't told me yet, but something's not right. She's all pale." She brings her hand to my forehead like I'm five years old. "You getting sick?" Her concern for me is so touching that it topples the flimsy dam I've erected to hold back my turbulent emotions.

My chin quivers, and my breathing hitches with the clawing

need to let out a sob. I don't want to worry them, but there's no way to hide this. I have to tell them.

"One of Biba's men took me to see him." My voice is no more than a whisper, a sliver of sound escaping past the fear constricting my throat.

Another breath catches, this one more pronounced than the last.

My mom's face hardens to stone. "What did that man do to you?"

"Petra," Gran scolds. "Can't you see she's already upset?" She lumbers up off the sofa and joins us. "Come here, sweet girl. Give me a hug and tell us what happened." Her familiar arms circle me, shredding my defenses. Tears pour like a summer rain down my cheeks as the sobs finally take over.

Mom encircles us both in her fierce hold. "That *bastard*. Who does he think he is, walking away all those years ago, then suddenly waltzing back into your life? Well, I'll tell you one thing. I'm not afraid of him like everyone else around here. You tell me where he's hiding, and I'll put him in his place."

"Momma, no," I sniffle, lifting my blotchy face to look at her pleadingly. "He already threatened to hurt you if I don't do what he's asking."

Outrage flashes gold in her brown eyes. "What *exactly* is he making you do?"

I hear the words in my head and know they will be atomic when I drop them.

"An arranged marriage. Some man named The Reaper," I whisper.

Gran holds me even tighter, murmuring in Slovak. She was born here, but English was her second language, not that you'd know it. She sounds like any other New Yorker.

Mom spins away from us, openly cursing. "I fucking knew it! That goddamn bastard wanted nothing to do with you the second he found out you were sick, but the minute he needs something, he acts like he owns you. One month old—the most precious, perfect little baby in the world—and he gave it all up because of a little hearing loss. You don't get to throw away a child like that. I told him never to come back, and I meant it. Men like him don't get second chances." She paces like a madwoman while she rants, eventually putting on her shoes, then hunting down her purse.

Mom has always advocated for my abilities at the top of her lungs since I lost hearing in my left ear as a baby. She was also the first to come to bat the moment anyone doubted or teased me. And she has never—not even for a second—forgiven Biba for using my hearing loss as an excuse to abandon us. This latest turn of events only adds fuel to her fire.

"Mom, stop. What are you doing?" I call out.

"I may have just been the other woman, but that doesn't mean I'm powerless. I can still go have words with him."

"*No*, Mom." I rush across the room and block the front door. "I don't know what he was like before, but he's not the sort of man you argue with now. I looked in those hollow eyes of his, and nothing was staring back. The man has no soul."

"I'm the mother here—" She only gets the first part of her sentence out before Gran finally steps in.

"*No*," she barks loudly. "*I'm* the mother here, and you will do no such thing. Both of you will come sit with me at the table, and we will talk this over rationally before anyone does anything. Understood?"

Gran is so loving and chill that in the rare instances when she asserts herself, compliance is the only option. The tension in the room reduces to a simmer as we walk to the kitchen table, each taking our unspoken assigned seats.

"Now, let's figure out what we know, then we can work on a plan to deal with the situation. Dani?"

"Yes?"

"When is this wedding supposed to take place?"

"I don't think it's set in stone, but he said his plan is to have me married in a week," I say meekly. I wish I had her strength, but I feel so defeated. So powerless.

Gran nods.

Mom glowers. "Okay, so we go off the assumption of one week." She shakes her head. "You know, this is exactly why I never got married. Men only make your life more complicated—they only care about themselves."

Mom's opinion about marriage is less than favorable in the best of circumstances. This situation doesn't help matters. In her words, there's no worse decision a woman can make than to marry a man. Her romantic interests never panned out well, and it's left her a bit jaded about men in general.

Gran sees things very differently. She adored Grandpa Miro, or so I'm told. I was young when he died, so I don't remember him. What I can say for certain is that every time Gran mentions him, her smile is infectious, and the corners of her eyes crease with love.

"This is not the time, Petra," Gran chastens, then looks back at me. "And you say this man is called Reaper?"

"That's what Biba said." I shrug. "I really don't know much more about any of it."

Again, Gran nods. "Then we have a week to get you somewhere safe."

"But Gran," I say warily. "He said if I run, he'll come after you guys. I can't let that happen."

"Sweet Dani." She places her wrinkled hand over mine. "I understand how hard this is for you, but try to imagine you have a precious little girl with a full life ahead of her. You've raised her from a little baby and want to give her the world. Would you be willing to let her become the property of a monster while you sit home and watch *Jeopardy*?"

I bite my bottom lip, realizing she has a point. "I hadn't thought about it like that."

"I know, and that's okay. You don't have any little ones yet, but one day you might, and then you'll see. We'd rather be dead ourselves than let something happen to you."

"What if we all go together?"

"Then he'd be that much more apt to find you. I'm an old woman and have no business living on the run. Besides, this will probably all blow over soon enough, and that way, you'll have a home to come back to."

Gran and Mom stare earnestly at me until I nod my acceptance. "Okay, but if I do this, you have to do something to protect yourselves as well. I can't just leave knowing you're in danger."

My seventy-three-year-old grandmother smiles warmly and squeezes my hand. "I have a cousin who'll help. We'll be fine."

"They'll let you stay with them?"

"They might if I ask, but I meant he deals in guns. We'll make sure we're well protected."

I gape, at a loss for words. "Gran, you don't even know how to hold a gun."

"Says who?" she tosses back with a wry grin. "It's been a few decades, but we'll go to the range for a few practice shots. Petra here will need the practice."

Mom shrugs as if to say, *I hate to admit it, but you're probably right.*

I stare dumbfounded at the two of them, thinking that this day can't get any crazier. Sure, Gran grew up during a tough time in the city, but she's *Gran*. She bakes banana bread and does large-print Sudoku. And Mom has never said one word about ever having shot a gun before. She hates opening biscuit tubes because the pop makes her jump.

"Who are you people?" I say with equal parts wonder and jest. The funny part is, I shouldn't be shocked. Gran is a wild card, for sure, and Mom is feisty as hell when she gets riled. I wouldn't even be all that surprised if they already had a gun hidden in the apartment somewhere. I've come to expect the unexpected with the two of them. If I had to label my own role in our little family unit, I'd say I'm the glue that binds us. Growing up with two such bold personalities and my own personal challenges to overcome has made me rather adaptable and even-tempered. For the most part.

Mom smirks. "Dad liked knowing we could protect ourselves. Probably should have done the same for you."

I see a warm glint brighten Gran's eyes. "My Milo was one of the good ones. He was always looking to take care of us."

"Too bad there's not more like him," Mom mutters as she gets up to start cooking dinner. "So what's the plan? Where can we hide you for the next six months?"

"You really think he'll let it go by then?" I ask with a degree of hope.

"I think we only plan for six months at a time."

Oh. Okay. I suppose that's reasonable.

"I don't have any idea where to go." I prop my elbow on the table and rest my chin in my hand. "Sachi would be happy to help, but I'm scared to endanger her. Plus, her place is tiny. She and her roommate are already packed in there."

"It needs to be somewhere unconnected to you," Gran offers.

"What, like a shelter?" I ask warily. I shouldn't be choosy, but a homeless shelter sounds scary.

"No," Mom says adamantly. "I'd rather empty my savings to pay for a motel before sending you to one of those places."

"I don't like that option, but I'm not sure how else I'm supposed to know of a place if I have no connection to it."

"A shelter is too visible, anyway," Gran adds. "Definitely not an option."

The room goes silent as we all contemplate the dilemma until a screeching sounds from the television. I look at the screen and see a bald eagle gliding over water before snatching a fish from below the surface. Gran had been watching PBS when I got home, and a nature show has come on after her program.

Seeing the spectacular creature gives me a flicker of an idea.

It's crazy—ludicrous even—but it's all I've got.

"When I was at school, we had an adjunct professor teaching photography," I start to explain. "He was young and really cool—he had us call him Ricky instead of Professor Auburn, and he hosted parties when he was in town—stuff like that. As part of his photography career, he goes away on long expeditions to shoot random animals like tiny frogs in the Amazon or the rutting season for a rare species of deer in China. His adventures are fascinating, so he sends out a sort of email newsletter updating friends and family on occasion. I just got one of his emails a week ago saying he was spending the next month in Iceland chronicling the migration patterns of the narwhal. I bet he'd be willing to let me stay at his place while he's gone, but I'm not sure I'll be able to reach him. He's usually off-grid on his trips."

"Best not to leave a trail anyway," Gran says as though she's worked secret missions all her life. When this is over, she and I are gonna have a talk.

"I guess that's true, but it means I would have to break into his place."

"What other choice do you have?" Mom asks softly.

Reluctance tugs my lips into a frown. "I have a week. I'll go by and see if anyone is staying there first. I don't have to decide right this second."

Gran stands, then disappears to the bedroom she shares with Mom. The two generously offered to give me my own room when I graduated from high school. I couldn't afford to go out on my own. Now, Gran sleeps in the twin bed against the wall in Mom's room that I occupied for so long.

I really do love these two women with all my heart. We may get on each other's nerves sometimes, but we are always there for one another when it counts. I will never forgive myself if something happens to them.

A new round of tears is burning the backs of my eyes when Gran returns and hands me something like a bundle of metal toothpicks bound with a rubber band. I stare at the offering, my brows furrowed in concentration.

"What are these?" I ask.

"Keys," she tells me.

I raise my brows at her, prodding for more of an explanation.

"You know how those damn dryers at the laundromat are always eating my quarters?" She lifts her palms in a what-choice-did-I-have gesture. "The owners don't give me my money back, so I go in and take it."

"You break into the laundromat?" I blurt.

She looks at me like I'm crazy. "Of course not. I just let myself into the money part of the machine. I only take what it owes me—nothing more," she says innocently. "Sometimes you have to take matters into your own hands."

Mom rolls her eyes, and I can't help but giggle.

"You practice a bit, and those'll get you in anywhere," Gran tells me nonchalantly.

"Okay, I think it's best if I don't know any more about your secret life of crime."

"That's just life, Danika. I've told you that."

"Yeah, Gran." I smile. "I suppose I should have listened better."

"Live and learn."

I get up and give each of them a kiss on the cheek. "I'm going to take a quick shower before dinner is ready. Is that okay?"

"Take your time," Mom tells me. "I'm just getting started, so you'll have at least an hour before it's ready."

"Sounds good."

I go to my room and close the door for a minute alone to process. Considering all that's happened, I could use a month to fully come to terms with my situation, but I don't have that kind of time.

One week.

I have one week to secure a place to stay, pack, and disappear.

I sit on my bed and stare at a painting of mine hanging beside my closet door. Two white calla lilies on a black background. Gran's favorite flower, and ironically, a symbol of death. They're one of the most popular funeral flowers, and a perfect reminder that I have to run. I can't let Biba take me.

I get up and start rummaging around my room. I'm not even sure for what. A genie in a lamp? Maybe a fairy godmother. Where can a girl buy a miracle in this city? No miracles, but I should probably get a prepaid phone so I can keep in touch with Mom and Gran.

Excellent thinking! See, you got this.

I find a scrap of paper to start making a list when I hear two sharp knocks on the front door. The apartment is small and not particularly soundproof, so I stand close to the bedroom door and listen. I'm not sure why. I don't normally care when someone comes by, but this stuff with Biba has me paranoid, and for good reason. When Mom opens the door, I hear a man's voice.

Please let it be creepy Mr. Wood from downstairs trying to hit up Mom for a date again.

Why I think I have any luck left at this point, I don't know because I've clearly drained that bucket dry. A man's rumbling voice sounds from the other room with an unmistakable Russian accent. As soon as he speaks, I hear my mother tell him that I'm not home.

I stand frozen with fear and indecision, my heart beating as fast as a hummingbird's wings.

What does this guy want with me? I assume Biba sent him, but why? Should I hide in the closet? Maybe I should already be out on the fire escape making my way to ground level. That's probably best, but when I hear the man shout aggressively, followed by a squeal from my mother, I instinctively charge into the living room.

"I'm here. Leave her alone," I demand, hands on my hips. "What do you want?"

He snarls, revealing the most cliché gold tooth imaginable. "Time to go."

"Where? Biba said I had a week to get ready."

"And you would have, had you not gone crying to the police. Such a disappointment to the Vor. Now, you spend the week at his place to make sure you no do anything stupid."

My mask of false bravado falls to the floor. "What? I didn't even say anything. I left before I talked to anyone."

"But you might not next time. Pack a bag, we're leaving."

I have no choice but to follow his orders. When I turn, Mom tries to follow me, but one harsh command from him stops her in her tracks. Fingers trembling, I throw together an overnight bag and make sure to grab my tablet computer. It's a crazy mismatch of clothing and toiletries because I can't think clearly enough to pack appropriately. I don't even know what is appropriate—is this a one-night bag until he sends men for the rest of my things? Will I be stuck in his house all week, or will he expect me to go out and put on a show? I'm so utterly bewildered that I just grab whatever comes into view first and stuff it in the bag.

When I return to the living room, Mom stares at me fiercely and completely ignores the man's fussing when she crosses the room to hug me. I try to draw from her strength. A part of me desperately wants to break down in her arms and beg her to keep me safe, but I know that isn't an option.

She empowers me with one final parting gift. A few words whispered hastily in my ear to calm and focus me.

"Stick to the plan. Don't let him take you. Run."

4
Danika

ADRENALINE FLOODS MY VEINS AS THE ELEVATOR plummets to the ground level. I know my chances are slim, but I have to try to get away. I just wish I knew how. I'll never win a foot race with a man nearly a foot taller than me. I'm an artist, not an athlete.

What else, then? Do I push him in front of oncoming traffic? Effective if I'm okay with possibly going to prison and living with the fact that I killed a man. Urgency bleeds my brain of all thought. The harder I push myself to come up with an idea, the more blank my mind becomes.

Come on, Dani. Think!

The rev of a motorcycle draws my gaze behind me. The light up ahead has turned green, and traffic is inching forward ... including a motorcycle not far from me.

I have no clue if I can pull this off, but it's the only idea I've got. I'll only have about half a second to make it work.

In three...

Two...

One...

I shove the Russian away from the street, then launch myself onto the back of the motorcycle. I burn my leg in the process but hardly register the pain.

"Drive, *please*! I need your help," I cry next to the man's helmet. My body tightly clutches his with my duffel still dangling from my shoulder. By some miracle of God, the bike revs to life, skirting around the cars in front of it and away from the furious Russian screaming at our backs. We zoom in and out of traffic, even going on sidewalks to avoid stopping, until we're a good mile or so away from my apartment building. Far enough that I feel safe asking the driver to stop. Again, my luck holds up, and the guy pulls his bike over in the loading zone for a corner market.

"Thank you so much," I say as I slide off the bike, careful not to burn myself again, and turn off my cell phone before I do anything else. Now that I've escaped, I don't want them using GPS somehow to track me down.

My rescuer takes his helmet off to reveal a middle-aged man with kind eyes. "You okay? I can drop you at a police station if you want."

"No, that's okay. Thank you." I offer a gracious smile, and while he returns the gesture, his eyes are full of pity. I don't like the idea of anyone worrying about me, but my situation probably warrants concern.

I give one more wave and watch as he puts his helmet back on and disappears into the night. Despite all that's happened in the past twenty-four hours, I'm bolstered by the reminder that decent people still exist in the world—people willing to help a total stranger. It gives me a tiny ray of hope that maybe an answer to my problems will present itself. In the meantime, I need to hide.

After using the only cash in my wallet to buy a blue Yankees ball cap in the corner market, I head to the subway. My best friend lives two stops away. I can spend one night with her, then move forward with my plan in the morning.

"Well, this is new." Sachi studies the way my trademark red waves are crammed under a ball cap—an unusual style for me, even more so considering the sun isn't out. Her eyes pop wide open. "Oh God. Tell me you did not try to give yourself bangs."

I have to chuckle as I push past her into the one-bedroom apartment she shares with another girl. "I wish."

"Then what's up with the incognito mode?"

"Ria here?" I try to peek into the bedroom but don't see signs of Sachi's roommate.

"She's out for the evening, why? What on earth is going on?"

I set down my duffel and have Sachi sit with me on the small futon sofa. "This is going to sound absolutely insane, but every word of it is true."

My best friend of the past five years sobers, the normally

serene skin of her forehead creasing with unease. "Are you in some sort of danger?" she blurts.

"You know that my dad isn't in my life, but I sort of left out the part about him being head of the Russian mob."

"Oh my God. You're not joking." If possible, her eyes widen even further.

I shake my head slowly, then launch into an explanation of the past twenty-four hours of my life. She listens raptly, asking questions like a soldier gaining intel before going on a mission.

"Sach, I don't want you involved in this," I tell her at the end. "I just need to stay here for the night, then I'm going to disappear for a bit and hope this whole thing blows over."

"You may be staying here, but you are *not* disappearing. Not from me, anyway," she counters sharply. What Sachi lacks in height—she's barely four-eleven—she makes up for in spunk. We usually complement each other nicely, but right now, I just need her to listen for once.

"No, it's too dangerous—" I try to argue before she cuts me off.

"All I'm saying is we're going to get a couple of disposable phones so that we can keep in touch. No reason for you to be totally on your own if you don't have to be."

I slump back against the cushion behind me, realizing she has a point. "I guess that's okay. I turned off my phone so he can't track me, not that I have any clue how that stuff works."

"Not good enough, hand me the phone." She takes my lifeless device, removes the case, and pops out the SIM card. "This is the real culprit." Her eyes light up as she snaps the tiny square in half.

"This is a product of all that true crime stuff you watch, isn't it?"

"You mean my survival research? Yes, and as you can see, it's paying off. Now, we need to get burner phones. I'll run by the electronics shop around the corner in a minute."

"Okay, but the phones are only for emergencies."

She holds up her hand as if swearing an oath. "Scout's honor."

"Crap, what about my laptop?"

"Should be fine, just don't connect to the internet."

I have work due, but I guess staying alive is more important. I'll worry about my projects later once I know I'm safe.

Sachi scoots closer with a conspiratorial lean. "Tell me about this place where you're planning to stay."

"Nope. It's too dangerous. I'd like to think Biba doesn't know you exist, but if he does, I want you to be able to honestly say you have no idea where I am." I keep going when she starts to frown, hoping to distract her. "One thing I can use your help with is these." I take out the bundle of lock picks still in my pocket from when Gran gave them to me earlier.

"What are those?"

"Lock picks. Our mission tonight is to figure out how to unlock a deadbolt."

As I'd hoped, her eyes light up with excitement. "Let me run to the store to get those phones, and then we can get started. I'm sure there are tons of YouTube tutorials we can watch. You can learn how to do anything on YouTube."

"Exactly." The adrenaline filtering out of my system brings my attention to a throbbing pain a few inches above my right ankle. I remember the scalding pipe on the motorcycle and have a look.

"That a burn?" Sachi asks.

"Yeah, from the motorcycle."

"Who has a motorcycle?"

"Random stranger—I hopped on to escape the Russian thug." I lift my gaze to my best friend when she goes quiet and find her staring at me like I've just won an all-expenses-paid cruise to the Caribbean.

"Your life is totally insane, and I'm a little jealous."

I roll my eyes with a smirk because I know she doesn't mean it. Sachi grabs her purse and slides on a pair of flip-flops before pausing, then crossing the room to give me a big hug. "But for reals, I'm so sorry this is happening, Dani. I wish there was more I could do."

"Thank you, honey. Having you here for me is more help than you can know."

I give her one last squeeze before she leaves in search of phones for us. After getting a baggie of ice for my burn, I dig in my emails to see what I can learn about Ricky's travels, hoping for clues about a possible house sitter. Unfortunately, not much info is available. On the upside, we make decent headway on the lock pics after Sachi gets back with the phones. We practice for over two hours on her apartment door while watching video tutorials. I feel confident I could get in a lock like hers, but who knows what kind of lock Ricky will have. I never paid attention to that sort of thing when I went to gatherings at his place. I watch a few videos on other types of locks and learn what I can before deciding to call it a night.

The following morning, I slip out of the apartment without saying goodbye. It's just too painful. I prefer to believe I'll see her again very soon—the same with Mom and Gran. Losing touch with them is too unbearable to think about, so I don't.

How FITTING THAT today is Independence Day. The Fourth of July—the day I go in search of my freedom because spending my life in an arranged marriage would be a prison sentence.

I'm officially alone as I ride the elevator up to Ricky's apartment. Not only am I alone but I hardly recognize myself in the mirrored elevator wall with my hair under a ball cap. Wearing baggy jeans low on my hips and an oversized T-shirt, I look like a preteen boy, which was intentional. Very few people were out and about on the way over since it's a holiday, but I didn't want to take any chances. I'm committed at this point. I don't want to be careless and wind up back where I started.

But are you committed enough to break into this apartment?

I stare at the door and wait for someone to answer my knocking. It's been more than enough time. If someone were inside, they'd have come to the door, right? Right.

I wipe my sweaty palms on my jeans and pull out the picks.

Here goes nothing.

The lock has an electronic keypad along with a traditional keyhole like so many door locks these days. We learned last night that as long as the lock has a keyhole, it can be physically picked regardless of the electronic component.

Time to see if my lackluster skills are sufficient to prove that theory correct.

I take out the two picks needed and begin the process. With the straight stick inserted, I use a skinnier stick with a hooked end to feel for the pins inside. I need to get each pin raised and locked in place. Five times I try. Five times I fail and have to start over. My hands are starting to shake. Sweat beads on my forehead, and I'm battling a swell of frustration threatening to overwhelm me. On my sixth attempt, as I quietly plead with the lock to give in, I feel the internal mechanism click over. I freeze in shock.

I've unlocked the door and broken into my friend's apartment.

My chest swells with a deep breath of elation as I push open the door. No one confronts me. The lights are off, and the place is silent. I don't even hear the beeping of an alarm, which surprises me, but I'm not about to look a gift horse in the mouth.

I did it!

I've secured a safe place to lie low until I can sort out my next move. The relief is so intense that my head spins with dizziness. Or is it disorientation? Ricky has redecorated since I was last here a few months ago. The design is still masculine in its simplicity, and nothing much is on the walls yet. I imagine he'll have them full of his amazing photography when he has the chance.

I set down my bag and walk into the living room to stare out the floor-to-ceiling windows at the incredible view. This bird's nest in the sky is my new sanctuary. I don't know what comes next, but I'm safe for now.

No sooner did the thought cross my mind than an arm clamps around my neck to secure me in a tight headlock.

"You think you can break into my place, you little prick?" growls a deep voice at my back.

I gasp and tug at the corded forearm blocking my airway, only managing to get out a petrified squeal. As if caught off guard, my attacker suddenly loosens his hold.

"The *fuck*? You're not a punk kid, you're a woman."

I nod and wheeze, "I'm so sorry. Please, don't hurt me. I'm a friend of Ricky's."

I lift my hands to my sides in surrender and slowly turn

around to find a gun pointed at my head. Another onslaught of adrenaline has my one good ear ringing so loudly that I'm nearly deaf.

A *gun?* I wasn't sure what would happen if someone was inside the apartment, but I never really imagined a gun being involved. It's light out. I knocked. This man has a foot of height and probably a hundred pounds on me. Why is he holding me at gunpoint?

My eyes flit from the weapon to the man in front of me. This time, I'm not the only one in shock as recognition registers.

"It's *you*," he hisses in equal parts awe and accusation.

I totally understand because I feel the same.

What are the chances that the man from outside the police station is here in Ricky's apartment? Did he follow me and slip in behind me somehow? Who on earth is he, and how does he look so damn terrifying yet breathtakingly beautiful at the same time?

"I'm not breaking in," I assure him quickly.

"You and I must have very different definitions of breaking in."

"Ricky's a friend, and I was hoping to crash here while he's away. I would have asked, but as you probably know, he's off-grid."

Dark brown eyes study me with acute precision. "If you mean Richard Auburn, he moved out a month ago. This is my apartment now, and I never leave the door unlocked, which means you. Broke. In."

Oh *shit*. Shit, shit, shit.

What have I done? Is he a detective or something? Is that why he was in front of the police station? Am I about to go to prison?

"This has been a horrible misunderstanding. I'm so sorry. I'll just grab my bag and go." I take one lunging step forward to escape around him when his hand whips out lightning fast and manacles around my throat. He doesn't restrict my breathing, but the gesture isn't friendly either. It's also not something a cop would do—not a good one, anyway. He's making a statement about who's in charge, and I receive that message with perfect clarity.

"I don't think so, *Danika*," he says in an eerily calm voice, making a point to show that he remembers my name. "Considering this is the second time you've orchestrated a run-in with me, you're not going anywhere."

5
Tommy

SEEING THOSE WIDE GREEN EYES AGAIN MADE ME WONDER for an instant if my obsessive tendencies had finally escalated to the point of hallucinations. However, with my hand circling her throat and her feminine scent invading my lungs, I can't deny reality. Danika Dobrev, the feisty redhead with a man problem, is here in my apartment.

Why? What does she want, and who is she working for? Is she undercover for the DEA or sent by one of our rivals, and if so, for what purpose? Either way, she's shit at her job. She's drawn so much attention to herself that she might as well be wearing a neon sign. If she thought tossing out the name of the man I bought this place from was going to erase my suspicions, she's a fool. Anyone with a computer and half a brain could look that information up online.

She's come after me for a reason, and I'm going to get to the bottom of it.

Later.

Fortunately for her, I have somewhere to be.

I tuck my gun in my waistband, then spin her around to secure her hands in mine and direct her to the back bedroom.

"Please, I know it sounds crazy, but I swear it's all a coincidence," she pleads, panic flaring in her voice. She's shit at being covert, but her acting is spot-on.

"Nice try, but you'll have to do better than that." I nudge her forward.

"What do you mean? You can't keep me here."

"Says the girl who broke in."

She looks back at me pleadingly, resisting my prods forward. "I told you, it was a mistake. Please, don't do this. *Please.*"

Her voice pitches high with elevated fear, which pisses me off because I don't like it. She sounds terrified, and what's worse is she's probably just playing me. I shouldn't be the least bit affected. So why do I find myself begrudgingly reassuring her?

"Look at me," I instruct firmly, turning her as much as I can while still keeping her hands secure behind her. "I'm not going to hurt you if you don't give me a reason to," I bite out. "I have somewhere to be, but you can't leave until you tell me what the fuck is going on, so you're going to chill for a bit."

"What does that mean?" Her wide eyes dart around as though she's searching for a way to escape. "Maybe you should just call the police and let them sort it out."

I don't answer her and have to use more force to overcome

her increased resistance as we turn down the dark hallway to the two guest rooms. It doesn't get any easier when I stop at a closet and grab a roll of duct tape.

When the designer outfitted each bedroom with a random chair, I'd thought it was pointless clutter but let her do her thing. She probably hadn't expected me to tie a woman to one of them, but regardless, her idea was more practical than I realized. The compact yet cushioned corner chair in the far back bedroom will serve nicely to contain my little intruder until I'm ready to deal with her.

"Sit." I motion to the chair.

She looks like she's going to argue, then glances at the bed before scurrying over to the chair. I'm not crazy about her thinking I'm a rapist, but whatever gets her cooperation works for me.

"You don't have to do this. Just lock me in the room. Or call the police on me." Her words are rushed and urgent.

I ignore them and make quick work of taping her wrists and ankles to the arms and legs of the chair. When I rip one last piece of tape for her mouth, she's engulfed in panic. Eyes wide, her nostrils flare as I press the tape over her rosy lips. Within seconds, her breathing intensifies to rapid panting. She's straining against the tape and seconds away from hyperventilating.

I place my hands on either side of her face and draw her frantic stare to mine. "Danika, listen to me," I say quietly. "Breathe with me." I take a slow, steady breath in through my nose, then out. She does the same, her entire focus centered on me in a way that makes me feel like a king. Like I have the power to move mountains if only because she believes I can. It's a heady sensation that does nothing to dim my unhealthy fixation on this woman.

We repeat the process three times until she regains control of herself. Once she's no longer at risk of passing out, I force my hands away from her, which takes more willpower than I care to admit.

"I'll be gone for an hour—no more. Then we'll discuss what you're doing in my apartment, understood?"

She nods, tears welling in her eyes.

Fuck me.

I have to get out of here before I do something idiotic. I close the door harder than I intended and get the hell out of my apartment. Besides, I *do* have somewhere to be, and I don't go off schedule. Routines and schedules exist for a reason. Ignoring them makes my skin crawl. That's one of my compulsions that generally doesn't give me problems.

As a kid, I would go unhinged when the family schedule changed unexpectedly, but as an adult, I have all the control. Sometimes things don't go as planned, and age has helped me learn to cope with that frustration, but for the most part, I can avoid disruptions with careful planning.

Danika Dobrev was *not* in my plan.

The part I'm struggling with the most is determining whether my intense need to know more about her is a justifiable result of her reappearance or the rationalization of my obsessive brain. If anyone else in the world had broken in, would I have simply called the police? Maybe. Maybe not. I'm not the type to call the cops in general, so the question isn't particularly helpful.

What I'd rather ask myself is why *she* suggested calling the police. It doesn't make any sense if she's part of a rival organization, and I can't see her being an undercover cop. I'm not a fan, but even I can admit they're not incompetent enough to do what she's done.

Could she be a random thief who pegged me as a mark—followed me home and planned to rob me? One who carries around a large duffel bag of crap and stares vacantly out windows after breaking in. That doesn't add up either.

Something is off with this woman. I don't understand people in general, but this feels like something more than an inability to read her. Something isn't lining up, and I intend to find out the reason one way or another.

I'M NOT BACK at my place for five minutes when Sante texts to tell me he and his wife, Amelie, are on their way over. Not ideal, but I'm the one who asked him to come by, so I put my curiosity on the back burner and let my little captive stew a little longer.

I plan to deal with her as soon as Sante leaves, but I should have known things would get complicated. They always do when women are involved. The minute Danika hears our voices, she starts to make a ruckus. Of course, Amelie hears it and isn't about to leave anything alone. Not that I intended to hide Danika from Sante. He and I have no secrets from one another. I simply had nothing to tell him yet.

Amelie demands to know why a woman in the back of my apartment is screaming. Sante looks equally curious, so I indulge them.

"I caught her breaking in this morning."

Amelie's eyes practically bug out of her head before she bolts for the back bedroom. She swings the door wide open, and we all take in the teary woman duct-taped to a chair. I internally cringe because I know how bad it looks.

"Tommaso Donati, what on earth have you done?" Amelie glares daggers at me.

"*Me?*" I shoot back at her. "She's the one who broke into my apartment."

"So you tied her up and left her back here?"

"I had somewhere to be." I shrug, knowing if I tell her I went to a haircut appointment, she'll skewer my balls and roast them at one of today's Fourth of July barbecues. Some things are better left unsaid.

She whacks my arm. I glare at her husband because that asshole has the nerve to snicker at my abuse.

After Amelie has carefully removed the tape covering my captive's mouth, she asks in a sickeningly sweet voice if Danika is okay. I roll my eyes only because I know Amelie can't see me.

"I'm so sorry. This is all a big mix-up," the little liar pleads. "I thought the apartment belonged to a friend who was out of town."

"You steal shit from your friends when they're away?" Sante's suspicion gives me some hope that his new wife hasn't muddled his brain completely. I like the woman, but everything's changed because of her. I fucking hate change.

"I wasn't stealing," Danika shoots back defensively. "I just needed a place to stay."

"Ah, so you're a squatter, not a thief."

"Sante," Amelie says in warning. "You're not even letting her explain."

He gives her an incredulous stare, which withers to a pathetic grimace under the glare of her scrutiny. Looks like I gave him too much credit. The cretin rolls over in surrender.

"I have a photographer friend from school who used to live here. I didn't realize he'd moved, but I knew he was on shoot in Iceland, so I was hoping to use his place while he was gone. I would have checked with him, but the shoot is remote, and he couldn't be reached."

I study her as she explains, trying to assess every little nuance of her speech and movements for tells. It's a craft I've studied for years because it doesn't come naturally to me. I've had to work very hard to learn to read people. Either she's very good at lying or she's telling the truth. But even if she is being honest, her answer only raises more questions.

"You don't look homeless," I point out. Nor does she look like someone who wouldn't have a single friend or family member to call on for a place to stay. Why would she choose to break into someone's home rather than stay with someone else?

"I'm not," she replies hesitantly. "I needed to lay low for a bit."

Sante is the first to respond, his answer mirroring my thoughts. "Lay low sounds an awful lot like hiding. Who are you running from?"

The woman's eyes squeeze shut with frustration before reopening. "It doesn't matter. Look, I made a mistake, and I'm really sorry, but no harm was done. Can you please just let me go?" She's genuinely scared of whoever has her on the run, which makes me even more convinced that she's not leaving until we get a name.

"*Who?*" Sante demands.

"You wouldn't know him." Her voice is suddenly weary with defeat. "And trust me, you wouldn't want to if you did. He's dangerous—that's why I needed a place he would never look."

I don't like it, but not for the reasons I shouldn't not like it. I should be pissed she's mixed us up in someone else's drama, but instead, I feel surging rage that someone has instilled this fear and despondency in her. It's not my place to care. I don't know this woman, and her problems aren't mine, yet I find myself pulling out my gun and pointing it right at her face.

"Who?" I demand with deadly calm.

Silence presses against my eardrums. Or maybe that's my thundering pulse. Either way, my blood pressure skyrockets.

"Who ... who are you?" she whispers with dawning realization. Whoever she's running from isn't the only monster in the city. She's leaped from the frying pan straight into the fire. Her paling skin highlights her freckles, making her look sickeningly innocent. How am I supposed to walk away from a face like that?

Fury over this turn of events sharpens my tongue when I answer her. "The last person you'll ever see if you don't give me a name." It's an empty threat, but she doesn't know that, and I want answers.

She squeezes her eyes tightly shut again. Tears roll down her freckled cheeks this time, and she whispers, "His name is Biba."

The single word ricochets like gunfire inside my head.

"Fuck!" Sante roars beside me.

She's got the Russian mob after her. This isn't just a case of a domestic dispute or some asshole loan shark looking for his money. She's got the boss of the whole Russian mob looking for her.

Jesus Christ.

I don't realize Sante and Amelie are having a wordless conversation until he addresses her in a frustrated tone. "What am I supposed to do, Mel? We don't know what the hell she's gotten herself into. This could draw us into a full-blown war."

"We can't send her out on her own," Amelie returns in a pitiful tone that I instantly know will trump any argument Sante or I might make. "I know what it's like to feel hunted and alone. Please help her."

Yup. Checkmate.

"I can get her a plane ticket. I hear Colombia is a great place to disappear," he suggests dryly. He can read the writing on the wall as well as I can.

"Is that what you would have wanted for me?" she prods, hands now hiked on her hips.

He grimaces, arms spreading wide. "What else do you suggest? I can't put her up in a hotel forever."

"No, but we could hide her while we figure out what's going on and see if there's a way to help."

"You and I hardly have room for ourselves in our tiny apartment, let alone a guest. Not that I'd let you bring that sort of danger into our house anyway." He pauses, then, as if in slow motion, turns to me. "You've got plenty of room, though, don'tcha, Tommy?" His knife slides as easily into my back as the grin across his face.

Fucking traitor.

"No fucking way. It's not happening." I haven't shared a living space with anyone since he and I were forced to spend a month in a barn with a dozen pigs back in Sicily. What he's proposing sounds just as distasteful. I don't share my space with anyone, let alone someone I know nothing about. And besides that, keeping Danika near me will eliminate all hope of scraping her from my mind. I'll be just as much a captive as she is.

Amelie turns to face me like a cat angling itself to look larger than it is and injects every ounce of authority she can summon into addressing me. "You owe me, Tommaso Donati, for pretending to be my stalker. Don't think I've forgotten about that."

I can hardly believe what I'm hearing. "*Owe* you? I took a fist to the face for that." And I was only doing what her damn husband asked me to do.

"That was between you and your delinquent friend over there." She nods toward Sante, then presses a finger into my chest, brows narrowing. "This is between you and me. It's not forever. Give her a place to stay while we figure this out, and we'll call it even."

"Un-fucking-believable," I breathe. "You going to say something, Sante?"

The traitor shrugs. "Yeah, happy wife, happy life."

Amelie grins, and I know I've lost.

After bellowing my frustration, I turn to my friend and level him with a scathing glare. "You fucking owe me."

He bites down on his lips to keep from laughing.

Amelie interrupts before I have a chance to sucker punch him. "You two quit standing there and get that tape off her."

We end our stare down and do as we're told like fucking children. As we finish removing the tape, Sante asks the million-dollar question.

"Why is Biba after you?"

Danika looks at us while rubbing her wrists and seems to debate answering. "First, I need to know who you guys are and how you know Biba."

She's not in a position to make demands, but I suppose I understand her need to know. "I'm Tommaso Donati, and this is Sante. My brother is Renzo Donati—have you heard of him?" I watch her carefully for signs of recognition, but find none when she shakes her head. "How about the Moretti Family? Ever heard that name before?"

Her porcelain skin pales even further. "You're Italian mafia," she breathes.

"Now it's your turn," Sante pushes, all business. "What does Biba want with you?"

Danika looks from one of us to the other, wringing her hands with indecision. "I took something from him."

Sante and I immediately look at one another as we're reminded of a crazy day years ago when we too stole something from Biba. We didn't exactly mean to—we were kids taking a million-dollar car for a joy ride. How were we supposed to know it belonged to the head of the Russian mob? The thrill was unlike anything I'd ever experienced. Unfortunately, Biba wasn't particularly understanding, and the incident was a key factor in our extended stay in Sicily.

It wasn't so long ago, yet it feels like a lifetime. What are the odds that a mere handful of weeks after our return, this woman careens into my life having committed the same sin? It can only be explained in one of three ways: a lie, a coincidence, or karma. All three options suck.

"What did you take?" I ask her.

"Something that wasn't his to begin with, and it couldn't be helped. I had no choice, and the thing I took is totally meaningless to him. He's just upset and needing to make a point."

"You're really not going to tell us what you took?"

"It doesn't make a difference what I took. Biba's going to hunt me to the ends of the earth regardless."

"Man trouble," I muse, remembering what she'd said yesterday in front of the police station.

She stares at me with a degree of strength and conviction

that surprises me. "And just like I said, there is no solution to this sort of problem. All I can do is hide."

"Well, I hope whatever it is you took was worth it because it very well may cost you your life."

Golden-strawberry hair waving all around her, she lifts her chin defiantly. "That's a price I'm willing to pay."

She thinks I'm talking about Biba.

She has no idea there's a greater danger standing right in front of her. A man with shady morals and a penchant for taking what he wants. That man wouldn't just kill her; he'd keep her, and her life would be forever his.

6 Danika

Prisoner or refugee? Shouldn't I be able to tell if I'm one or the other? If I wanted to leave, would they let me? Where would I go if I did leave?

Exhaustion hits me like an ocean wave crashing onto the shore. The man and woman—Sante and Amelie—just left, and no matter how terrified I should be about being left alone with Tommaso, I have no energy left to fuel any fear.

I've escaped the grasp of the Russian mob only to end up in the hands of the Italian Mafia. I don't know what to think about that. Amelie seems sweet enough, and her husband clearly adores her, so that's a good sign.

Tommaso is a different story.

They called him Tommy, but such a boyish name doesn't fit around his hard edges. He's so severe. So rigid.

I would be sold on that perspective of him if it wasn't for the way he helped keep me calm after restraining me. What kind of monster comforts its prey? Either he's a very twisted creature or ... he's not a monster at all.

I'm bound to find out soon enough.

He watches me with inscrutable intensity like a jungle cat eyeing a snake for the first time, unsure if it's danger or dinner. I want to assure him I'm neither, but it won't do any good. I can already tell Tommy is the sort of man who isn't easily swayed.

"Bathroom is in there." He gestures to one of the two closed doors. "I'll bring dinner at eight." And with that proclamation, he's gone, shutting the door behind him.

The safety of solitude brings on another wave of exhaustion, but I don't let myself give in to it. I could be in more danger than I know, so I force myself to stay awake by checking out my new surroundings. The bedroom suite is equally as luxurious as the rest of the apartment—nicer than I've ever known. A queen-sized bed is fitted with soft cotton linens and plenty of pillows. The neutral colors and minimal decor create a modern aesthetic that is simple but not overly cold.

I'm just settling in when Tommy appears with a plate of food as he promised at 8 p.m. on the dot, according to the bedside clock. He doesn't say a word and is gone as quickly as he arrived. The lemon chicken with asparagus and pilaf rice is delicious. I don't realize until the smell hits me just how starving I am. I haven't eaten all day. Once I've downed every last bite, I decide to venture out of my room to return the plate to the kitchen. He never said I couldn't leave the room, and the door isn't locked. If I am, in fact, a refugee rather than a prisoner, I figure the least I can do is clean up after myself.

I don't see Tommy while I'm out of my room and have no idea where he is. I figure it's none of my business and plan to return to my room as soon as the dishes are cleaned. It feels safer back there. But when I see the last bit of sunshine melting into the river beyond his wall of windows, I can't look away. Going right up to the glass, I sit cross-legged on the floor and absorb the view. When the first firework of the night goes off, I startle out of my haze and remember what day it is. Independence Day. And this apartment has a perfect view of the city's fireworks show over the river.

I take a minute to turn off the living room lights, leaving the kitchen on so I'm not in total darkness, then return to my seat on the floor. I'm fascinated by the way fireworks can explode into shapes, but my absolute favorites are the giant glittery gold ones that sparkle as they fade.

I'm so engrossed in the show that I don't hear Tommy come into the room and have no idea he's joined me until he speaks.

"While you're here, you don't touch anything. I like my home in a certain order. I expect it to stay that way." The softly spoken words are a warning.

I peer back and see that he's sitting on the sofa behind me, eyes glued to the brilliant display out the window as though he can't even bring himself to look at me. I get it. This isn't how he expected his day to go, either.

"I understand," I return. "And I appreciate what you're doing. I really am sorry to have barged into your life."

Briefly, ever so briefly, his gaze flits to mine, then returns to the fireworks. He doesn't say another word, and when the show is over, I look back to discover he's gone.

It's time for this wretched day to end.

I go back to my room and find my bag sitting on the bed, which is an enormous relief. I wasn't entirely sure if I'd get it back or if my belongings had been confiscated. I check to verify that my tablet computer is still safely inside my duffel, then scrounge inside the bag to see what else I crammed in there. I was so disoriented when I packed that I have no idea what I grabbed.

I manage to find a pajama set and a couple of pairs of underwear, which is a good start. There are also two mismatched socks, a silk blouse, a pair of leggings, a sundress, and a tank top —a perfectly worthless capsule wardrobe. Oh, well.

When I pop into the bathroom, I see a travel-size toiletries kit on the vanity, which wasn't there before. It's an unexpected kindness. I still don't feel safe, but it's sufficient to help me relax enough to shower and head to bed. But before I do anything else, I get out the disposable phone Sachi got for me.

Me: Hey, Sachi, it's me. All is well.

It's a little white lie, but I don't want her to worry.

Sachi: Good! Man, I've been worried. What kept you?

Me: Just being cautious. It's all good, and I'm headed to bed. Exhausted.

Sachi: I bet. Night, babe

Me: Night 🌙

Next, I text Mom to let her know I'm okay. It's probably not the safest thing to do, but I'm sure she and Gran have been worried sick.

Me: Marco

To help minimize the risk to both of us, I decide to be

discreet and use a game we've played since I was a kid. I think Marco Polo is supposed to be played in water, but we never had access to a pool. I started playing the game with her while hiding in clothing racks at department stores, and it stuck with us, evolving into a silly thing we do when we're looking for one another.

She won't know the number for the disposable phone. All I can do is hope she sees the message and realizes it's me. She's not great about looking at her phone, so I know she must have been waiting for me when a message comes back almost instantly.

Mom: Polo 🖤

My relief is overwhelming. So much so that if I don't get in the shower now, it'll never happen. The absence of a lock on the bathroom door gives me the motivation I need to take a record-fast shower. Before crawling into bed, I set the chair in front of the bedroom door. I'm not sure what it will do because it's lightweight, and I can't get it to stay wedged under the handle, but it's better than nothing. Two minutes later, I'm fast asleep, but it doesn't last long.

I wake groggily at the sensation of ice on my wrist. When I try to pull away from the cold, I realize I'm not alone. A flood of adrenaline ensures I'm now wide awake.

"Get away from me. What—" I frantically try to figure out what's going on.

"Calm down," Tommy cuts me off harshly while struggling to keep hold of my hand. "I just need to—"

Something cold clamps closed around my right wrist. I instinctively yank my arm to get away and use my other hand to try to remove the hard metal cuff, but in the dark, I can't see what I'm doing. Hands flailing, mind in total panic, I pant as I struggle to free myself.

"*Fuck*, stop moving—" Tommy grouses.

"*Don't touch me*," I hiss back at him.

"I'm not going to hurt you." A sound of metal ratcheting together clinks through the blackness, and we both still. "Oh, fucking *Christ*. Do you realize what you've done?" he demands.

My hand is yanked against the iron headboard frame by the metal cuff circling it. "What *I've* done? No, I have no idea what's going on. I was asleep before you attacked me, remember?"

"I never attacked you," he bites back. "I wouldn't be able to sleep with you loose in my house, so I came to fix that problem."

I tug at my arm, my eyes adjusting to see the slightest silver glow around my wrist. "By cuffing me to the bed?"

"You're not cuffed to the fucking bed. You're cuffed to *me*." He waves his hand, showing me how he's attached to the other end of my cuff, which is wrapped behind the iron bar on the bed. "*We* are cuffed to the bed."

"You cuffed us together so that you could sleep better?" Okay, so maybe I'm not as awake as I thought. This isn't making any sense.

"No, Danika," he grumbles, his exasperation evident. "I was cuffing *you* to the bed, but you lost your shit, and now we're both handcuffed to the fucking bed."

I sit up, my thoughts finally clearing. "Well, unlock it, then."

"Genius. Why didn't I think of that?"

"Don't you have a key to your own cuffs?" I gape at him.

"I do, on my dresser, where I left it." Tommy's irritation is escalating as he explains the situation, and I probably shouldn't push him, but I can't help myself. It sounds too absurd to be true.

"You accidentally cuffed us together ... with no key?"

"Not me, *you*. It was your flailing that did it."

A heavy silence blankets the room before laughter bubbles

up from deep in my belly. Uncontrollable, tear-producing, cackling laughter.

"You think this is fucking funny?" he barks at me.

It only makes me laugh harder. "Oh ... my God. So funny," I wheeze between breaths.

"I fail to see the humor."

He's truly upset, so I try to collect myself. "I know it sucks, but it's okay. It's not like we're going to die here, right? Someone will come by eventually and help us."

"Eventually? You're okay with *eventually*?"

A second silence thickens the air as reality sets in.

"Do you have a cleaning service or anything?" I ask in a much more reticent voice.

"Yes, but they come once a week and were just here two days ago."

Five more days.

Oh, good God.

"Someone will come looking for you before then, right? Will your friends be back? What if I have to pee? Would someone below hear us if we screamed loud enough?"

Tommy must hear the rising panic in my rapid-fire questions because his tone is softer when he answers. "Slow down. Don't blow this out of proportion."

I think he's trying to calm me, but the damage has been done.

"You're the one who said we may be stuck for days," I say in a high-pitched squeal.

"My interior designer is supposed to come by in the morning. We won't be stuck for days. Now, move over." He tries to nudge me away from the edge of the bed, but my thoughts are still reeling.

"But we won't be able to open the door to let her in."

"She has a key. Now, *move*."

I absently shift to the side as realization sets in. "So we weren't in any danger of dying here. You were just toying with me?" I blurt.

He lies beside me, explaining himself as he tries to find a comfortable position with one arm forced over his head. "Who said anything about dying? This right here is what I was trying to avoid, and now I'll be awake all night, I'll miss my morning workout, and my entire day will be a mess," he grunts and grumbles until finally settling on his back with a sigh.

The heat from his arm resting against mine makes me suddenly aware that he's not wearing a shirt. We lie very still, both of us with an arm raised over our heads. Neither of us sleeping.

"I didn't mean to do it," I whisper into the silence.

"I know," he says on a weary exhale.

God, this is so uncomfortable. So awkward. I try to adjust my position from one side to the other, but it's pointless.

"Quit your wiggling," my irritable captor fusses.

"I'm trying to get comfortable."

Nope, the side I'm on is making my arm go numb. I return to my back only to have Tommy wrap his free arm around my middle and pull me snug into the curve of his body like we're some sort of couple.

Oh God. This is bad.

Every muscle in my body tenses in anticipation of a fight. This man is a criminal. And we're in a bed together. I'm clothed, but the thin fabric hardly seems like any barrier at all.

"Last time I'm telling you, woman," he says in a brooding grumble. "Get some sleep before I knock you out myself."

I'm not sure how I can tell, but my instincts assure me it's an idle threat. For all the scowls and posturing, Tommy Donati has yet to do a single thing to hurt me. The reminder helps me relax a bit, though I'm well aware our limited interactions aren't any real predictor. Technically, this man held me at gunpoint and has me in handcuffs. The fact that I'm not totally terrified of him has got to be a testament to my exhaustion. Once I get some rest, I'll go back to feeling appropriately petrified of the man. I can't allow myself to be fooled by a tiny bit of kindness.

Men like Tommy and Biba should never be underestimated.

If I am, in fact, not a prisoner, I'd do best to get myself out of here at the earliest opportunity. Who knows what might happen if they figure out who I really am. Even without that knowledge, they could easily decide to use me as a bargaining chip, but knowing my paternity could make me a full-fledged prisoner and subject to who-knows-what horrors.

Let's stay focused on the positives, or you'll never get any sleep.

Right. Sleep.

Hopefully, this go-around will be less traumatizing than the last. With my luck lately, chances are slim.

7
Tommy

Something wakes me. I'm instantly on guard until I remember the absurd situation I'm in. Handcuffed to a thief in my own home. I couldn't make this shit up if I tried. I'm certain she's inadvertently woken me, which is just one of the many reasons I don't do sleepovers. Rest is a crucial part of my routine. If I don't get sleep, my whole day can be thrown off course, and I can't see how anyone sleeps with someone else in the bed moving and making noises.

I will say, however, that I fell asleep with Danika tucked against me much more easily than I expected. I thought I'd lie here all night, counting my heartbeats until morning. I don't think ten minutes passed before I was out cold. Her body relaxing into mine had some kind of hypnotic effect on me—as if her touch muted the constant buzz of my thoughts.

I didn't check and recheck all my guns before bed. My phone isn't plugged in on my nightstand next to my watch, which means I'll have to charge it in the morning, and my morning will already be chaotic without my workout and breakfast. All those things and more would normally peck at me incessantly until I give in and do something about the situation, but with Danika next to me, I experienced an unfamiliar sense of acceptance.

It could be a fluke. Whatever the cause, it's the same reason I'm not entirely upset about being woken up and am halfway back asleep when a whimper from Danika stirs me wide awake. She makes the soft but unsettling sound again, prompting me to prop myself on my elbow as best I can since that arm is the one handcuffed to the bed.

"Danika," I murmur softly but firmly. "Wake up, Danika."

She lets out a painful mewl that carves a chunk out of my soul.

"Jesus, don't cry. I can't handle crying." I gently shake her shoulder and finally get a response from her.

"What?"

The raspy caress of her voice has my dick hardening between us.

"You were whimpering in your sleep."

"I was? Sorry," she says groggily. "It happens sometimes."

"It does? Why would you cry in your sleep?"

"Huh?"

I realize she's still not properly awake, so I give her one more little shake. "Danika, why do you cry in your sleep sometimes?"

It's none of my damn business. There is no good reason on God's green earth for me to need to know why this woman cries, yet I can't help myself. I need to know.

Finally, she comes to, stiffening as reality sets in. "What? No, I don't cry in my sleep. Why would I do that?"

"Don't know. You're the one who said it happens sometimes."

She lets out an awkward chuckle. "I was probably still asleep. There's no telling."

I don't believe her, though I'm not sure why or what part bothers me. Is it the crying itself or the knowledge of the crying that she doesn't want to admit to? Why try to lie about it when I clearly heard her? And what was she dreaming about that made her cry in the first place?

A part of me wants to suss out the truth, but there could be any number of causes, including being cuffed to a bed with the man who held her at gunpoint. Probably, I should just leave her the fuck alone—we'd both be better off if I did.

I huff and lower my head back to the pillow, then reflexively pull Danika closer as if I hadn't just chided myself to keep my distance. I can't seem to help myself where she's concerned. I tell myself one thing, then do the complete opposite.

I wish I could set my curiosity on fire until nothing is left but ash. Yet when given the chance, I find myself inhaling her scent —sweet berries and total anarchy. This woman has the potential to be world-ending. She'll turn my life inside out until it's unrecognizable, and I'm so fucking fixated already that I'll probably thank her for it.

When I feel compulsion sink its teeth into me, I have to decide early on whether I plan to own it or fight it. Do I want to live the rest of my life resisting the constant craving, or do I embrace the trigger and resulting compulsion as a new fixture in my world?

I could kick Danika out of the apartment the moment we unlock the cuffs and potentially free myself from a lifelong addiction.

I could, in theory.

But it would take an enormous effort, considering I haven't known her for twenty-four hours, and I can't seem to let her stray even a few inches from me in the bed.

If I'm unwilling or unable to fight the impulse, then that only leaves one other option.

I would have to own it and own her in the process.

THE SUN IS ALREADY bright in the sky when I wake, which is a new experience for me. I'm always up before sunrise. *Always.*

My internal clock is infallible—or so I thought.

Danika is like an electromagnetic pulse disrupting even the most finely tuned device with her presence. She doesn't even have to try. The air around her sparks and flickers with mischief. Even now, something as simple as looking at the clock behind me creates inner conflict because I don't want to wake her by moving. She broke into my house and got us locked up together —why the hell does it matter if I wake her? It shouldn't. It doesn't.

So why am I not moving when I desperately want to know the time?

This is bad.

I need to at least make an effort so that I know I tried to keep my world from crumbling. There's a big difference between admitting defeat after fighting an uphill battle and waving the white flag before shots are even fired. Am I really willing to cave so easily?

I like my life. I like doing exactly as I please and not having to take anyone else into consideration. If I want to eat the same goddamn thing for breakfast every day of my life, there's no one to stop me. Living alone means no unnecessary clutter, no television or music when I want quiet, and no need to worry about the occasional bloodstain on my clothes after an eventful day of work.

Allowing a woman into my world would end all of that. It would be a monumental shift, and I can tell by the knot in my gut that I'm not yet ready to embrace that change.

Time to get my head out of my ass and grow a pair.

I force myself to twist away from Danika and look at the clock on the nightstand behind me. 8:30. It's even later than I expected. Grace is supposed to be here by nine.

Good. It's time to end this ridiculous charade.

As if on cue, Danika lets out a little moan as she rouses from sleep. It's the sexiest fucking sound I've heard in my life, turning my morning wood to tempered steel.

Shit.

"What time is it?" she asks while rubbing her eyes and shifting to her back. Her nipples beg for attention, pressing stiffly against her nightshirt.

"Eight thirty." I clear my throat. "My designer should be here in the next thirty minutes."

"That's good."

We lie on our backs and stare at the ceiling for endless seconds before she breaks the silence.

"I like what she's done with the place. Should have known

Ricky had moved when I saw all the beautiful plants you have, but I wasn't thinking very clearly at the time."

"How'd you know him?" If she actually did know the guy. It's entirely possible she's working for Biba rather than running from him, and everything she's told us is a big fat lie.

"He was an adjunct professor for the photography class I took in my last year of school. He's a really nice guy, so we became friends."

Is that a polite way of saying they fucked?

Jesus, I'm a dumbass. Now I have the image of her getting fucked in my living room, only it's not my cock she's riding, and it pisses me off. Would she be in his bed right now if I hadn't moved in?

My entire body crawls with the need to hurt someone.

"I like plants," I grit out harshly. "They're simple. No fuss required."

"Glad you think so," she continues as if I didn't just bite her head off for no reason. "I can't keep plants alive for the life of me."

"All you have to do is be consistent." This time, I'm able to speak without sounding like a disgruntled man-child.

She peers at me from the corner of her eye and smirks. "Not sure if you've met many artists, but consistency doesn't tend to be our forte."

That has me intrigued. "What kind of artist?"

"I work in digital arts, but I prefer paint—oils and acrylics."

"I guess it works that you're here, then."

"Why's that?"

"Because that's the reason the designer is coming over. She's found a painting for my dining room wall and wants to see what I think, but I don't think anything about art." I may not know about art, but Grace does, and it's one way to test Danika.

"You don't think about it, or you don't enjoy it?" Her openly curious tone, absent of judgment, keeps me from getting defensive. Art has long been a sensitive subject for me.

"I don't see it. All the symbolism and designs that others say they see? It's all just blobs of color to me. I told her to just pick something and put it on the wall, but she insists on finding something that speaks to me. If art speaks, I must be deaf."

"If you ask me, I'd say you don't have to hear it to appreciate it. Blobs of color can be just as enjoyable as a well-crafted statement on the human condition. If it appeals to you, who cares about the reason?"

I think about that for a moment and realize she has a point, except she doesn't understand how hard it is to appreciate something when you know it has a secret meaning and you're the only one who can't decipher it. I don't need art to serve as an additional reminder of how my brain sets me apart from everyone around me. I've had enough of that in my life.

"I'll keep that in mind," I mumble, effectively ending our conversation. The silence that ensues would probably be categorized as awkward for most people, but it doesn't bother me. If there's nothing to say, silence is the natural result. Why should that feel uncomfortable?

I take the time to ground myself by mentally reciting the US capitals in reverse alphabetical order. It's a practice I started when I was young. To this day, I find it's still one of the best ways to clear my head. I'm midway through my second recitation when the door buzzer rings.

"That has to be Grace."

We both keep inhumanly still, straining to hear the door open. The second the lock clicks, I shout for her attention.

"Grace! I need you to come back here and help me."

"Alright," she calls back. "Let me set this thing down first—any bigger, and it wouldn't have fit in the elevator. At least it's light without a frame." Her voice grows louder as she moves toward us down the hall. "Where are you?"

"Back bedroom."

"Okay, I'm coming."

When she appears in the doorway, she takes in the scene with a surprising degree of calm. "Oh! I see. I remember those days." Grace is in her early seventies. The last thing I want to do is picture her doing whatever it is she thinks we were doing.

"It's a long story," I say in lieu of an explanation. "I need you to get the keys—they're on my dresser in the master bedroom."

"Primary, Tommaso. I keep telling you, we call it a primary bedroom now." She raises her carefully manicured brows at me.

"Please, just get the fucking keys, Grace."

As a designer, she came highly recommended, but what I appreciate about Grace is her pragmatism. Despite her generational tendencies and her perfectly coifed appearance, she doesn't stand on ceremony. Grace calls it like she sees it and isn't afraid to get shit done.

"Here we go." The platinum blonde in a black leather pencil skirt waves the key with a grin. I take it from her and unlock the cuffs.

"Let me throw on some clothes, and I'll meet you out there," I tell her before heading to my bedroom. I don't want to make Grace any more uncomfortable than she may already be by meeting with her in my underwear. Once I've got on joggers and a T-shirt, I join her in the dining room, where she's eyeing the painting that now rests against the wall.

"What do you think?" she asks brightly.

I look at the muted colors blended to varying degrees with all manner of brushstrokes and see ... paint on a canvas. I sigh. "It's a painting."

Unfazed, Grace pats my arm. "We'll let it simmer there for a few days. I think it looks amazing here."

"Oh, *wow*." Danika's reverent admiration of the canvas announces her presence. "That is absolutely *stunning*."

"Better be, considering the price," I note.

Grace tsks. "I told you, think of it as an investment."

Danika moves up close to study the painting. "I thought so—it's a Todorovic. His work is exceptional. This one reminds me of Central Park in the fall." She peers back at me before continuing. "These gray strokes here are like the surface of the reservoir on a foggy morning. Absolutely stunning."

So she knows art. I'm still not letting my guard down because she could be an artist *and* a thief.

I look back at the canvas and can see what she means, but I never would have seen it without her explanation. I'm suddenly curious to see her artwork. She must be decently talented if she makes a living off it.

"The painting works as well as any other. You can bill me for it," I tell Grace.

She beams. "Excellent, and I'll get it framed, too."

"Leave it for now," I say, eyeing Danika as she continues to study the canvas. "There's no rush."

Grace gives me a funny look, knowing as well as I do that for someone like me, there's always a rush when it comes to getting work done at my house. I hate disorder. Even a painting set haphazardly against a wall is an annoyance. My comment doesn't make any sense, so I choose not to analyze it. I'd be better off beating my head against a wall.

"Alright," Grace concedes. "You know how to reach me. And Dani, it was lovely to meet you."

I stand frozen as the two say their goodbyes. Her familiarity with my little thief startles me before I remember I left them in the bedroom together while I put on clothes. Did Danika introduce herself as Dani, or did Grace take the liberty of a nickname?

It doesn't matter what her name is or what I call her. The ID I took from her could have been fake. Danika Dobrev may not even be her real name. I have to remember that. This woman walking freely in my home is not to be trusted.

I'm suddenly in a foul mood as I head to the kitchen to start breakfast. Never in my life have I suffered such internal conflict, and I hate it.

"You eat eggs?" I ask briskly when I notice her leaning against the wall beside the fridge.

"Yes, thank you. I really appreciate all you're doing for me."

I start cracking eggs into the skillet with my back to her. "Just keeping you alive so I don't have to deal with the body."

"I hate getting stuck with a dead body."

I'm not great at reading between the lines, but I sense she means something more than her words are saying. It pisses me off. Sometimes I feel like people are speaking in another language, and I'm stuck without an interpreter. It puts me at a disadvantage, and I hate that, especially around someone as potentially dangerous as Danika.

On impulse, I take the paring knife I set out for my avocado and throw it in one swift motion as I spin toward her so that it punctures the wall inches from her head. Partially out of frustration. Partially to make a point.

Her eyes open wide, but the rest of her is frozen. I slowly stalk toward her until I'm close enough to pull the knife from the sheetrock, then touch the tip of the blade to my finger for emphasis.

"It's not a good idea to make fun of the only man between you and the Russian mob," I tell her in a low, even tone.

She swallows, and I'm mesmerized by the movement of her throat—so delicate. So vulnerable.

"I ... I wasn't making fun of anyone but myself and the mess I'm in. I figured my death would be the best-case scenario for you. No more inconvenient disruption to deal with."

My gaze is locked on the feminine slope of her neck, pulse point flickering like an erratic flame. We're close. Too close. It makes me want to be even closer.

"The disposal of a body is more of a pain than people realize," I say distractedly as I give in to the temptation and allow the backs of my knuckles to trail down the soft skin of her neck.

"I suppose you'd know about that sort of thing." She swallows again, her eyes finding mine. "What would you do with my body?" Her words hang in the air, and even I can hear the double meaning. I can't imagine what would bring her to make such an innuendo, but it's dangerous for both of us.

"Don't ask questions unless you're willing to learn the answer." My gravelly warning lingers between us for a handful of heartbeats before I drag myself away and back to cooking.

Neither of us chances conversation again during breakfast. She helps with the dishes, though I take over to make sure everything is cleaned properly. She goes back to her room while I wait for Sante to arrive. I'm not about to shower or leave my place unsupervised with her here. My cousin and his wife can babysit since they're the ones who put me in this mess.

As soon as they arrive, Amelie goes in search of Danika. I half expect Sante to object to his wife being alone in a room with an unknown threat, but I seem to be the only one who sees the potential danger. I still sense that something about Danika doesn't add up.

"How was your night?" Sante asks, fighting back a smirk.

"You don't want to know." I glower at him, refusing to admit I spent the night handcuffed to Danika in her bed. I'd never hear the end of it.

His brows climb on his forehead. "Didn't figure she'd be too much of a handful, but I get it. I know I told Amelie we'd look into things before we sent the girl packing, but I was thinking. This could be a really great opportunity for us to gain some leverage with the Russians—or even just some goodwill."

"What are you saying?" I think he's talking about handing her over to Biba, but I hope I'm wrong because just the suggestion has rage coiling deep in my muscles.

He shrugs. "I figure if she got herself into this mess, it's her own fault. We might as well use our good fortune to our advantage. Who knows what it could be worth for Biba to owe us a favor."

"It's not happening, so forget about it," I ground out harshly.

Sante stills, his eyes narrowing. "What? Last night, you couldn't wait to get rid of her."

"Yeah, that doesn't mean I want to hand her over to Biba."

"Something goin' on I should know about?"

"Nothing going on so long as you don't do anything stupid."

"And turning her over would be stupid," he says slowly as if mulling over the words as he says them.

I nod, satisfied.

My cousin grins, confusing me.

"What?" I demand.

"Just never thought I'd see it happen."

"See what happen?"

"You fall for a girl."

I step closer, my patience worn down to a ragged thread. "I'm going to go shower before I decide to break your face instead."

"As if you could." His eyes dance with challenge.

It's a temptation I can't refuse. I start to turn away as though retreating, then spin back and sucker punch him in the gut.

"That's for yesterday, you dickhead."

He bends at the waist and wheezes through a chuckle. "Now *that* I shoulda seen comin'."

"I wouldn't be too hard on yourself. You always were a little slow."

"Fuck you, Tommy," he calls at my back as I head to my bedroom.

"Fuck you, too, Sante," I echo, a satisfied grin spreading wide on my face.

8

Danika

I don't know how to process what just happened. Technically, it's been an hour since Tommy flung a knife at my head, but the emotions cling to me as though I can still see the blade out of the corner of my eye—the shock and fear washing over me like a December rain. But the chill only lasted for the briefest second before Tommy's scalding touch brought on a very different storm of emotions.

The palpable desire in his eyes—the reverent caress of his hand—there's no denying Tommaso Donati desires me. It's so confusing because I know he resents my presence. Last night, I was certain he was holding me out of irritation. But now ... I'm not so sure.

A strange pull exists between us. It's heady and intriguing and incredibly dangerous.

It's the reason I made that ridiculous body comment. I wish I could say I mentally blacked out during those few seconds and wasn't to blame, but I was all too aware of what I asked. I tasted the words on my tongue, and they were too delicious to resist.

I should *not* be crushing on this man.

The fact that I'm giving it any mental energy at all is inexcusable. Tommy is unpredictable at best and possibly unhinged. He's Mafia. That alone should repulse me. And it does, when I think about it, but my body responds to him without thought. Something about this complicated man speaks to me on an elemental level, and I don't know how to turn that off. Regardless, I have to find a way because having one deranged killer in my life is one too many. I refuse to invite more fear and corruption into my world.

"Danika?" Amelie's quiet call at my bedroom door startles me from my thoughts. I hurry over and let her in.

"Hey, how's it going?" It's such an odd question, considering our situation, but she's been kind, and my manners are too ingrained to be rude.

"I'm good—how about you?" She looks me over worriedly as we sit on the end of the bed facing one another.

"I'm okay. Spent the night cuffed to the bed and had a knife thrown at my head this morning, but otherwise, I'm good."

Amelie stares wide-eyed. "Oh my God. Please tell me you're joking."

I shake my head.

She takes my hands in hers and leans close. "I swear he's not a bad man." She seems to reconsider her words before continuing. "Let's just say this, I'd bet my life that he'd never actually hurt you."

I withdraw my hands, not liking the comfort they give. This woman is Mafia just as much as her husband. It would be idiotic to trust her.

"How long have you and Sante been married?" I ask, hoping to change the subject and learn a bit more about the people who hold my life in their hands.

Her answering smile is a mix of joy and embarrassment. "A little over a month. Our families are close."

I'm not sure why she'd feel compelled to explain being newly married. I get the sense she's implying their relationship isn't conventional, but I'm not sure why.

"Was the marriage arranged?" I ask.

"Oh! No, we just got married quickly. I've gotten used to having to explain the whirlwind romance."

Ah, thus the mention of their families being close. "I see."

"We may not have dated long, nor have I known Tommy for long, but I've known the Donatis for years. They truly are decent people."

My answering nod is far from convincing, inadvertently prompting her to continue.

"Tommy may come off as harsh," she offers quietly, "but that's only because he interacts a little differently than some people. These guys aren't the type to go to doctors or therapists, but if I had to guess, I'd say Tommy is neurodivergent in one way or another. You can't jump to conclusions where he's concerned, that's for sure."

I consider how impeccable he keeps his apartment—the way he insisted on cleaning the dishes himself—and the seemingly confrontational questions he asked the first time we met. I think about how hard it is for me to read him and the conflicting signals he sends, abrasive one minute and kind the next. It would all make a bit more sense in that context.

Then I remember what he said when he threw the knife at me. *It's not a good idea to make fun of the only man between you and the Russian mob.*

If he is somewhere on the spectrum or otherwise cognitively outside the norm, he probably was teased all his life. Any possible mockery could easily be a trigger for him, and if he has trouble catching on to sarcasm, he could easily misinterpret it as a joke at his expense.

I'd been so caught up in his actions that I hadn't truly focused on what he'd said. He thought I was laughing at him. I sigh heavily because while it shouldn't affect the way I see him, it does. He was simply protecting himself. If anyone can relate to that right now, it's me.

"I suppose I see what you mean," I finally say to Amelie. "But he and Sante—all of you—you're Mafia. That hasn't changed." I probably shouldn't admit my fears, yet I want to trust her. To trust all of them. Having someone to rely upon would be a huge relief.

"True, but that means something different for every organization. I can't promise you safety, but I know for certain that the Moretti family is nothing like the outfit Biba runs."

For her, maybe. I'm a different story.

If the Russians are their enemies, they could also see me as the enemy.

"Do you think they'll let me go?" I ask softly, scared there is no good answer to my question.

"I'm not sure," she says hesitantly, her lips pursing. "But I'm confident they won't turn you over to Biba without good reason." She means her words to be reassuring, yet they're far from it. Even she would have to agree that Biba's paternal relationship to me would qualify as a good reason to turn me over. It's enough to solidify my resolve to escape. I have to find a way out.

9
Tommy

Turn her over. Sante's lucky we have so much history together, or I would have beaten him to a fucking pulp for suggesting such a thing. The savage rage that I felt was so overwhelming that it took all my willpower to keep myself under control.

Even now, I can still feel it slithering under the surface, waiting to strike.

My temper has always been a struggle, but this is unlike anything I've experienced in the past. Like a feral alternate personality has clawed its way to the surface and refuses to stay quiet. It could be problematic since I'm already a surly asshole with questionable morals.

Maybe I'm being hard on myself.

I always send my mother flowers for Mother's Day. It may not fully offset the lives I've taken, but it's got to count for something, right?

What the actual fuck is happening right now?

I've never in my life worried about my reputation or conscience. This is all her. My desire for her is twisting me inside out until I don't recognize my own thoughts. All it took was the flash of a mental image of her green eyes framed in ugly purple bruises, rosebud lips split and bleeding, and my visceral reaction was instantaneous. Biba cannot get his hands on her. I won't allow it.

Where does that leave me?

I have no fucking clue, except I know I need more information before I can make any decisions, which is the reason Sante is back at my place babysitting, and I'm meeting up with a colleague.

DiAngelo Farina is a capo that I would normally avoid because of his reputation for being impulsive and because he's my brother's closest friend. But in this case, he has contacts in unlikely places from doing time when he was younger. He's my best shot at getting info on the Russians from the inside. I want to know if what Danika says is true—is Biba hunting a thief? What did she take? How badly does he want her? Does her nightmare have anything to do with why she's on the run?

That last one should be irrelevant, but I can't erase her haunting cries from my mind. Not even the best actress performs when she's asleep. That anguish was real, and I want to know the source. Maybe it has nothing to do with Biba. It's possible.

It's also possible that she's in a whole lot more trouble than she's letting on, and I want to know the truth.

It takes me a few minutes to track down DiAngelo. He told me which pier he'd be at, but that still left some ground to cover. I find him overseeing the docking of a giant cargo container ship. It's important to be present even though we don't play an active role in the daily functions of the ports—if only to make sure the workers know we're watching.

The cranes slowly lumber overhead in preparation to unload while tugboats help position the rig for docking. It's impressive to watch, no matter how many times I see it happen.

DiAngelo gives me a brief, dismissive glance when I stand at his side. "Gotta admit, you got me curious."

"Why's that?" I ask coolly.

"You haven't been back from Sicily long. Can't imagine what you'd need to talk to me about."

"I know you're a man with connections, and I'm looking for information."

Finally, he gives me his full attention, his formidable stare taking my measure. Our fifteen-year age difference would give him a notable advantage if we were to square off. He's built of solid mature mass that can't be duplicated with creatine and trips to the gym. Of course, spending your final teenage years in prison has a way of maturing a person. I had it tough in Sicily, but not that tough. I imagine securing allies was the only thing that kept him alive. Or sane. I can respect his grit, but I'm still not interested in being his friend.

"Your brother know you're digging?"

I have to take a deep, even breath before I can answer because fuck him for treating me like a child. "Can't say that he does. He doesn't know I took a shit this morning either, but that's because he's not my babysitter."

DiAngelo drops his chin a degree, a tiny hint of a smirk tugging at the corner of his lips. "Alright, so what sort of information are you after?" He looks back at the ship, signaling his willingness to hear me out.

"I hear Biba's crew has been under attack."

"It would seem that way."

I think carefully about what I say, not wanting to give away any more than necessary. I have to assume anything DiAngelo hears will go straight to Renzo, and I'm not sure I'm ready to tell him about Danika.

"I also hear it's this Reaper character behind it. They any closer to figuring out who he is?"

He eyes me, probably surprised I know as much as I do. "Don't believe so, but I haven't asked either. You know something?"

"Not about The Reaper. I've heard someone stole something from Biba, though. Heard he's pretty pissed—that's what I'd like to know more about."

"What's it to you?"

"If Biba's facing threats on multiple fronts, the pressure could make him erratic. As someone who's had run-ins with his men before, I'd like to stay informed as best as I can."

DiAngelo considers what I've said, then gives a nod that seems to signal his approval. "I've got a friend not far from here. Let's see what he has to say." He takes out his phone, says a handful of murmured words, then disconnects. "Come with me."

I'm not sure what I expected, but a grizzled old fisherman wasn't it. An arthritic hand gnarled with bulging knuckles holds a burning cigarette while he stares out over the water. Long white hair and whiskers fly every which direction, and he wears a stained white apron over loose-fitting clothes that appear nearly as old as the man himself.

"Grisha, you're still not dead yet?" DiAngelo's greeting surprises me. He knows the man well, and the respect is mutual, judging by the grin that now lights the old man's eyes.

"Not for lack of trying." He raises a glass containing two fingers of clear liquid and downs it in one seamless swallow. "What's this? You bring me a gift?"

I'm not sure what the fuck that means, but it sure as hell puts me on guard.

DiAngelo chuckles. "Not today. This is Renzo's kid brother. He's looking for some information."

Grisha takes a long drag from his cigarette. "And what? You thought you'd bring him here, and I'd spill my guts, as they say?"

Without using his hands, he emits an ear-piercing whistle through his lips. Two men appear at our backs. No, not *our* backs—*my* back. DiAngelo steps aside like a bystander watching a street performance.

I've been set up.

He's not even trying to de-escalate the situation, which tells me he fucking knew this would happen. I don't understand and don't have time to riddle through it. The second a hand clamps down on my shoulder, I shift into survival mode.

I grab the man's wrist and spin around, twisting his arm and eliciting a cry of pain while simultaneously kicking the other man in the gut. My quick reaction gives me the advantage I need to stay on the offensive. I punch the first guy, dodge a jab from the second, then give him a wicked right cross. When I look back at the first, he's slipped a set of brass knuckles onto his fist.

Russians and their goddamn brass knuckles.

So uncouth, but they seem to love the brutality. Fortunately, I'm never unarmed. I slip a switchblade from my boot and stand guard.

The old man squeals with delight.

"That's enough, Grisha. Call it before someone loses an eye," DiAngelo says in a bored tone.

I don't understand what's happening, but I can't afford to take my eyes off my opponents. The old man laughs behind me. "Eh, you never were any fun, but I suppose he's proven himself enough." He barks an order in Russian. The two men stand as if released from a spell and walk away like our fight had never happened.

"The fuck?" I lower my hands but keep myself alert as I look at DiAngelo for clarification.

He pats my shoulder. "Relax, kid. Grisha here doesn't talk to just anyone. You have to prove yourself first."

"A heads-up would have been nice," I say through gritted teeth.

"Not how life works. You have to earn your place."

"Trust me, I know that as much as anyone."

"Ohh, yes," the old man coos. "I think I like him. Come sit down and tell me what you want to know. I may not have any answers, but we can see."

I watch warily as DiAngelo takes a seat on a large wooden spindle with rope coiled around it. Only after the two men stare expectantly at me do I relent and join them.

"I've heard Biba is looking for someone."

"Is that what this is about?" Grisha says gaily. "You're after the reward?"

Reward? Would Biba want Danika badly enough to offer a reward? Or have we miscommunicated, and he thinks I'm talking about The Reaper? That would make much more sense, especially after the triple murder.

"No, this is about a woman," I correct him, ignoring DiAngelo's stare boring into me.

The old man laughs. "Yes, the woman. Biba's put out word that he'll give a million dollars to the man who finds her."

Fuck, this is bad.

Aside from the fact that Biba wouldn't offer a million dollars to catch a simple pickpocket, I can almost hear DiAngelo's teeth grinding together at my side. He's probably dying to grill me about what I know and why I kept it a secret. He'll have to wait.

"He say why he wants her?" I ask.

He gives me a patronizing look. "Biba does not explain himself to no one. You should know that. His business is his alone."

Not what I wanted to hear, but at least I'm not leaving empty-handed. I nod and stand. "I appreciate your time."

"You go as unexpectedly as you come, like a shooting star." He peers down at my boot, where I sheathed my knife. "You're comfortable with knives, are you?" His question is heavy with meaning, and for once, I know exactly what's being implied.

"I'm not The Reaper, if that's what you're asking."

The old man bursts out laughing. "Yes, I like him. Sometime, you come back, and we'll have a drink."

I give him a thin smile and make my exit, hoping to disappear while DiAngelo says his own goodbyes. No such luck. A minute later, he jogs up beside me and pulls me to a stop.

"Whoa, little brother. You're not getting away that easily."

"I'm not your little brother."

"No, but you're Renzo's brother, and I take family seriously—mine or my friend's."

"Look, there's nothing to tell. Sante's cop friend Malone is working the murder of those three Russians. He was asking questions, which I didn't answer, but I learned Biba was after some woman. I wanted to know the score."

Again, his withering stare tries to break me down, but I hold firm. He has a long way to go until he reaches the status of Uncle Lazaro, our guardian in Sicily. That man's scowl could strip paint right off the wall. He took care of us—taught us everything—and did it while being the scariest motherfucker I've ever met. If I can look him in the eye, I can stand tall to anyone.

DiAngelo caves, sighing heavily. "I know I don't have to tell you, but I'm gonna do it anyway. Be careful butting your nose into Biba's business. The man's a lunatic."

"You're right. Your warning is unnecessary, but I appreciate it anyway. And thanks for the introduction. I owe you."

We shake hands and part ways. I'm glad because I'm antsy to get back to my apartment. It's time to make Danika give me some answers, but first, I have one more stop to make. Especially knowing what I do now, it's past time I got a lock on that bedroom door.

"How'd it go?" Sante asks when I return home. He's on his laptop in the living room by himself, and the place is quiet.

"I won't know until I ask her some questions, but it's not

looking good." I speak quietly since I'm not sure where she is. "The girls in her bedroom?"

"Amelie's gone. One of the others picked her up to go see Pippa and the twins in the hospital. She had them early this morning." Sante closes the laptop screen and stands. "Good luck, man. And call me later. I want to know what's happening."

He lets himself out, and I go in search of the little thief. Her bedroom door is open, allowing me to watch her for a moment before she notices my presence. She's sitting on the bed with her knees up, supporting her tablet while she holds a pen to the screen. Her hair is piled in a messy clump on her head, stray tendrils lending her an innocence that I fear she doesn't deserve.

Maybe not, but there's no denying her beauty. Something about the white sheets around her makes me think of a Grecian goddess—like she should have a lyre in her hands rather than a computer. It doesn't seem right that she should be so disarming yet so deceitful at the same time.

I could get the truth from her. I wouldn't enjoy it, but I could do it. Everyone caves eventually with the proper motivation.

I set that thought aside and walk to the bedside to see what she's working on.

"Oh! I didn't realize you were back."

I ignore her comment and motion for her to hand over the device. I can already see the image, but it's so unexpectedly poignant that I need to take a closer look.

"You did this?"

"Yes, I've been working on it for a few weeks."

Her gift is exceptional. And I appreciate the realism of the piece. Everything she's depicted is drawn in perfect detail so there can be no question about what it is. A city street so busy with detail I can feel the energy, every bit in black and white save for a small brown teddy bear abandoned on the curb. The most striking part of all is the sadness it elicits without even knowing why. She's making some sort of statement. As usual, I'm clueless, but I don't have to understand the specific message to be affected by it. Such loneliness and despair—sentiments I know well.

"That's impressive."

"Thank you. I—"

"Stand up," I interrupt, dropping the tablet on the bed.

She follows my orders despite the worry that creases her brow. Her gaze drifts to my right hand and the bloody knuckles she likely noticed when I took the tablet from her.

"You make people see what you want them to see when they look at your artwork. Does that gift extend to other aspects of your life?"

"What do you mean?" Her attempt to scoot backward is thwarted by the nightstand. "What's this about? You're scaring me, Tommy."

It's the first time she's spoken my name. I hate how perfect it sounds on her lips. Her lying, deceitful lips.

I bring my hand to her throat, slowly wrapping my fingers around her. "I spoke with a Russian man today. A man who knows Biba well."

Her face blanches, and I could swear she sways in my hold. "Please, stop," she whispers, sparking my fury.

"No, *you* stop. Stop fucking lying and *tell me the truth*." I need to know what's really going on, and I need her to trust me. I know this isn't the way to gain that trust, but fuck if I know how else to do it.

"I told you—" Again, I cut her off, but this time it's with a kiss.

No, not a kiss.

There's nothing romantic about my desperation. My demands. I use my lips to beg in the only way I know how. I devour her. I worship and plead and rage with the sweep of my tongue and the graze of my teeth. I give her a window into the crippling desire I feel for her—an admission I do not take lightly—in the hope that she might allow me past her defenses. Because if she doesn't find a way to trust me, the consequences may kill us both.

10
Danika

Tommy's kiss is brutally savage yet infinitely tender because while his mouth claims me, the hand he keeps wrapped around my throat stays perfectly still, not once threatening to harm me. The duality is intoxicating. The cuff around my throat a kindness, coupled with a kiss meant to consume.

It's a hypnotic storm I'm helpless to resist.

I've never been a part of an exchange of such intense emotions with another person—not like this. I swear I can see down into the black velvet cave of Tommy's soul, and it's filled with sparkling diamonds. The beauty is breathtaking, and I never want to leave.

When he finally draws his lips away from mine, a hollow ache radiates in my chest.

"The lies have to end, Danika," he breathes, his lips only a breath away from mine.

"I'm not lying," I plead weakly because it's the truth. I did steal something Biba couldn't care less about—I stole myself. And I had every right to do that. He doesn't own me. No one does.

Tommy releases me, his eyes suddenly void of emotion. "Biba doesn't have a million-dollar price on your head because you stole some silly trinket. Sante and I stole a goddamn Lamborghini from the guy when we were younger, and he didn't put a reward out for us. Cut the bullshit and tell me what the *fuck* is going on."

Words escape me.

My jaw hangs open without a sound for endless seconds. "A million dollars? For *me*? I ... I don't know what to tell you."

"How about you start by telling me exactly why Biba would be so consumed with getting his hands on a little artist who stole something meaningless to him? A million dollars is a lot of money over nothing. What did you take—or is there more to it?" His voice is stilted with distrust and frustration.

I understand because I feel the same. How can I possibly give any more information without endangering myself? If he knows I'm Biba's daughter, there's too great a risk he'll turn me over. I have to find a way to keep my identity a secret.

"I'm telling you, it doesn't matter. A priceless necklace. The identity of an informant. Or maybe just a banana from a fruit bowl—something ordinary and seemingly disposable that he's decided he wants back. All he's worried about is his ego, and that won't be mended by simply handing over an object. He wants me to pay, regardless, and that's the bottom line." My rant escalates in intensity with each word as days of bottled emotions swell in a frothy mess to the surface and spill over.

Tommy turns his back to me and roars while he fists a hand in his hair. After several heaving breaths, he spins back around. "You're going to drive me absolutely fucking crazy, you know that?" For someone so seemingly structured and methodical, he's a raging storm of emotions. Like a majestic wild stallion rearing back onto its hindquarters—savage yet regal in its beauty.

He takes my breath away.

And worst of all, the allure of telling him everything is almost overwhelming. How easy it would be to hand over my troubles to someone else—to a warrior like this man—and absolve myself of responsibility. But that's not an option. I am the one and only person who can see this through to the end, whatever that end may be.

"I'm so sorry, Tommy. Truly, I am," I whisper.

A shutter comes slamming down behind his eyes, closing him off from me. I feel it like a slap to the face, the sting intensifying as he turns and walks away. When I hear the echo of a slamming door, I grab my computer and walk quietly down the hall. I'm fairly certain he's shut himself in his bedroom, a suspicion I confirm as I stand alone in the vacant living room.

I look down at my computer, then up at the door. If I want to run, this would be a perfect opportunity. If I disappear from the city, I can't hurt anyone else, and that's all I'm capable of doing lately. I'm not even sure how or why. Tommaso hardly knows me, but I can sense I've wounded him, and that guts me.

Where would I go if I left? This apartment was my only plan. I have nowhere else.

Defeated and overwhelmed, I do what I always do when life

is too much. I draw. Curled in a large armchair, I sketch the image I can't scrape from my brain. The harsh angles of betrayal and desire war on Tommy's face. So much passion. So much discipline. A fierce and deadly battle, all because of me.

I wish I understood why, but even more, I wish I could take it all away. The best I can do, however, is own what I've done, so I immerse myself into my drawing to memorialize the pain I've caused.

I'm so engrossed in my work that I don't notice his return until the click of clamps releasing ricochets through the room. Tommy's sitting on the sofa opening a long, hard case he's placed on the coffee table. When the lid lies flat to expose what's inside, I can see it's a gun case. A rifle? I have no clue except that it's long and very sophisticated. This type of gun looks like something from the military rather than a simple hunting rifle.

I watch raptly as he begins to dismantle the weapon and clean it without any regard for me. Each movement is performed with such ease that I suspect this is something he does often. Like the gun is an extension of his person.

"Are you doing that to scare me?" I ask quietly.

"Don't flatter yourself," he murmurs dryly. "This is what I do every afternoon when I'm not dealing with a home invasion."

Every day? That seems excessive. Guns don't need to be cleaned that often, do they? I can't imagine so, but I also know next to nothing about them. I've gathered that Tommy likes routines and order. He's Mafia. And apparently, he prizes this very expensive-looking gun. I wonder if his interest is personal or business.

"Tommy?"

He gives me the tiniest flit of his gaze before returning to his work.

"Are you a hitman? Is that what you do?" Mafia is a broad term. A man who sits at a computer and facilitates online gambling is very different from the man who goes out and collects the debts. Tommy's made it clear he's dangerous, and I suddenly need to know exactly what that means.

He doesn't keep me guessing.

"It's not just what I do, little thief. It's who I am. Back in Sicily, they called me Death." The words are spoken with such frigid indifference that my entire body would have chilled had I not seen the same man rocked with passionate emotion an hour earlier. He'd like me to think he's a stone-cold killer. And to some extent, he is, but not all of him. Contrary to what he claims, that isn't *who* he is. I feel it down to my bones.

He's trying to push me away, the same as I did to him. And because that's probably best, I let him have his wish. I go back to my sketch of a man at war with himself and hope for my sake that the better man wins.

11
Tommy

How could silence be awkward? Silence is simply the absence of someone else intruding on my thoughts, vying for my attention. That sort of peacefulness has never bothered me. I thought I was immune to what others describe as the discomfort of an awkward silence.

I thought wrong.

Two hours pass before Danika retreats to her room. Two long hours of warring thoughts bombarding me with demands to say something—do something—fix it. I hate how inept I feel at navigating this standoff. Danika isn't telling me everything. I know there's more to her story, but I can't find a way to coax the truth from her.

I told myself to put fear into her when I confronted her in her bedroom—that having her fear me was worth our safety. Fear and pain are powerful motivators, but I couldn't bring myself to do it. I couldn't hurt her with those wide evergreen eyes staring back at me.

So where does that leave me?

I have no fucking clue, which made the silence between us so undeniably frustrating. I felt this oppressive pressure to say something that would convince her to trust me, but without any idea what words might work, that pressure had no outlet. The atmosphere between us felt dense and stagnant like ocean air trapped on the coast before a storm pushes through.

I couldn't even be relieved when she retreated to her room because it left me with no choice but to make the call I'd been putting off all afternoon. I'd used her presence as an excuse. Now, I have none. It's time to tell my brother what's been going on, especially after today's adventure with DiAngelo, though Renzo has probably already been given a debriefing, considering how close those two have become since I left for Sicily.

I take a minute to put a precooked meal in the oven before dialing Renzo's number.

"Yeah?"

"You have a minute?" I ask.

"Sure, I'm just leaving Terina's place. What's up?" Renzo has kept an eye on our sister ever since she lost her husband and then our dad died within a matter of months. That was years ago, but she's never fully recovered.

"She okay?"

"Yeah, she's fine. Just checking in with her. What did you need?"

"I wanted to talk to you about what's going on with the Russians."

"Yeah." He sighs. "That doesn't seem to be going away. D and I were just talking about it earlier."

Interesting. DiAngelo, or D as my brother calls him, must not have told my brother about our excursion this morning, or Renzo would have mentioned it right off.

"What's your take on the situation?" I ask.

"If I had to put money on it, I'd say Biba's on the brink of war with Reaper's crew. I'm curious if the two have met and whether we can find out what Biba knows about the guy. I'd rather be two steps ahead should the dominos start falling in our direction."

"You think we'll feel the effects?"

"Don't see a way around it. Something that big is bound to spread. Why're you asking?"

I weigh my words carefully. "I've got some information, but I don't know how it fits in the picture. It may not be relevant at all except that it has to do with Biba."

"Okay..." he prompts me to continue.

"Two days ago, a woman broke into my place."

"No shit?"

"She told me Biba was after her for taking something from him. She claims she knew the guy who owned my apartment before me and the fact that she happened into a Moretti home is pure coincidence."

Renzo stays quiet. If there's one thing we can agree on, it's that coincidences are bullshit.

"I wasn't ready to release her until I knew more about the

situation, so I did some digging. Turns out Biba's got a million-dollar reward out for her."

"Fucking Christ, tell me you don't still have this girl stashed at your place, Tommy. The last thing we need is to involve ourselves in Biba's mess."

I'm fairly certain anything he could have said would have irritated me, but his quick reprimand and dismissal of my judgment on the situation are especially abrasive.

"For all I knew, she was sent by Biba or some other faction in an outright attack. You saying I should have just sent her on her merry way without asking a few questions?" Each word cuts with my growing anger.

"What I'm saying is you should have run it by me. Something that sensitive needs to be handled carefully."

"And I'm not competent enough to do that on my own, is that it?"

"That's not what I said," Renzo bites back.

"Check again, big brother, because that's exactly what you fucking said." I'm too pissed to keep talking. I hang up, knowing it won't help matters, but I'm unable to care.

Fuck him.

He and our father, back when the man was alive, always questioned my abilities and motives. In their eyes, if they couldn't understand my rationale, it must have been wrong. If I didn't have the right words to explain myself, I didn't know what I was talking about. Even compulsive behaviors irrelevant to my critical thinking skills somehow became excuses for dismissing my opinions.

I didn't have the understanding or confidence to rebuke them back then. I'm not a kid anymore, and I'm done being overlooked and dismissed. If Renzo wants me to prove myself, then I will. I'll prove myself by not rolling over. I'll show him that I'm just as capable as he is, and I'll do it my way.

All that leaves me to do is figure out what *my way* entails.

Fantastic.

I sit at the kitchen bar and lay out my situation as objectively as I can. Biba is after Danika. He's so intent on getting his hands on her that he's offered a million-dollar reward. His motive must be substantial, which means she didn't just take something insignificant. But she refuses to tell me what she took. Why?

The most logical reason for her silence is fear. Fear of what? That I'd take the item from her? That I'd turn her over to Biba if I knew what she'd taken? At this point, she's seen that not even a million dollars is incentive enough for me to turn her over. What then? What has her scared enough to risk her own life because that's what she's doing. I could have killed her multiple times over, yet I haven't laid a finger on her, and it still hasn't been enough to convince her to surrender her secrets.

The only way any of it makes sense—the only thing worth protecting with your life—is the life of someone you love. Maybe what she stole isn't a what; maybe it's a who. Could she be hiding someone?

Man trouble.

The realization hits me with the force of a city bus.

Was I mistaken in assuming the man in her "man trouble" was Biba? Could she have been referring to a lover instead? Someone whose location she's protecting with her life?

How had the thought not occurred to me? I'm absolutely livid with myself. With her. With the entire world. Danika Dobrev is not allowed to belong to someone else. She can't come crashing into my world on behalf of another man. I won't allow it.

She can't belong to another man, not if she stays here with me.

With that sentiment echoing poignantly in my head, I take dinner out of the oven, make a plate for her, then take it to her bedroom. "Dinner," I announce flatly, setting the plate on the dresser with a clatter.

"Oh, thanks." Uncertainty coats her words.

I take a subtle look around. She has everything she could need in here for the night, so I don't feel bad when I leave the room and lock the door behind me. I bought the lock so I could sleep without feeling in danger. That still applies, except now there's more to it. Now, I'm locking her in because I don't want to risk losing her.

"Tommy?" The sweet innocence in her voice freezes me mid-motion.

"Just locking the door for the night," I explain, hoping to keep her from panicking.

"You're locking me in?" she asks, her voice moving closer with each word until I know she's only a step away. The door handle jiggles. "What if there's a fire or something?"

"There won't be." And even if there were a fire, I'd burn alongside her before I'd let her die alone.

For the first time since she careened into me in front of that police station, I'm blanketed by a sense of certainty. Of purpose.

I want Danika Dobrev.

Everything else is superfluous. Her motives and secrets. The danger surrounding her. I don't care whether my reason for wanting her is rational or not. Even my obligation to my family pales compared to my driving need to protect this woman and make her mine.

I've only experienced a similar sensation once before, and it led me to spend four years of my life away from home because I knew I needed Sante in my life more than I needed anything else.

I don't regret that decision one bit. I listened to my gut, and I'm glad I did.

It's time to do that again. I'm done making excuses.

Feeling a renewed sense of certainty, I eat my dinner before allowing myself to give in to my curiosity. A new door lock wasn't the only thing I bought earlier today. I gave in to a rare impulse and bought a nanny cam. Is it an invasion of privacy? Sure, assuming someone has a right to privacy. Danika signed away those rights the minute she broke into my home. Besides, if she won't give me answers, she's giving me no choice but to go in search of information.

I open my laptop in my office and launch the software I installed right after placing a tiny camera in the fake floral arrangement on her dresser. It was the only viable option given the short notice and my minimalistic decor preferences. Regardless, it works perfectly.

The second she appears on my computer screen, something primitive deep inside me uncoils. Danika sits on the side of her bed looking at a phone. She's texting someone.

The darkness lurking within me bristles.

Who is she texting? If she's protecting a man, could she be texting him?

There goes any semblance of a good mood. I want to snap that phone in half, then hunt down this asshole to punish him for putting her in so much danger. What kind of worthless sack of shit would hide and let his woman act as a shield for him? The sort who doesn't deserve that woman in the first place.

She eventually sets aside the phone and stands at the

window at the edge of the camera's reach. I glance at the wall of windows nearby and see that the sun's departure has left tangerine ripples across a sapphire sky. I wonder if that's what she's looking at or if she has her sights and thoughts focused elsewhere. What I wouldn't give to know what she's thinking. Rather than assuage my curiosity, the camera seems to be making it worse.

I didn't think I could sleep knowing she was free to roam my house. Now I *know* I won't be able to rest until she's already fast asleep. I don't want to miss a moment of her movements. How could I possibly sever the one tenuous connection I have to her?

I can't, which is why I end up with soap in my eyes while showering with the laptop on my bathroom vanity. Probably serves me right for watching her. I still don't fucking care.

12 Danika

My door is still locked when I wake in the morning. It's early, but not too early to call Sachi. I think it's time to tell her what's happened since we parted.

"I know you said for emergencies only, but you gotta keep a girl in the loop!" My best friend jumps right into a lighthearted scolding.

"I know, Sach. That's why I'm calling."

"How are you? Is everything okay?"

I scrunch my nose, though she can't see me. "I'm good, but things are ... complicated." I launch into the crazy story that has been my life over the past two days. Sachi listens raptly, occasionally inserting a gasp or a single word of disbelief.

"You are going to make a *fortune* when you sell the movie rights to your life," she says when I'm done.

I have to laugh because the outlandishness of it all is truly astounding. "Assuming I make it out of here," I add, sobering both of us.

"What are you going to do?" she asks in a hushed, worried voice.

"I can't stay here, Sach. It's too risky for everyone involved. Even if Tommy is truly intent on helping me, this is so much bigger than he knows, and he could end up getting himself killed. I'm not okay with that. And if I make the wrong call and stay, and they end up turning me over, I'll wish I was dead."

"No, Dani. Don't say that."

My body wilts with a weary sigh. "The point is, I've got to run."

"Okay, then let's make a plan."

"I've been thinking ... he's got a lock on my bedroom door, and the lock picks were gone from my bag when he gave it back to me, but I have a ton of bobby pins. Knowing what I do now about how locks work, I think I can use those to get free."

"Do you know where you'd go from there?"

"That's the biggest problem, and I've been afraid to look online for ideas since I'm stuck using his internet connection. Can he use that to see my search history?"

"I'm not sure, but it sounds like something that would happen in the movies, so it's probably best to avoid it. How about this? When you leave, go to a nearby hotel and text me where to find you. In the meantime, I'll look into ideas. We could set you up at a women's shelter outside the city somewhere just until you can sort something else out."

"That sounds more appealing than a homeless shelter."

"For sure. Okay, do we have a plan, then?"

"Yeah. I'll buzz you as soon as I'm somewhere safe."

"Perfect." She pauses, her voice earnest when she continues. "Be safe, Dani. Love you bunches."

"Love you, too, Sach."

I disconnect and look at my text messages before stashing my phone back in my bag. My mother still hasn't responded to my text from last night. I don't want to panic, but I can't imagine why she wouldn't have texted me back. The possibilities clamp tight around my chest and squeeze until it's hard to breathe.

I get lost staring out the window, desperately wishing I could check on her. I hate that she could be in danger because of me, but she was adamant that I ran. Honoring her wishes is yet another reason I need to get out of here. If something has happened to her, I can't let that be for nothing.

A throat clears, making me realize I'm no longer alone. My bad ear was toward the door, and with my turbulent thoughts distracting me, I didn't notice Tommy unlocked the door and was now leaning against the doorframe.

We watch one another for long seconds. The pulsating tension between us hasn't dissipated. If anything, it's only gotten worse, and the fact that he's not wearing a shirt isn't helping. His chiseled torso is covered in sweat. It's clear his affinity for routines includes working out. The man has hardly an ounce of fat on him.

Come on, Dani. Keep your head in the game.

"Am I allowed out?" I ask.

"Told you, it was only for the night." His rugged voice sends a cascade of tingles down my spine.

"Because you think I might try to kill you in your sleep?"

He shrugs his broad shoulders. "Better to be safe than sorry."

"I don't get it. If you don't trust me, and I'm such a pain, why not let me go? Honestly, I'm having trouble understanding why you haven't turned me over for the reward. None of this makes any sense. And I know I'm not in a position to make demands, but the uncertainty makes all of this that much harder for me." I'm not sure why I'm confronting him like this. Frustration. Maybe a twinge of hurt. I don't like him thinking I'm some sort of diabolical criminal. Is it so bad that I haven't told him what I stole? Is that the reason for his glacial demeanor ever since our kiss?

Tommy prowls closer. My heart stutters and stumbles with anticipation. I'm never quite sure what he might do, and the suspense is oddly invigorating.

Once he's close enough, he weaves his fingers into my hair at the nape of my neck. "Maybe I've decided to keep you for myself," he says distractedly, his eyes slowly roaming across my face.

Keep me? As in ... *permanently?*

His admission stuns me.

Does he mean keep me as a prisoner? Is that the real reason he locked the door last night—not to protect himself but to prevent me from leaving? Maybe, but as I stare deep into his tempestuous eyes, I don't feel like a captive. If anything, I feel like a siren under Tommy's fiercely determined gaze.

"Is that what's happening here?" I breathe. "Are you planning to keep me?"

"All that matters is that, for now, you're mine." He pauses as if wanting to do or say something but thinks better of it and releases me.

My body sways. I might have quit breathing—his proximity does that to me. And to hear him say I'm his ... it's surreal. I knew he desired me, but this feels like more than attraction, and I'm not sure how I feel about it.

While I'm still reeling, he surprises me again when he extends a black credit card toward me between two fingers. "I know you weren't able to bring much when you ran, so you should order new."

I take the card and stare at it in confusion. "You mean ... you want me to buy clothes?"

"I mean, you should get whatever you want. Whatever makes staying here feel more comfortable for you."

God, I'm so confused. He locks me away and tells me he's keeping me, then gives me carte blanche to use his credit card? This man is an ever-changing riddle that I have no chance of solving.

When I look back at him, I see that his gaze has wandered down to my chest. I realize I'm wearing a thin camisole without a bra. As if preening with satisfaction, my nipples pebble and pull in his direction. The physical response is so sudden and arousing that I inadvertently gasp. Our eyes lock, and his dilated pupils remind me of a jungle cat ready to pounce.

Tommy lifts his fingers to the pulse point at the base of my neck before slowly lowering them to the neckline of my camisole, sliding them from one side to the other as if testing his restraint.

His touch has my body so greedy for more that my legs tremble.

"You could always forgo clothes," he murmurs. "I wouldn't complain."

My gaze shamelessly drifts over his sculpted chest. As an artist, I can't deny the exceptional beauty of his masculine form. As a woman, I'm tempted to lick the beads of sweat from his skin. This man twists my thoughts and insides into such knots I have no idea what I think or how I feel. I shouldn't want him, but my own selfish desire has me asking myself if this man didn't enter my life for a reason. He's Mafia. That should end the discussion entirely, except ... only someone like him has a chance at fending off Biba. If I didn't run, I'd need someone like that to keep me alive.

And if you get him killed in the process?

That thought is enough to finally slap some sense into me. I clear my throat and step back, dissipating the electric chemistry buzzing in the air around us. "Thanks. I'll have a look online after breakfast."

He doesn't respond. When I look up to see his reaction, I'm left wanting because his fathomless stare is as guarded as ever before he walks away. If he does have feelings for me, one way or another, he's unwilling to share them. I wonder if he ever shares that sort of thing with anyone.

I have to wonder if I'm overcomplicating the matter. Maybe he's attracted to me, and that's all there is to it. Hell, perhaps he's just horny. Could be, but Tommy strikes me as a man of action rather than words. I suspect he'd be more direct if that were the extent of his interest. Keeping me implies a degree of commitment, doesn't it?

Not if he wants to keep you as his sex slave.

Okay, that's enough of this delightful little dive down the rabbit hole. Instead of guessing at his thoughts and motives, perhaps I should focus more on his actions. Or maybe I shouldn't. Because when I think of all the little ways he's shown me kindness, I feel even worse about the danger he could be in. He doesn't deserve that, and if I have any self-respect at all, I'd free him of my presence sooner rather than later.

Finally, something all the voices in my head can agree upon. The only problem? I didn't expect sooner to arrive quite so quickly. I find myself locked in my room after breakfast so Tommy can shower and decide it's as good a time as any to run. If I truly believe leaving is best and that time is of the essence, I need to go. Now.

I throw my things back into my bag, making sure to leave his credit card on the dresser.

I can hear the faint thrum of water running, so I get to work. Bobby pins aren't nearly as easy to work with as Gran's "keys," but they suffice. Interior locks aren't exactly made to thwart trespassers. In less than a minute, I get the door open and hurry from my room and out of the apartment. I press the elevator call button at least fifteen times before it finally arrives, and a minute later, I'm walking free on a busy Manhattan street.

Of course, free is relative.

I'm no longer physically captive, but paranoia is my new prison. Each person I pass is suspect. Every glance in my direction is a possible threat. I am completely unprotected out here in the open. It's terrifying.

I keep my head down and make a beeline for the first hotel I see. Once inside, I pull out the small stash of money I still have from home. I'm a little surprised Tommy didn't take it along with my lock pick tools. It's things like that that make me think he's a decent man beneath it all, which is why it's best that I'm gone.

I book a room for a single night and head upstairs, not

breathing easily until I'm safely tucked away in my room. I did it. I'm in the wind. Sitting on the white cotton duvet, I look at my new sanctuary and discover that I don't feel the relief I expected to feel. I'm free, but I'm also alone.

I get out the phone and text Sachi the hotel name and room number. At least I get one last visit with her. After today, I'm on my own.

Sachi texts that she'll be by shortly. I prop myself against the headboard, cuddle the down pillows, and scroll through daytime TV until a knock sounds at the door. I hurry over to let in my friend, but when I open the door, it's not Sachi on the other side. It's six feet of bristling Italian, hands clenched furiously at his sides.

13
Tommy

THE SOUND OF MY ALARM STINGS MORE THAN I THOUGHT IT would. I knew Danika would try to run. She's too terrified not to. So why do I feel a stab of betrayal knowing she did exactly what I expected her to do?

I must have been holding on to some shred of hope that it wouldn't happen. That kind of irrational nonsense only adds to my irritation. The one silver lining to this turn of events will be getting to gut the man she's protecting, should she lead me to him.

I towel off and check my phone. The trackers I placed in her things triggered my geofencing perimeter alarm when she exited the building. All three are still on her and sending a strong signal from down the block. Time to get dressed and see where she's going.

Most people would jump on a train and be halfway to Philly by the time I caught up with them. Not Danika. She's two blocks over at a Holiday Inn Express.

I swear to Christ, if I find her in a room with a man, I'll bury the motherfucker.

A hundred bucks buys me the room number. GPS works great on flat ground but can be a nightmare when it comes to high-rise buildings. Fortunately, money helps fill in the gaps.

As I ride the elevator to the third floor, I check my weapons one last time. I came prepared. When the elevator door chimes my arrival, I envision the bell ringing in a boxing match. Time for the show to begin.

I knock on the door to the room number given to me by the dickhead kid at the registration desk. Danika swings the door wide open as if welcoming a long-lost friend. She didn't even check the peephole, for Christ's sake. She was expecting someone, and judging by the sudden horror on her face, it wasn't me.

"Tommy?"

I push past her and scan the room for other occupants. If she planned to meet a man here, her reaction to my arrival leads me to believe I got to her first, but I'm not making any assumptions. I don't see any signs of anyone else, just an empty room with a TV playing an old 90s sitcom.

"Did you track me?" she demands from behind me while I check the bathroom.

"Of course I did." I peek under the bed next, but like most modern hotel beds, it's enclosed. She's alone, but she was definitely expecting someone. Good. I'll be waiting when he gets here.

Satisfied, I turn my attention to her with a withering look. "Care to tell me who it is you're meeting?"

Her brows knit together, and she nips at her bottom lip. "No one?" she asks as if that might suffice.

I step forward. She takes a step back.

"Don't lie to me, Danika. I know you were expecting someone other than me at that door just now. Who is it?" I bite through clenched teeth.

"Just a friend who was going to help me get out of town, okay? It's no one to you."

"No one? It's someone you're willing to trust over me."

"I barely know you, Tommy." Her shoulders sag. "I don't understand why you're doing this. Why not just let me go?"

"Because that's not the kind of man I am. Why not have waffles for breakfast or skip my morning run? Why clean my gun when I just cleaned it last night and the night before? Because I have to have things a certain way, or I feel like I'll crawl out of my skin."

"What does that have to do with me? If I'm gone, you can get back to having things the way you want them."

"Not if you're the thing I want." My words linger in the air like a single delicate snowflake. "You made me a part of this, Dani. I can't just erase you from my mind." She's rooted herself more deeply inside me than she could ever know. Moving on wouldn't just be a matter of erasing her. I'd have to lobotomize a part of my brain.

"What do you want from me, Tommy?"

"I want you to let me help you."

"Help me ... or keep me?" she asks hesitantly.

I use the pad of my thumb to free her bottom lip from between her teeth. "Would it be so bad to be mine?" I ask quietly, cursing myself the moment the words are out because they reek of vulnerability.

"That depends," she answers honestly. "If by yours, you mean lock me in a room and control—"

"No, Danika," I cut her off, engulfed in frustration. "I know it's started off poorly, and I can't explain any of it except that I don't want you to go. I want to see you paint and watch the funny way you spread jelly on your toast. I want to stare at the tiny hint of ass cheek that peeks out from under your shorts, but most of all, I want to know that you're safe. I locked the door because I was scared this exact thing would happen, and Biba would get his hands on you before I could stop him."

My tirade ends, blanketing us in a suffocating silence.

"Oh." One syllable, two letters, and a world of meaning encapsulated in the tiny word.

"If I promise no more locked doors, will you come back?" It's my only concession and the only time I'll ask, and I'm only doing so because I'd rather have her return of her own free will than force the issue. Not just because it would be easier. I want the damn woman to want me.

"But you and your family are going to end up in danger. You may not believe me, but that's a big part of why I left. I'm terrified someone will end up hurt because of me—it's not right for me to let that happen."

"It's right if I say it is." I step closer, and this time, she doesn't retreat.

"I don't understand, Tommy," she whispers.

"Neither do I," I admit before pulling her close and kissing her. It feels so incredible to have her in my arms that I'm able to set aside my desperation and relish the taste of her. While her tongue is sweet, her surrender is the most delicious thing I've ever known. Her body molds into mine on a sighed breath that I devour with ardent intensity. I try to show her with each press of my lips that I don't care about the danger surrounding her or the limited time we've known each other. I don't care that none of it makes sense. I'll walk through fucking fire for her.

A knock on the door turns our blistering kiss into a pile of smoldering ashes. Her eyes lock with mine, a flash of fear turning emerald irises to evergreen. We turn toward the door at the same time. She reaches for the handle, but I angle myself in front of her and take the lead.

"I don't think so, little thief," I tell her quietly.

"It's just my friend," she says with a note of urgency in her voice.

"Good, I love meeting new people," I say dryly, then open the door to a tiny, doll-like woman with black and purple hair gaping up at me.

"Sach, I'm here." Danika pushes past me and hugs her friend. Her very female friend.

"*That's* who you were meeting?" I ask, unable to hide my surprise.

"Yeah, why? Who did you think it would be?"

I slip my mask of composure back into place. "No one."

The woman continues eyeing me like she expects me to pull out a machete and massacre them at any second.

"Sachi, this is Tommy," Danika introduces. "Tommy, this is my best friend, Sachi."

"This who you've been texting?" I ask.

She studies me for a second, probably wondering how I

know what she's been up to. "Yeah, and my mom, except I haven't heard back from her. It's got me worried."

Sachi leans in and whispers something to Danika.

"He's okay, really," Dani says with a tiny glance in my direction. "We've been talking, and I think there's been a bit of miscommunication."

Her friend continues to watch me warily. Smart of her except gaining her approval would probably go a long way in convincing Danika to trust me.

"Okay, so what does that mean?" Sachi asks.

"It means ..." Danika peers at me again. "I think I'm going to stay with Tommy for a bit."

I swear to God, relief has me sprouting wings and lifting three feet off the ground.

Sachi nods. "In that case, I can run by and check on your mom and gran."

Danika chews her lip, something I've noticed she does when she's uncertain. It's fucking adorable and highly inconvenient because it makes me hard.

"I'd love that, but I'm also worried about putting you in danger."

"You won't. I'll borrow my roommate's Instacart lanyard and roll up with a bag of groceries. Easy peasy." She grins broadly.

"I don't know. I'm still not crazy about it. What if he's watching the place?"

"Then he learns your mom needed grapes and a loaf of bread. It's going to be fine, trust me."

"Okay, but you better be careful." Danika gives her friend another hug, then looks back at me. "No more locks, right?"

"No more locks," I agree.

Sachi narrows already slender eyes at me and points a finger in warning. "You better not hurt her, you hear me?" The girl's got balls for someone so tiny.

"Only did it for her own good. I knew she'd take off the first chance she got, and she's a hell of a lot safer at my place than on the run."

She grunts as if to say we'll see about that, then turns back to Danika. "I'll go check on your mom as soon as I leave here, okay?"

"Sounds good, and thanks again. You be safe."

"Ditto, babe." The two hug fiercely. I'm glad Danika has a friend like that and fucking thrilled that the friend doesn't have a dick.

We head out at the same time. Sachi goes south while we head north back to my place.

"I've got some emails to catch up on," I tell her once we're back in the safety of my apartment. "You good?"

"Yeah." She nods, then takes her things back to her bedroom before returning to the living room. We spend the next couple of hours on our computers in a companionable silence. I think we both appreciate the break from constant tension and chaos.

She keeps her phone beside her the whole time, and I make a mental note to get her a real goddamn phone. The piece of crap she's using isn't remotely reliable enough. It serves its purpose, though, chiming halfway through our sandwich lunch.

As she reads a long message, her chin starts to quiver.

My entire body goes rigid, ready to shred whoever or whatever has upset her.

"Sachi says Mom was hurt. She hasn't answered my text

because she was at the doctor getting checked out. Sach says Mom has a black eye and claims she's fine, but Sach can tell she's moving stiffly." Tears stream down her cheeks. "I knew this would happen."

"You think it was Biba?"

"I know it was," she says hoarsely, emotions choking back her voice. "He threatened to hurt them if I ran. This is a warning, and I'm scared to death of what he'll do next. I didn't even want to run because of this exact reason, but they made me. They said they'd rather die than let him take me, but how am I supposed to live with that?"

She's inadvertently given me a world of information, her distress hampering her inner filter. I'm not sure what to make of it, though. Biba warned her not to run? Did he do that before or after she stole from him? How does he know her well enough to find her mother? They had to have had contact prior to the theft—maybe even an ongoing connection. And if he wanted to use Danika's mom to draw her out, why not kidnap her mother?

I did a basic background search on Danika already, but I think I need to dive a little deeper into her family. With her Slavic last name, her father might even work for Biba—there's no telling how she might be connected to the man. The city hasn't digitized the records I want to access, and working hours are almost over, so I need to hurry if I'm going to get this done today.

"Here's what's going to happen," I tell her in a calm but firm voice. "We're going to find a safe place for your family to stay while we sort this out. I need to look into a few things to get that all sorted, though."

"What kind of things?" she asks, her anxiety creasing her forehead.

I smooth the skin with the caress of my thumb. "Nothing you

need to worry about, but I need to know that if I leave, you'll still be here when I get back."

Once Biba knows I'm involved, I won't want to leave her unprotected, but at this point, he has no clue where to find her. She should be safe, so long as she stays put.

She nods, and while I can sense she's scared, I think she's telling me the truth. I suppose I'll find out when I get back.

I lean in and allow myself a brief inhale of her sweet scent, then murmur, "I'll be back soon."

14
Danika

I GIVE MYSELF OVER TO THE TEARS FOR THE FIRST TIME since my life careened off the tracks and detoured straight into a ravine. I haven't had the luxury of letting myself fall apart. With Tommy gone and my mother in danger, I can't fight back the emotions any longer.

I cry deep, uncontrollable sobs that leave me exhausted on the sofa, which is where Tommy finds me fast asleep when he returns home.

"Wake up, Danika. You have some explaining to do."

The words slowly filter into my consciousness. "Huh? What

are you talking about?" I sit up and rub my eyes, trying to get my bearings.

Tommy stands over me, arms crossed stiffly. "I've done some digging, and it doesn't take a genius to connect the dots."

"What do you mean?" I'm finally feeling awake but still clueless.

"I'm talking about you. Danika Dobrev. That's your mother's maiden name. It's what's on your birth certificate because your father is listed as John Doe." He cocks his head to the side. "You said you stole something, but after seeing your birth certificate, there's another much more plausible explanation for Biba's willingness to pay such a huge amount of money for you, but I don't want to believe it. Tell me I'm wrong, Danika. Tell me you're not Biba's daughter."

His words are eerily calm like the glassy surface of a dark lake concealing a terrible monster below. Tommy's not a monster, is he? He said he wanted to keep me safe. Would his opinion change if he knew the truth? I'm terrified to find out.

"I have no idea what you're talking about." I pull my knees to my chest as if they're a shield. It's laughable because I'm at this man's mercy in every way.

He stalks closer, eyes narrowing as he towers over me. "I'll ask you one more fucking time." His savage words slash at me as he holds his phone out. "And I want the truth, or I'll call Biba myself right goddamn now. Are you his fucking daughter?"

Desperation is quicksand tugging at my body, its unrelenting weight pressing against my lungs and blurring my vision. I'm terrified to tell him the truth, yet I have no choice. I see it in his eyes. He'll do it. He'll hand me over in a heartbeat if he thinks I'm lying to him. My only hope is that telling the truth doesn't end in the same fate.

"Yes." The single word is nothing but a whisp of air. A shameful, ugly exhalation.

Tommy waits as I collect myself to explain.

"Biba's technically my father, but he's never played any role in my life. As you probably know, he has two sons with his wife. My mom and I were his dirty little secret. He walked away not long after I was born, refusing to acknowledge us even in private. And now?" Tears burn the back of my eyes. "Now that he's found a use for me, he seems to think he owns me."

"A use for you?" Tommy asks with a sneer.

"He summoned me five days ago to inform me he'd arranged my marriage to some terrifying man named The Reaper." I shake my head. "I can't let that happen, Tommy. I won't do it. Please, *please*, don't turn me over to him." My voice is reed-thin, emotion clogging my throat.

Tommy takes an unsteady step backward. "When you said you stole something from him, you meant yourself." The words are a soft realization.

"At first, it was the easiest way to explain why I was hiding, but once I realized you knew him, I was scared you'd turn me over ... or worse."

"Worse?"

I bite my bottom lip, hoping I don't anger him. "If you were his enemy, I wasn't sure what you might do to me thinking you were hurting him." The possibilities are too horrific to even think about.

I take a risk and go stand in front of Tommy, my gaze hesitantly lifting to his. "I'm not his to give away. Please don't tell him where I am. If you want me to leave, I'll go. No one ever has to know I was here—"

Tommy's hand gently but firmly fists in the back of my hair, cutting off my plea. His grip is secure but not painful, as though his purpose is purely to claim my attention. His eyes glint with a primal savagery I've never seen before, and I can't make sense of it because he doesn't know me well enough to elicit such emotion, does he?

"Is there someone else?" His snarled question catches me off guard.

"What do you mean? Someone else after me?"

"No, is there a man in your life? Is there ... someone ... else?" He says each word as if it tastes worse than the one before.

"No. I'm not seeing anyone." I'm so confused as to what that has to do with anything.

"Look at me," he demands, waiting to continue until my searching gaze meets his. "You're right. You can't be his to give away if you're already mine."

"What?" It's more of a shocked exhale than an actual question. "What does that mean?"

"It means you're going to marry me."

Words escape me.

He can't be serious. I can't marry him. Biba would be furious, and I know what happens when Biba is angry. And that's not even taking into account that I hardly know Tommy. "No, I ... I can't do that."

His hands cup either side of my face before he brings his lips close to mine but not to kiss me. The intoxicating uncertainty of what he might do next has me entranced. My breathing quickens to shallow pants as he slowly nips my bottom lip between his teeth, then allows his tongue to drift languidly over the heated flesh. My core warms and pulses with need so intensely that my body instinctively sways toward his.

"You can, and you will, and not just for your protection." His hand slips under my shirt, then down inside my shorts and beneath my panties. He keeps me rooted in place with the intensity of his stare. Not that I want to flee. His touch feels incredible as he cups my sex, his thick middle finger easing itself deep inside me.

I gasp for air, my hands clinging to his shirt for support.

"You'll agree to be mine because that's what your body wants." His finger glides in and out of me a couple of times before he retracts the hand and brings it up between us, displaying the shameful degree of arousal coating his finger. Eyes locked on mine, he inserts the finger into his mouth and sucks it clean.

It's the hottest thing I've ever seen. My lips part as I watch him, enthralled.

"Want to know what you taste like, little thief?" His voice is worn leather and the smoldering embers of a fire. The scent and sound and texture invade my senses to demand my allegiance.

I nod because I have to. He wants me to say yes, and at that moment, I want to give him anything and everything he wants.

He brings his finger to my lips as though to give me a taste, then detours at the last second, his hand dropping to cuff my neck. He brings his lips a breath away from my ear and whispers, "*Mine.* You taste like mine, little thief."

Oh, holy hell, I'm in trouble.

It's the most combustible, delicious thing I've ever heard a man say, real or fictional. How does logic stand a chance when up against that sort of temptation?

What's to say marrying him doesn't make sense?

And that's exactly why a man like Tommy is so dangerous. He's everything I shouldn't want and everything I desperately need.

"Being yours and getting married are two different things." I try to carve my way through the haze of desire and think rationally, though I'm not sure I've accomplished my goal. I'm not even sure what I'm trying to say. I just know I need to think this through.

Tommy's chin lifts the tiniest fraction. Is that an acknowledgment that I'm right, or a recoil out of irritation? I can't tell. He's too hard to read.

"Where Biba is concerned, there can't be any wiggle room. You have to be mine in every way." His voice has an edge. A wariness. Or is it a warning?

"What does that mean, Tommy?" Is he talking forever? Or does he mean for us to put on a convincing show? It seems so presumptive to think he's pushing for a real marriage. He wouldn't want that, would he?

"Everything, Danika. It means you bind yourself to me—give me every piece of yourself—and in return, I'll give you your life back. As my wife, you'll have not only my protection but the strength of the entire Moretti family as well." His voice is cool and clinical, and the heat in his stare from seconds ago is now shuttered behind an impenetrable wall. "But what I'm offering is all or nothing. I'm not a man who deals in concessions. Think carefully before you make your choice, but remember, time is ticking."

Tommy walks away, leaving me dumbstruck in the living room, my entire life teetering in the balance.

15
Tommy

I RUN SO HARD MY LEGS THREATEN TO GIVE OUT. THEN I run a little harder. It's the only way I know to burn up the radioactive energy blistering my insides. That damn woman is going to drive me insane.

Danika is Biba's daughter. I thought that realization was enough to give me an aneurysm but add to it the fact that Biba wants to force her into a marriage with The Reaper, and I was blacking out with fury. The fucking Reaper.

Never.

Going.

To happen.

I'd rather kill her myself than hand her over to that psychopath. Not that it would come to that when marrying me would remove The Reaper from the equation. Biba's going to be pissed, but he can suck a bag of dicks. Piece of shit motherfucker using his own daughter as a bargaining chip—makes me sick.

Danika deserves so much better, and I'll give it to her if she'll let me. If being the keyword. I could see the shock and despair written all over her face after my proposal. Okay, so it wasn't exactly a proposal, but the point is, she was horrified.

Her rejection was a spoon carving out my insides.

I know we've only known each other a week. I know that I've held her hostage and threatened her, but I've tried to explain myself. I've tried to show her the things I'm not good at saying—that I want to help her. That I desperately want her to want me. I'm beyond obsessed with her. Every minute I spend with her, every touch and taste of her, only solidifies my madness.

Jesus, the taste of her.

And the way she responded to my touch? Everything I ever could have dreamed of, only to be dashed away when she tried to mince words and squirm away from a life beside me.

The problem is, I'm not made to charm. I'm logical and practical and blunt. I tend to see things in black and white, which is why reluctance on her part feels like complete rejection. My defenses were up before I had a chance to calm myself, which only made me sound that much more frigid. Not the ideal way to convince her I'm worthy of her surrender. Now, I don't know what she'll choose, and I hate the uncertainty.

As if you'll give her up if she chooses to go.

True. I've already started planning for the fallout of our marriage. It'll create ripples. Renzo's going to be furious, but he can share that bag of dicks with Biba because he married a woman from the Irish outfit. He has no room to argue about me wanting a woman linked to the Russians. This is happening, even if I'm the only goddamn person on board.

When I get back to the apartment, Danika is cooking breakfast. We didn't talk much during the rest of the evening, so I'm not sure what she's thinking regarding my offer. I want to demand an answer to alleviate my suspense, but that would be selfish. I've already been an ass. The least I can do is not force the issue any further. Besides, now that I'm back in the apartment, I'm plenty distracted, keeping control of my dick while she walks around my kitchen in those tiny pajama shorts she wears. When she reaches for an upper cabinet, I can see the tiniest bit of ass cheek peeking out. It makes me hungry for a hell of a lot more than eggs.

"Hey, I hope you don't mind." She flashes a shy smile. "I was hungry and thought I'd get breakfast started."

Smile at me like that and you can do whatever the hell you want.

As soon as the thought drifts across my mind, I realize it's true. She's frying the eggs rather than scrambling them, which is how I make them, and she's using the wrong pan, yet I hardly notice. My fixation on her is practically rewiring my brain. Things that seemed important a week ago aren't even registering.

I wipe up a dab of raw egg on the counter—some things are too ingrained to be overlooked. "If you're going to be my wife, my home is your home." Okay, so I didn't leave it alone, but I didn't force an answer, either. I'll call it a win.

She turns toward me as though she's going to say something before her gaze sweeps down my sweat-soaked body. Gold-flecked heat flashes in her eyes when they return to mine.

"Um..." she says distractedly. "Okay."

Yeah, Danika Dobrev is mine. She just doesn't know it yet.

When the phone rings, she answers, and I take over at the stove as though we've been together for years. A natural transition that is so minor in the grand scheme of things but fills me with hope.

"Mom, I told you when we texted earlier, it's not safe there." She listens to her mother's reply before continuing. "This new friend I'm staying with, his name is Tommy. He said he'd find a place for you guys to stay. Listen, he'll tell you." She puts the phone on speaker and stares at me pleadingly.

"Danika's very worried for you. I'm happy to help get a place and make sure you and your mother are safe while we deal with Biba." I meant to work on it yesterday but was too distracted by the evening's bombshell of revelations.

Petra Dobrev's voice is firm when she responds. "That's very generous of you to offer, but we don't want to go into hiding. This is our home."

"Mom," Danika says with exasperation. "You know it'll only get worse if Biba sends one of his men over again. He could kill you next time."

"He won't do that," Petra counters.

"You don't know that," Danika insists. The two are both adamant, and I have no idea who will win.

"No, you don't know him. I do. While I don't like to admit it, I spent a year with that man. I know him, and I'm not scared of him. Besides, Gran's cousin is helping us install a security system. We'll be safe, I promise."

Danika sighs and slumps against the counter. "I know how bullheaded you are, so I'm not going to fight with you about it, but I think you're making a mistake."

"Wouldn't be the first time, sweet girl," her mother says

gently. "If something changes, I promise you I'll reconsider, okay?"

"Okay," she says in a weary voice. "I better get going. Breakfast is ready. Love you, Mom."

"Love you, baby."

Danika ends the call and takes the plate I've made for her to the bar. It's on the tip of my tongue to point out how frustrating it is to have the person you're trying to protect defy you and endanger themselves, but I have enough sense to keep that thought to myself.

"She'll come around," I assure her as I join her with my plate.

"You don't know my mother. She's stubborn like you wouldn't believe. It's one of the best and worst things about her."

"You guys get along, though?" I'm genuinely curious. I haven't heard her talk much about her family.

Danika takes a bite of eggs, waiting to answer until she's swallowed. "Yeah, we do. It helps that I'm pretty chill. But maybe that's why I go with the flow. If I didn't, we probably would have killed one another a long time ago." Her gaze drops to her plate, worry wafting off her in waves.

"Biba's not going to kill his only leverage—that wouldn't help him get you back," I remind her. "But if it would make you feel better, I could always force the issue."

"What do you mean?"

"I mean, you may not be able to force them into hiding, but I can. I could take your mom and grandmother somewhere safe and make sure they stay there."

"You'd do that for me?" The gratitude in her eyes sinks hooks deep into my heart, anchoring me to her in ways I can't explain.

You'd be terrified if you knew the lengths I'd go to for you.

"Just say the word."

Her gentle smile deconstructs the world as I knew it and rebuilds it with her at its center. "Not just yet, but I appreciate your offer. Thank you, Tommy."

I grunt and fill my mouth with food before I can tell her in graphic detail all the ways she can thank me. No need to fuck up the progress I've just made by giving her a front-row seat to the twisted shit in my head. I'll save that for later, after we're married.

WE BOTH SPEND the day working. Well, I assume she's working. I'm too busy dealing with all the crap on my plate to be sure what she's doing. I have a wedding to plan, a war to prevent, and a job that still demands my attention. By evening, I'm exhausted. Not the best timing for Sante to show up and pick a fight.

"I get where you're coming from, man. I do. But she's his fucking *daughter*," he argues, wearing on my last fucking nerve. "You can't steal her like that. He'll come after the entire organization to retaliate."

I'm quickly regretting the decision to update him on the Danika situation.

"It's only genetics. She'd never even met the man until he tried to sell her off to The Reaper." I'm on my feet, my hands out wide in exasperation.

"Doesn't make a difference, Tommy, and you know it."

"So I'm just supposed to hand her over? That's fucking bullshit, and *you* know it," I yell back at him.

"Don't get pissy with me. I'm just trying to talk some sense into you. I know how you can get."

I stiffen. His words sound an awful lot like something my brother would say.

"Did I try to talk you out of moving across the globe to claim a girl you hardly knew?"

"No, but you called her a piece of ass," he bites back bitterly.

"Yeah, and you put me in my place for it. That's what I'm doing here." I point an angry finger and practically hiss at him. "I'm telling you she's fucking worth it—whatever *it* is. If you can't back me on that, then get the fuck out of my house."

Sante stills as he studies me, his hands propping resignedly on his hips. "You're telling me this is it?" he asks in a solemn tone.

I'm not entirely sure what he's asking, but either way, the answer is yes. I give a single nod.

"Alright, then. If she's the one, I'm behind you one hundred percent." He extends a hand, and I take it, relieved to know my best friend still has my back.

"Renzo's gonna be pissed," I warn him.

"We wouldn't be family if we didn't piss each other off. Now, come on. Let's have a drink."

16 Danika

I'd already gone to my room when the yelling started. It's quiet now, but the shouts still echo in my mind. Not only am I putting Tommy in grave danger, I'm coming between him and his best friend—probably his entire family.

I feel wretched.

Tommy's life is being turned upside down. My mom has already been attacked once and is living in constant danger. I'm not sure Gran would survive a run-in with one of Biba's men. They're all suffering, and I'm curled up in a lush, cozy bed like a princess in the top of her storybook tower. It's not right.

I don't want to give in to Biba's demands, but I'm not sure I can stand the alternative either. It all feels so hopeless. A viscous, suffocating sense of desolation drags me into a fitful night's sleep. When I wake the following morning, the sun is out, and I feel more tired than when I went to bed. I consider staying in bed all day until the savory smells of breakfast manage to coax me back to life.

"Hey," I offer quietly as I sit at the kitchen bar.

"Good morning." Tommy gives me a glance over his shoulder, then turns off the stove. "Cleaners will be here today, just so you know."

"Okay, I'll stay out of their way."

He brings over two fully loaded plates of breakfast and begins to chow down on his. Despite the delicious smell, I'm suddenly struggling to find my appetite.

"Something wrong?" He pauses.

I use my fork to move the eggs around my plate, struggling to find the right words. "I've just been thinking that maybe I'm being too selfish by running away from reality. I mean, maybe this Reaper guy isn't all that bad. I could be putting everyone in danger for nothing."

His fork clatters onto his plate. "It's not for nothing. It's your fucking life."

"I know, but who am I to put so many others at risk to avoid a future that might not be so bad? This Reaper guy could be a lot like you—" My words die as I realize I'm only making things worse. "I just meant, you guys may live outside the law, but that doesn't necessarily mean you're horrible people."

Yeah, I'm definitely making it worse.

Tommy stands abruptly, his chair screeching backward. He goes to the fridge and pours two glasses of orange juice.

"I'm sorry, Tommy," I say softly. "I'm not trying to offend you. In fact, I'm trying to protect you."

"Don't need your protection." He plunks the juice glasses down in front of us angrily.

I have a tiny urge to smile. For a grown man who can be plenty terrifying, he has a hidden boyish side that tugs at my heart.

"You're helping me. Am I not allowed to do the same for you?" I ask gently.

"Not if it means putting yourself in danger."

"That's just the reality I was born into. There's no changing it."

"There will be once you're my wife." He says the words just as I take a swig of juice, causing me to choke and spill some down the front of me. I cough a few times, then look down to see what damage I've done to my pajama top. It's going to need a wash for sure. I reach for a napkin to wipe the sticky juice from my chest when Tommy's single-word command slices through the air.

"*Stop.*"

He turns his chair, then pulls mine closer until I'm practically wedged between his open legs. His eyes lock on mine as he slowly leans forward, then lowers his head to lick the sweet juice from my chest. He lavishes three languorous strokes of his tongue against my now flushed skin.

My lungs and heart forget how to work in tandem, making me breathe in short, irregular puffs of broken air. Every nerve ending in my body comes alive, and my head angles back to allow him room when he trails a series of claiming kisses up my neck to my jawline.

With his lips seductively close to my ear, he whispers, "I

suggest you get used to me calling you my wife because it *is* going to happen. Forget the name Reaper ever existed." He leans back and pulls out his phone. "In fact..."

I watch with curiosity as he dials a number.

"DiAngelo, I've got the girl. Make sure it gets to Biba that he can call off the hunt. She and I are getting married." He lowers the phone and hangs up despite the clipped male voice barking commands on the other end of the line.

My eyes are as round as saucers, and my mouth hangs open.

A satisfied smirk tugs at the corner of his lips. "Now there's nothing to debate. Eat your breakfast; it's getting cold."

Dear God. What have I gotten myself into?

17
Tommy

I HAVE A TEMPER, BUT I'M NOT IMPULSIVE. I ACT IN A strategic, methodical fashion in almost every facet of my life. I live by the mantra "measure twice and cut once." That's how I quickly became the man to call upon in Sicily when someone needed a problem resolved … permanently. I research and plan until I'm absolutely certain I've accounted for all possible variables, leaving only a small margin for error.

Yet today, I didn't just poke a hornet's nest. I knocked it to the ground and lit that motherfucker on fire.

Life is about to get very, *very* intense, and I have zero regrets.

I feel as though all of my fixations and neurosis have somehow decided to join forces and focus on a single subject. Danika. She's all I can think about. I don't think I could breathe without her. Therefore, despite the chaos I've invited into my life by impulsively announcing my intent to marry her, I'm blanketed in a calm certainty that I'm doing the right thing.

It's the same reassuring sense of peace I get when I have a target in sight and pull that fateful trigger. *Success.*

I don't expect Danika to feel the same about me as I do her, though I'd prefer the idea of being with me doesn't repulse her. So long as she's mine, I can deal with the rest. That's what I've decided.

To further that goal, I have a few errands to run. I wait for the cleaners to leave before I go so that the apartment is locked tight. By the end of the day, it'll be too dangerous to leave her home alone. I'll have to arrange for protective duties.

I add it to my mental list before heading out. When I get back a few hours later, I find Danika on the sofa watching television. It's so foreign to have someone else living at my place, yet so unexpectedly comforting, but only because it's her. She has the eerie ability to make me feel centered and whole.

"Hey, there," she greets me warmly.

I'm constantly amazed at how optimistic and courageous she is despite all the shit life is throwing at her. Anyone in her position would be justified in being withdrawn and bitter, but not Danika. Effervescence is her natural state.

"Watching anything interesting?"

"Depends on how you feel about *The Golden Girls.*"

I shake my head incredulously, then hand over my shopping bag. "This is for you."

The contents shouldn't be a surprise, considering the apple on the side of the bag, but she still seems shocked.

"You got me a phone?"

"You can't keep using that piece of crap." I nod to the burner phone on the coffee table.

"Yeah, but..."

"But what?"

"But ... it's just a very expensive gift."

I close the distance between us and place my hands on the back of the couch on either side of her to lean in close. Her gaze stays locked on mine, her face angling up. Our noses are only a few inches apart.

"If you think that's expensive," I rasp. "Things are going to get very awkward when you see what else I've ordered for you." The tease of her sweet scent has me placing a kiss on the top of her head just to get one more smell before I pull away.

"What do you mean? What have you ordered for me?"

My only answer is a smug grin. "I have more work to do. I thought I'd put in an order for dinner. Does Thai work for you?"

"Um, yeah. Wait—Tommy! You didn't answer me," she calls after me as I retreat to my office.

"Text me what you want to eat. My number's already in your phone." I can't remember the last time I smiled so broadly. Something about surprising her makes me feel like seeing a rainbow for the first time. And she's going to be shocked because the engagement ring I've just bought couldn't be any more spectacular.

When my phone chimes with a text minutes after sitting at my desk, I'm eager to see what she says.

Danika: Thank you for the phone. I hope you know you didn't have to.

Me: If I do something, it's because I chose to. Remember that.

Me: Your order?

Danika: Chicken yellow curry, please

My girl likes a little spice. Good to know. And I do want to know—all of it—every little thing about her. I want to count the freckles on her nose and hear the story behind every one of her scars. I want to know what cartoons she watched as a kid and whether she prefers white wine or red or none at all. I want to make a mental dossier of her entire existence—color-coded and tabbed for easy reference. I want to eat, sleep, and breathe Danika.

Now that I think about it, maybe I should let her think she's an inconvenience because if she knew the truth, she'd be terrified, and I wouldn't blame her. My need for her isn't normal. And I don't care one little bit.

It's been thirty minutes, and I'm still wide awake. I can't get comfortable. I know what's wrong and have tried to fight it off, but it's not fucking working. Danika and I had dinner together, then watched television. Everything was perfect until it was time to go to bed. She went to her room, and my skin started to crawl with the need to keep her close.

I can't take it a minute longer.

I fling off the covers and march across the apartment to her room. The door is shut. I try to open it quietly so as not to startle her, but it's no use. She pops up and looks around.

"What's going on? Tommy? Oh God. Not the handcuffs again."

I'm not the best judge, but I'm pretty sure there's humor in her tone.

"Not unless you want them," I jab back before tossing back her sheet and scooping her into my arms.

"What are you doing?" she gasps, holding tight around the back of my neck.

"Taking my wife to bed."

"I'm not your wife, Tommy," she scolds without any real fire.

"You will be soon enough. Now, quit arguing."

"I'm not arguing. You'll know if I start to argue."

I grunt and take her to my bedroom—*our* bedroom—then situate us on the bed. Her on her side. Me on mine. Finally, I can relax.

"Tommy?" Her melodic voice lingers in the dark.

"Hmm?"

"What is this?" she asks hesitantly.

"This is us trying to sleep if you'll quit asking questions." Am I being a dick? Probably, but I'd rather not define this thing between us because I'll most likely scare her shitless. I'd rather take her hand and coax her down the path until she's hopelessly lost without me.

"A week ago, you couldn't sleep with me free in the house, and now you want me in your bed?"

"That about sums it up."

"What changed?" Her voice is no more than a whisper.

I consider my answer carefully before saying, "You, little thief. You've changed everything." Then I do what I told myself

I wouldn't do and pull her into the curve of my body the same way I held her when we were cuffed to the bed. I had hoped simply having her an arm's length away would be enough. It wasn't. Fortunately, she doesn't object, and I fall asleep feeling like the fucking king of the world.

18
Danika

Having grown up in a one-bedroom place housing three of us, I'm no stranger to sharing a bed. I often found myself sneaking into bed with Mom or Gran even after I got a twin bed of my own because I preferred to be snuggled up next to one of them. I'd forgotten how good it feels.

I woke up halfway through the night to find myself doing my best koala bear impersonation around a Tommy tree. I was embarrassed, so I untangled myself as best I could without disturbing him and went back to sleep. The next time I woke, he was up and gone.

I took a leisurely shower in the primary bathroom. His

apartment is incredible. I felt like I was in a movie using his heated towel rack and multiple shower heads. By the time I got out, Tommy was back from his run and cooking breakfast. Scrambled eggs, the same as he's made every morning. I get the sense he doesn't stray from that dish very often. It's strangely endearing.

We chatted a bit through breakfast like a normal couple. It's so odd to think of how things have morphed over the past week. I'm not sure how to tell if my changing feelings are genuine or some shade of Stockholm syndrome. He's been surprisingly sweet in a gruff way and unquestionably protective. I can't avoid seeing him as more than his Mafia label. I have no idea what that means, especially considering he's convinced we're getting married. It seems crazy.

Even crazier? I don't hate the idea.

It does worry me, though. And Biba worries me. A lot. I worry what he might do to Tommy. Biba is ruthless to a degree that probably qualifies as psychotic. As far as I can tell, he doesn't have an ounce of empathy in his body.

It's a good reminder that I should check on Mom and Gran. Now that breakfast is over and Tommy's gone back to shower, it's a perfect opportunity. I add Mom's number to my contact list in the new phone, which already contains Tommy's and Sante's numbers. I add Sachi's as well while I'm at it, then ring Mom.

"Hello?" she answers in a terse tone.

"Mama, it's me."

"Oh! Dani! How are you, sweet girl?"

Hearing the relief in her voice has me grinning ear to ear. "I'm good. Tommy's taking good care of me."

"Is that right? I'd like to hear more about this *friend* of yours. He seems to be awfully understanding of your situation."

"It's kind of a crazy story, but he's actually part of the Moretti family." I internally cringe as seconds tick by.

"You kidding me?"

I hear Gran in the background demanding Mom put the call on speakerphone.

"What did I miss? What's happening?" Gran interjects.

"Tell her," Mom demands.

"It's a long story, but I'm sort of staying with an Italian—one of the Morettis."

"And?" Gran asks.

"Ma!" Mom balks at her, making me smile.

"What? If he's giving her a place to hide out, what's wrong with that? He's not hurting you, is he?" Gran's voice takes on an edge.

"No, not at all. This number I'm calling from is a new phone he got for me. He's been very thoughtful."

I can almost hear Mom's grimace. "I don't like it. That's how they lure you in. Trust me, I've been there."

"Ignore her," Gran says. "Everything else okay?"

"*I'm* fine. How have you two been? Biba hasn't sent anyone else around to harass you, has he?"

"No, that really was no big deal, which is why I wasn't even going to mention it until Sachi came by. No reason to worry you." She's trying to downplay the situation so I won't bug her about hiding out.

"Well, I do worry, and I will keep bugging you to let us keep you safe."

"You just take care of yourself, Dani," she replies in a voice weighted with concern. "I know you think this man you're staying with is different, and for your sake, I pray that he is, but be careful. They hide their true nature."

Images of Tommy come unbidden to my mind—tender kisses on my forehead, the awe on his face when he looked at my artwork. Even when he first took me hostage, he couldn't help but guide me through deep breaths when I panicked. Those aren't the actions of a monster. And more to the point, those are the glimpses of Tommy at his most genuine self. I'd say she's right. Both Biba and Tommy wear masks, but where Biba puts on a charming front to hide the lack of a soul, Tommy's mask serves as armor to protect the goodness he hides down deep.

I could try to convince her, but she won't believe me about Tommy any more easily than I'll believe Biba isn't a threat to her.

"I know, Mama. I'm going to be okay. I promise." As I say the words, I realize that with Tommy helping me, I believe them. "Gran, you doing okay?"

"Yeah," she answers breezily. "The doctor said the dizziness was just heart palpitations and nothing to worry about."

"*What?*" This is the first I've heard of Gran having heart palpitations.

"It's nothing for you to worry about," Mom tries to assure me. "Seeing Biba's goons here got her agitated, and she had a little arrhythmia. The doctor said that's not unusual in high-stress situations. She's fine now—feisty as ever."

I breathe deeply. "Please, be careful, you two."

"You know I will," Mom says, "but this old woman here has never listened to either one of us, you know that. She went to the laundromat yesterday after I told her I'd handle the laundry this week. She waited until I was in the bathroom and took off."

I can picture the entire scene in my mind—including Mom ranting to herself in an empty apartment. The two of them are more alike than they want to admit. I have to smile. I love both of them so much. "Do your best, and Gran? Behave," I chide playfully.

We exchange I love yous and say goodbye. I disconnect and try to decide whether the call made me feel better or worse when I realize I'm no longer alone. I look over at the man leaning against the entry wall, expecting to see Tommy, only to find a terrifying stranger watching me. He's enormous—like the Brawny man but with tattoos and a scowl.

So many thoughts flood my brain that I freeze, my mouth hanging open like a fish yanked from the water with no idea what's just happened.

My first thought is Biba. He's found me.

But how? Could someone in Tommy's organization have leaked my location?

The man comes off the wall, snapping me out of my stupor. I jump to my feet and stumble backward in retreat.

"Get away from me. I'm not letting you take me." I look around frantically for some sort of weapon. Anything to stop him. Yesterday, I had considered letting Biba win so that my family would be safe. When faced with the reality of actually being stuck in a forced marriage, my survival instinct is screaming at me to fight. To do anything I can to get away. Only, I don't know how. There's nothing at all that remotely resembles a weapon. Tommy doesn't have *things*.

I grab a small potted plant and hold it in one hand as I continue to inch backward. My pursuer watches me, his head angling a fraction to the side as though studying a newly discovered species. "Take you where? To Tommy?"

I freeze, my eyes widening. "Tom—? Tommy?" His name is a benediction falling from my lips. "You're not one of Biba's men?"

His head falls back with a bellow of laughter, but it's short-lived. When he looks back at me, the deranged edge in his stare steals my breath. "Nah. That bastard can go fuck himself."

My relief is instantaneous and overwhelming. I plunk the plant back on its table, then try to steady myself as my vision blurs and my legs threaten to give out.

"Fucking Christ." The clipped curse barely penetrates the ringing in my ear before I'm swept off my feet. Though I don't know this man from Adam, I cling to him because every ounce of strength has left me, and I'm seconds away from passing out.

"Sorry," I mutter. "Just need ... to sit ... for a second."

"No shit."

He takes two steps toward the sofa when the primary bedroom door bangs open, and a buck-naked, soaking-wet Tommy charges at us, a gun in his hand.

"*What the fuck is going on here?*"

19 Tommy

"Easy, Tommy. Put the gun away." DiAngelo slowly sets Danika back on her feet but doesn't let go of her completely.

"I think I'd like to hear what the fuck you're doing here, first. I know my door was locked." I didn't turn the alarm on after coming back from my run, but I'm religious about locking the door. That means either Danika let in a man she didn't know, or this muscled-up asshole broke into my house. I'm not thrilled about either option.

"I came by to see if it was true—if you really did have the woman Biba's looking for." He takes a quick glance at Danika, who skitters away from him. "I knocked, and no one answered, but I could hear a woman's voice, so I let myself in."

Danika lifts a hand to her ear, looking bewildered. "I was on the phone with my mom. I never heard a thing."

DiAngelo studies her for a second, probably wondering like I am how she could have missed him knocking. "She thought I was sent by Biba and nearly passed out. I was trying to get her to the couch. Now, it's your turn to A, put your gun and your dick away. And B, tell me what the fuck is going on."

I don't like him giving me orders in my own home, but I can hardly argue. I *am* still standing here with my dick on display, after all. I sneer at him so he knows I'm still pissed, then grab a throw blanket off the sofa and wrap it around my waist.

"There's not much to tell. This is Danika; she's Biba's daughter. We're getting married, like I told you." I called him yesterday to pass along the word to his connections, not come interrogate me over my decisions.

DiAngelo goes still as a marble column. "His fucking *daughter?*" He looks over at Danika, who pales.

"Did I forget to mention that part?" I wanted to demonstrate that he doesn't know everything, but I'm second-guessing myself when I see the way he's staring at my bride-to-be.

"And what's your role in all this?" he asks her.

"This used to be a friend's apartment." She shrugs weakly. "I came by, not realizing he'd moved."

Thank God she doesn't tell him she broke in. That would just complicate things even more. I also make a mental note that it's time to invest in a new fucking lock.

DiAngelo prompts her to continue with raised brows. "And why are you on the run from your father, who, might I add, has never told anyone he has a daughter."

"He isn't my father. He's a sperm donor. My mother isn't his wife." Her voice finds a bit of strength. "I'd never even met him until he decided he wanted to marry me off to some guy named Reaper."

D finally turns his attention back to me. His gray stare stabs at me accusingly, saying, *and you think you're going to save her by marrying her.*

I take a tiny step forward, sending back a glare that says, *I'm marrying her because she's* mine.

He looks from me to Dani and back. "*Fuck,*" he hisses under his breath, then lumbers to the door, slamming it behind him.

"Holy crap, who was that?" Danika asks while releasing a breath that sounds like she might have been holding it throughout the entire exchange.

"That was DiAngelo. He's my brother's best friend and an important figure in our organization. He also has contacts with the Russians, so I had him help me gather a little information." I finally set my gun down and cross to Danika. My hands frame her face, bringing her wide gaze to mine. "You okay?"

"Yeah, though I don't like all the trouble I'm causing you."

"I'm a hitman for the mob. You think I can't handle a little trouble?" I ask softly, my eyes devouring her delicate features. At that moment, something very unexpected happens. The blanket around my waist falls to the floor, exposing my raging hard-on.

She sneaks a peek, then swipes her pretty pink tongue across her parted lips.

"Oh, little thief. You shouldn't have done that."

I slant my lips over hers, devouring the moan she releases. She's so damn intoxicating that I can't resist pulling her close so that my cock is pressed against her belly. She wraps her arms around my neck, and my hands drift to the bottom of her shorts.

"Do you have any idea what these fucking shorts do to me?"

Danika gives two small shakes of her head.

"Let me taste you, Dani. I need to taste you again so fucking bad."

Our gazes stay locked until she finally nods, and I swear to Christ, I feel like I've been given the gift of immortality.

I suck in a lungful of air, then take a step backward. "Lie on your back."

She peers at the sofa.

"No, here on the rug. Down where I can see you—all of you."

Fuck if my dick isn't screaming for me to stroke myself, but I resist. This isn't about me. This is about trust. I need Dani to know she can trust me, and if that leads to an exploding dick, so be it.

20
Danika

Tommy stands over me, so intent on taking in my every movement that I'm not sure he remembers he's stark naked. Every smooth curve of skin pulled taut over hard muscle is on display, including the sight of his engorged cock jutting out over me as I lay on the floor. His damp hair is unusually mussed, and his brown eyes have gone dark as a moonless night. They watch me as though I am the embodiment of heaven above. I wish it were true if only so he'd never look away.

"Take off the shorts. Only the shorts," he orders quietly.

I do as he instructs, mesmerized by the movement of his corded neck as he swallows.

"Now your panties."

I remove them slowly, playing along with this game of his because I'm enjoying it just as much as he is, even though I shouldn't. This is the very last thing I should be doing. But I can't stop. I'm desperate to know what he'll do next.

"Bend your knees. That's it. Now, slowly, *slowly* spread your knees to the sides. Show me what's mine, Dani. I want to see that beautiful pink pussy on display, just for me."

He hasn't even touched me, yet my clit already hums with pleasure at his words and the way his ravenous stare licks across my skin. I'm in awe of what this man does to me without even trying. I want his touch so badly, I can hardly keep still.

"Please, Tommy. I need you to touch me," I give in and plead.

The satisfied rumble that reverberates from his chest has my insides clenching tight. The sight of him dropping to his knees practically undoes me.

"You smell so fucking sweet, you may have to beg me to stop." He lies flat on his stomach and takes a long, languid lick up my slit.

I hiss and arch at the zing of pleasure shooting from my core.

"*Goddamn*," he murmurs to himself. I hardly register the exaltation because I'm too concentrated on my need for more. Tommy's intense nature and inherent mystery have me almost instantly perched on the precipice of a pleasure avalanche. He licks along the side of my clit, then along the other, before circling his tongue directly on the head of the sensitive bundle of nerves. The pleasure is blinding.

A wanton moan claws its way out from deep in my chest. My thighs start to quiver and shake. Tommy instantly pulls away.

"No! I was so close," I cry.

He nips at my inner thigh. Once. Twice. The graze of his teeth so close to where I need his touch only intensifies the ache for more.

"I hated seeing his hands on you." Another nip, this one with a tad more bite.

"I was about to pass out," I remind him distractedly.

"Doesn't matter. I still hated it." He teases me with a slow sweep of his tongue along my center. "I want to hear you say you're mine." Another languorous lick.

"I'm yours, Tommy. Only yours." The words come unbidden as though they already existed and were simply biding their time. I'm too overwhelmed with need for caution or misdirection. I might be shocked at the ease with which I spoke the words if that same preoccupation didn't have me too distracted to care.

"Damn right, you are," Tommy growls before worshipping me with the gift of his tongue. He doubles down his efforts, and in a matter of seconds, I'm crying out a cataclysmic release.

I've never come so fast or so hard in my life.

My entire body clenches and vibrates as I absorb the shock waves of physical elation. Tommy helps me milk every last ounce from the orgasm by continuing slow, gentle strokes around my clit. When he finally stops, I no longer have a care in the world. Biba could be in the other room, and I wouldn't even flinch I'm so blissed out.

"That was so much more addictive than I imagined it would be," Tommy says, now seated between my open legs.

His words drift amorphously through my consciousness, not fully taking shape. "Addictive? What's addictive?"

"All of it. I've never really wanted to taste a woman like that before. It was better than I imagined, and the way your body responds to the lightest touch—you're magnificent." His eyes remain locked on my core while his hand trails up my inner thigh. It almost feels like he's talking to himself, but I think it's just because he's so genuinely surprised.

"Are you saying you've never gone down on a woman before?" I ask, my clarity resurfacing as shock registers.

"That's exactly what I'm saying."

"I don't see how ... I mean ... why not?" I'm flabbergasted. Utterly stunned. He's so erotically possessive that I don't see how he could be with a woman and not want to own her in every way possible. And I have no delusions about his past. The man knows his way around a woman's body.

"Because putting my mouth on a woman like that felt too intimate." He taps my foot for me to lift so that he can slide my panties back on.

"Is it the emotional or physical intimacy that you didn't like?" I ask curiously.

"Both."

"I would normally have been a bit more ... prepared ... down there." I wish I'd had a chance to shower before this—I wasn't exactly keeping myself performance-ready. It's hard not to be self-conscious about that sort of thing.

"Look at me," Tommy says firmly. "How often do you think I hand out empty compliments for the fun of it?"

I survey his severe expression. "Never."

His eyes crease the tiniest bit in the corners. "Exactly, so if I say you're fucking addictive, I mean it."

"Okay." That's a relief, I guess, but also, I'm desperately curious about his past. I hadn't considered it before. Has he ever been in a relationship? Do I really want to know? Probably not. "Well, if that's your first go, I'm highly impressed." I sit up next to him, my cheeks flushing. I scoot a bit closer and run my hand up his thigh. His hand wraps around mine to stop me.

"What about you?" I ask. I've only been in a couple of long-term relationships, but a certain degree of reciprocity was always assumed.

Tommy shakes his head. "I'm not coming in your mouth or hand. The first time you wring me dry, I want my cum inside you, and that's not happening until you're my wife." Before I can argue, he brings his lips to mine, stealing my thoughts with a seductive kiss. Once I'm thoroughly mindless, he stands and helps me to my feet. "I'm going to finish getting ready, but first..." He starts tapping at his phone.

"First what?"

"First, I'm arming the damn alarm. No more unexpected visitors," he grumbles.

Once he's done, he turns for the bedroom, then pauses to look back at me. I'm standing in the same place, chewing on my lip. His brows furrow in a deep crease.

"What is it?" he asks.

"Nothing, I guess." I look around the room, wondering what on earth I'm going to do with myself all day.

"You guess? I'm not good at reading between the lines, Danika. If there's a problem, you have to tell me."

"Not a problem, I'm just a little stir-crazy. I've been stuck here in the apartment for a week. Another long day inside feels a little daunting."

"I suppose you can join me today if you want to." His voice bears a note of uncertainty—a hint of insecurity, as though he's not sure he should offer.

I smile warmly to reassure him. "I'd really love that, thank you."

Tommy grunts and resumes his walk back to the bedroom. He doesn't coddle me or feel an artificial need to make me comfortable. In his eyes, it's time to move on to the next task. Knowing that his behavior isn't meant as a personal slight, I find it unexpectedly refreshing. I can take his words and actions at face value, and I appreciate that.

This Mafia captor of mine is an incredible duality of simplicity and complexity. So straightforward yet so unusual. I can't wait to see what more I can learn about him in his work environment. I shouldn't be so excited to spend time with him, but I can't deny the eagerness exists. Tommy Donati has me utterly spellbound, for better or worse. I can only pray it's for the better.

"Are we at a company picnic?" I look around at the families carrying plates of food and playing carnival-style games inside the large conference center. The predominant theme among them is a familiar brown delivery service logo.

"It's a benefits fair for the local branch of the Teamsters Union." Tommy has to project his voice over the ruckus of the crowd. With bounce castles at the back of the room, this is definitely a family-focused event. Lots of kids. Lots of noise.

I have to strain to hear clearly, and I make sure to walk with Tommy on my right side—the side of my good ear. Crowds aren't my favorite, but I'm intrigued about why we're here. A union gathering would explain the information booths, but it doesn't help me understand our purpose here.

"Sooo, what exactly are we doing here?" I ask as we walk past a man making balloon animals in front of a cluster of children—not at all what I expected a workday with Tommy to look like. I don't know what I *did* expect, but this wasn't it.

"My family plays an active role in the Teamsters and other mall onions intensity."

Mall onions intensity?

I play over his words and can't make sense of them. "The Teamsters and what? I didn't catch that last part."

"I said, the Teamsters and other smaller unions in the city."

That makes more sense linguistically, but I'm clueless as to why a Mafia family would care about unions. I doubt they're concerned about fair wages or comprehensive healthcare. I decide to take a chance and push for a bit more information.

"Can you elaborate on your family's role with the union?"

He stops strolling and pulls us aside. I'm grateful because I want to make sure I hear his answer.

"Each of the Five Families has a sort of ... specialty. A focus on one of the main power centers in the city. The Lucciano family is involved in real estate—construction in particular. Nothing gets built in the city without their knowledge and approval. The Gallos handle waste management. You piss them off, your garbage doesn't get picked up for a month. That's a surprisingly powerful bargaining chip. The Russos are into banking—loans, to be more specific. The Giordanos are all about politics. They know what goes on behind closed doors among the elite. My Moretti family takes a more salt-of-the-earth approach and keeps the pulse of the working class. Nothing goes into or out of this city that we don't know about."

Absolutely fascinating.

"I had no idea things were so clear-cut among you."

"It keeps the peace. No room for turf wars when territorial boundaries are clearly defined. In this case, we're talking about the division of the main power hubs rather than actual geographic territory. Same rules apply. Of course, everyone has their own profit centers like online gambling or other pursuits, but as far as control over the city, those separations of power have been in effect for decades—ever since the RICO laws forced the Families to keep a lower profile." He takes my hand and resumes our stroll through the busy exposition hall.

"I appreciate your explanation," I tell him. "And honestly, I'm a little surprised you're willing to share that much."

"You're about to be just as much a part of that scene as I am. No reason to keep you in the dark," he says casually, eyes scanning the crowd.

I'm about to correct him when a large bald man with a long goatee beard steps in our path.

"Mr. Donati, glad you were able to make it by." The man shakes hands with Tommy, then grins at me. "And I see you've brought a guest. An exceptionally beautiful guest." He reaches forward to shake my hand. "Name's Mario. And you are?"

I open my mouth to tell him my name when Tommy uses two words to slice through the air like a deadly sword.

"My fiancée."

I smile and try to ignore him. "I'm Danika. It's good to meet you."

Mario's eyes cut from Tommy to me and back as he gives me the briefest handshake in the history of handshakes. It's as though I've suddenly acquired the plague, and he can't get away fast enough.

"Well, I don't want to keep you," Mario says sheepishly. "It was lovely meeting you, Miss Danika. And Mr. Donati—a pleasure, as always." He nods his head and does a runner, disappearing into the crowd.

"What on earth was *that*?" I snap at Tommy in a hushed voice.

"He's the current president of the group."

"That's not what I meant. Why are you introducing me as your fiancée, and why did it send him running in panic?"

"You've answered your own questions." Tommy looks at me, rich cappuccino eyes swirling with mirth.

He's telling people I'm his so that they'll stay away? Or, more pointedly, he's using his reputation to scare people away from me—something only someone with an exceptionally terrifying reputation could do. And here I am, about to argue with him because I'm a special kind of stubborn.

"Tommy," I start softly. "You've got to stop assuming we're getting married. I appreciate your efforts to protect me—I truly do—but marriage is a big deal. It has lifelong implications that I wouldn't jump into for some short-term fix."

He stops walking and leans in to bring his lips close to my ear. "There is nothing short-term about my intentions, I assure you, but this isn't the time or the place to argue."

I'm still analyzing his comment before I realize we're walking again.

Nothing short-term about his intentions? What does that mean? Is he expecting a *real* marriage—a lifelong commitment? Surely not. We've only known one another for a week. When he tossed out the idea of marriage, I figured he meant for show. Was that not the case?

I walk around in a distracted fog, my thoughts stuck imagining what it might be like to be Tommy's wife. The concept has a certain appeal I wasn't expecting. It's confusing because I know I shouldn't want to be with a criminal. But he's so much more dynamic than just a Mafia man.

I watch him carefully when he interacts with the occasional event coordinator. He's confident, demands deference while still being respectful, and his ever-present touch tells me I am always a central focus of his thoughts. He doesn't give me a single cause for admonishment the entire hour we're at the event. It's not a reason to marry him, nor does our time here give me any grounds for objection.

A marriage seems so outlandish that I suppose I hoped he'd give me a reason to balk at such a proposition. Even looking back on our week together, I can't find much of anything to justify my knee-jerk reaction to refuse him except the obvious—the brevity of our relationship, and the fact that Tommy is Mafia. Both are valid concerns. They could also both be completely irrelevant in the right circumstances.

In other words, I'm no closer to knowing what to do about Tommy when we leave the exposition as I was when we arrived. I don't like it. Something as important as a marriage should be entered into with full confidence. Tommy has me so confused that I don't know what to think.

When we head out, he opens the car door for me, which I silently chalk up as half a point in the pro column. A little chivalry is never a bad thing, right?

I'm considering making an actual pros and cons list when a call comes through over the car speakers. The screen says unknown caller. Tommy answers anyway.

"Yeah?" His finger hovers over the disconnect button in anticipation. It's the first time in my life I wished the call had been about an extended car warranty. Instead, a graveled

Russian accent comes across the line, instantly skyrocketing the pressure around us.

"Little Tommy Donati," Biba tsks condescendingly. "This is the second time you have stolen something of mine—either you're as stupid as they say, or you have a death wish."

21
Tommy

They say redheads are born with a fiery temper. I was starting to think that didn't apply to Danika. Her instinctive response to uncomfortable or threatening situations tends to lean toward passivity. However, the moment Biba makes his verbal jab at my expense, her feisty side flares to life. It just needed the right trigger.

To see rage flash in her eyes on my behalf is a sight I will never forget.

While I would prefer to kiss her, I clamp my hand over her mouth instead to prevent her from saying whatever scathing words are primed on the tip of her tongue. I see the sentiment reflected in her eyes, and while I'm immeasurably grateful, I don't want her to give away her presence.

"Maybe you should take better care of your possessions," I prod back in response to his comment that I've stolen from him again.

Danika narrows her eyes at me. I give her a look to say *please, just let me handle this*. Damn if the woman doesn't roll her eyes at me. I withdraw my hand from her mouth but make a mental note of the eye roll.

"Maybe you should give me my daughter back before I return the favor. You have two sisters, yes?" He says the last part in a calculated, menacing tone.

"Why should I give her back? You didn't want her in the first place—never even bothered to meet her."

He makes a dismissive scoffing noise. "She was defective. Men like us can't show that kind of weakness—you know that. I had no way of knowing she'd overcome. Either way, she's still my daughter, and I want her back."

"I'm afraid that's not going to happen, Biba. As you've heard, we're going to be married. Soon. I suggest you go back to ignoring her and pretend she never existed." I move to disconnect the call when an eerie laughter comes through the line.

"You'll regret this, boy, and so will she," Biba says in a voice that's pure malice.

I end the call. The Russian asshole is responding as I expected. We'll need to up security among the family until this blows over, and I need to get with Renzo to map out a game plan, assuming he doesn't officially disown me when I tell him what I've done.

"Tommy? I'm scared," Danika says in a voice so tiny that it breaks my heart. "What do you think he'll do?"

I place my hand on the side of her face and project every ounce of confidence I possess. "Biba will figure out he doesn't want to make an enemy of all five Italian families, and he'll back off. He can't afford a war on two fronts. Everything's going to be okay, you hear me?"

She nods despite the tears pooling in her eyes.

It's time to go home. I finally pull away from the curb and ask something that snagged my curiosity. "When Biba said you were defective, did he mean because you were illegitimate?" His insinuation didn't seem to fit the circumstances, but I could be wrong. It's hard for me to predict people's emotional responses, especially a batshit-crazy Russian like Biba.

"He means my hearing loss."

"What hearing loss?" I have no clue what she's talking about because the woman can hear just fine.

"When I was a month old, I got sick with a virus called CMV—it's one of those things that isn't a big deal for adults but can be harmful for babies. Getting the infection at such a young age caused me to lose all hearing in my left ear. Most people never notice because I've worked hard to compensate, but it still causes issues sometimes. That's why I'm not a fan of loud, crowded events. It takes a lot of effort for me to follow conversations. It's also the reason I didn't hear DiAngelo at the door. I had the phone to my good ear, so I never heard him knock."

I don't know what to say. She manages so well that I never suspected.

"Biba knew enough about you to know you'd lost your hearing?"

"Yeah, Mom says he was thrilled to have a daughter until I got sick. He walked away at that point. Didn't help support her or anything, which is when she figured out he was already married. The fallout left her pretty jaded, but she never blamed me. My mom and grandmother are amazing. I've worried about them more than anything during this ordeal."

"Then maybe it's time to push the issue."

Danika looks over at me like I hung the moon in the sky just for her. "You mean take them somewhere safe?"

"Yeah. I bet we can make it happen if we show up in person."

"Thank you," she whispers.

"Why don't you call your mom and let her know we're on our way?"

"Good idea." She places the call, her shoulders sagging with relief when her mother answers. "Hey, Mama. You guys doing okay?" She sits taller in her seat until her spine is rigid, every ounce of relief erased. "Where is she? What do you mean you don't know? How long has she been gone? Oh God. Okay. We're coming to get you and take you somewhere safe. No more arguing."

I listen to her half of the conversation with growing unease. Something's clearly wrong. I start to weave more urgently through traffic, knowing exactly where I'm going after memorizing the address that first day when I snagged her ID.

"Already headed that way," I say as soon as she disconnects the call.

She doesn't ask how I know where to go. She simply nods and wills the car forward.

Two hours later, we arrive back at my apartment with her mother in tow. The two women console one another despite obvious signs of worry. Gran hasn't been seen or heard from for four hours. She'd gone out for her daily trip to the market to pick up food for dinner and never came home. She isn't answering her phone, and from what I'm told, this behavior is very unusual. There's little doubt that Biba has followed through with his threat, likely even before he ever called me. He better hope for his sake he's only taken her hostage because if he hurts her, there's going to be hell to pay.

"I'm going to arm the alarm—do *not* open the front door for anyone. I've got a man guarding the hallway. Don't even let him in. No one. I'll only be gone for an hour or so." I speak softly so as not to be overheard even though we're alone in the primary bedroom. Danika's mother is settled into the guest room across from what has become Danika's paint studio, hopefully just for the night.

"We won't go near the door, I promise. And thank you, Tommy. Just saying thank you doesn't feel like enough, but I have no other way of repaying you for all this." Her teeth give a worried graze over her bottom lip.

I'd love to tell her she can thank me by wrapping those fuckable lips around my cock, but we don't have time for that right now. Plus, she may not feel so inclined when I tell her what I'm about to say.

"I'm happy to do it, but there's a price, Danika," I tell her in cool, simple terms. It could be a defense mechanism in anticipation of her refusal, or maybe I'm just as heartless as some people say, but I don't sugarcoat my demands. I want her to know I'm deadly serious. "I will get your grandmother back and keep the two of them safe, and you will marry me immediately after. Those are my terms."

It's simply too good an opportunity to pass up. She's

expressed reluctance at the idea of marriage from the moment I mentioned it. If I don't take advantage now, she might never agree to marry me. I can't risk it. I must make Danika mine, no matter the cost.

Shock registers in her wide eyes, shining an emerald green thanks to shafts of sunlight streaming through the windows. "You're serious," she whispers.

"I am."

"But why? I still don't understand, Tommy. Why would you do all this for someone you hardly know?"

"Because I don't have to know every little thing about you to know *me* and know I will *never* stop wanting you." I stand stock-still, waiting for her to tell me what I said doesn't make sense. It's what a rational person would do, which is why my heart stutters when I hear her gift me with the most perfect single word anyone has ever spoken.

"Okay," she says in a soft but firm voice. "I'll marry you."

22

Tommy

S**HE SAID YES. D**ANIKA SAID YES—IT'S ALL I CAN THINK about on my way to Renzo's place. Was her response coerced? Sure. Does it still count? Abso-fucking-lutely.

Danika is going to be my wife and sooner than she realizes. But first, I need to get her grandmother back. To do that, I'll need help.

I've always hated asking for help. Admitting a lack of knowledge or ability only reinforces the doubts others have about me. If at all possible, I try my absolute hardest to handle things on my own, but that simply won't work this time around. I reached out to DiAngelo to get help locating Gran. He insisted on looping in my brother. To keep the numbers even, I roped Sante into joining me for our little sit-down. I can face my brother on my own, but having Sante beside me makes it a hell of a lot easier.

I wait out front of Renzo's place for Sante to arrive so we can enter as a united front. DiAngelo's already inside when Renzo opens the door with a thunderous expression.

"Get in here and tell me what the fuck is going on."

We head into his brownstone home, following him to the living room like two kids sent to the principal's office, taking a seat and awaiting our lecture. Sante sends me a questioning glance, wondering what bug has most recently crawled up my brother's ass. Now that we're all here, I'm thinking I probably should have told Sante about the engagement before we arrived.

Renzo stays on his feet, hands propped on his hips. "Want to tell me why the fuck I'm hearing from my best friend that you're getting married?"

Out of the corner of my eye, I see Sante's head perform an *Exorcist*-style swivel in my direction.

Yeah, I'm definitely going to get my ass chewed out when this is over.

"Things have moved quickly. I haven't had a chance to tell you."

"Bullshit," he barks at me. "You have a goddamn phone."

I swallow down the argument I'd like to shoot back in my defense, knowing it would only make things worse, and try to move the conversation in a more productive direction.

"As you know, Biba wants Danika back. When I informed him that wasn't happening, Danika's grandmother went missing. It's safe to assume Biba's taken her as leverage after roughing up Danika's mother didn't get him the results he wanted. We've yet to hear from him, though. I've got her mom over at my place to make sure she stays safe, but we need to find an alternative place for her to hole up until this all blows over. You know I don't do houseguests."

"Except for the one woman who could put our entire organization at war." Renzo glares at me. "You've not only taken her in but decided to *marry* her, apparently."

My anger flares like wildfire at his blatant disregard for Danika.

I rise to my feet. "You're goddamn right I'm marrying her, which means that's my future *wife* you're talking about. I suggest you remember that."

He starts forward. "You threatening me?"

DiAngelo inserts himself between us, ushering my brother backward. "This isn't getting us anywhere, and I'm not here to listen to you two argue. Tommy, you need to be more respectful of your *boss* by keeping him informed. Renzo, Tommy's doing the best he can in a shit situation."

Doing the best he can—as if either one of them could magically handle the situation any better.

"If you don't like my decisions," I direct at my brother in a voice carved from stone. "You're welcome to cut me loose, but Danika is mine. I'm not walking away from her simply to avoid pissing off Biba. You need to make a call about what's best for the organization. If that means us parting ways, so be it."

Sante is a brick wall beside me, arms crossed and support unyielding.

Renzo looks from me to Sante, then back before looking away with a sigh. "This is Sicily all over again, isn't it?"

"If you mean I'm refusing to abandon the people I care about, then I guess so."

He studies me long and hard. "If she means that much to you, I suppose we need to come up with a plan."

"About fucking time," DiAngelo mutters. "I need a drink. Anyone else?" He heads to the liquor cabinet at the behest of three grumbled requests.

Sante and I ease back onto the sofa, a degree of tension melting from my shoulders into the soft cushions. The worst part is over, and I haven't been disowned. I would have been surprised if Renzo cut me loose, but it was a possibility, and I was more concerned about it than I realized.

"So," Renzo begins, "as I see it, we have two immediate concerns: getting Danika's grandmother back and finding a way to appease Biba. Any other major issues we need to plan for that I'm missing?" He looks at me pointedly, getting in one more silent jab.

I mentally roll my eyes. Technically, I needed to come up with a place to stash Danika's mom as well, but I can't bring myself to mention it now. I'll figure that out on my own. "That's it. I'm good to retrieve Gran on my own if I can just get some help figuring out where she is." I look over at DiAngelo, taking my turn at a silent prod.

He brings over four highball glasses of scotch and distributes them. "I don't like to make promises, but I can probably figure out where they've stashed her."

Renzo sniffs at his glass. "If anyone can find her, it's you."

"I'd owe you," I tell D gratefully.

"You already owe me," he mutters.

I nod, ready to own my obligations. "I think it goes without saying that Biba will be angrier than ever if we pull this off."

Renzo nods. "I'll reach out and see what I can do to negotiate peace terms, but not until you get her back. We don't need him sending her back to us in pieces as a warning."

Silence grips the room as we all digest the horror of that scenario.

Sante clears his throat. "I can always give Malone a call to see if the cops have any new info that might be helpful."

"You think he'd give you anything?" Renzo asks.

"It'd help if I had something to offer in return." His eyes lock with Renzo's in a wordless conversation that makes me uncomfortable because if there are lines to read between, I don't see them and have no clue what's passing between my brother and my best friend.

Eventually, Renzo ends the communication with a drink from his glass. "I got word recently that the man known as Reaper has a scar across his throat. Seems he's as hard to kill as they say."

Interesting. Something like that should help identify him. It'd be pretty noticeable unless he runs around wearing a turtleneck in July, which would be equally as unusual.

Even more interesting is that Renzo has offered information to give the cops on a rival organization ... for me. He's set aside one of his steadfast rules, which he never would have done if I hadn't needed help. Despite all our disagreements, my brother is putting my needs above those of the Moretti family—it's a move that could get him killed if word got out, and a risk taken on my behalf that I won't soon forget.

I lift my chin in silent appreciation.

Sante takes out his phone and dials a number. "Malone, you got a minute? Good. We're dealing with a situation and could use an exchange of information, if you're willing." He stands and starts to slowly pace. While he talks, the rest of us sip our drinks and listen. The second he disconnects, I down the last of my drink and lean forward.

"He have anything useful?"

"Not sure. They figured out those three Russians killed by Reaper were trafficking kids—primarily little boys."

The air thickens with disgust. We may not follow the law, but we aren't completely devoid of a conscience. The shit some people do is plain cruel. We have zero tolerance for that brand of evil.

"I wasn't aware Biba was into that sort of shit," Renzo comments. "But I also wouldn't put it past him."

D swirls the remaining liquid in his glass. "Could be a side hustle that his crew was running without his knowledge."

"Either way," Sante continues, "Malone says it looks like their deaths put a serious dent in the operation. He's still questioning if this Reaper character isn't some sort of vigilante."

DiAngelo shrugs. "From what I can tell, his outfit is about fifty strong—tiny in comparison to some, but they're all skilled. He's selective about this recruiting. Never heard of a vigilante running with a crew like that, but I suppose it's possible."

"True," Renzo adds, "and as far as we know, those kills could have been a takeover rather than justice. I don't think it's safe to assume anything about him."

"Fortunately, he's not our concern at the moment." DiAngelo stands and stretches. "Time to start the hunt."

"How long do you think it'll take?" I ask.

A predatorial glint lights his eyes. "I'd keep my phone close, if I were you."

23
Danika

WHEN TOMMY GETS HOME, HE'S CARRYING A LARGE BOX IN his arms with Sante in tow, doing the same.

"What's all this?" I call from the kitchen as they march through the living room toward the primary bedroom hall.

"Your stuff." The words are tossed over his shoulder before he disappears around the corner. A few seconds later, the two walk purposely back to the front door and disappear again.

I sneak a glance at my mom, who is staring at me with her eyebrows riding high on her forehead. "Oh! The gravy is boiling." I rush back to the stove and turn down the heat, stirring the viscous liquid to keep it from getting lumpy. Mom and I have been stress cooking for the past hour. We've managed to make enough food to feed a small army. "Check on the rolls," I tell her in part to distract her from asking me questions I'm not sure how to answer.

When the guys return, they're both pulling hotel-style luggage carts full of my things. Boxes. Canvases. My pink bedside lamp.

"Are you moving me in here?" I blurt, completely forgetting about my mother.

"That's usually how marriage works," Tommy answers distractedly.

"*Marriage?*" Mom blurts.

I cringe, squeezing my eyes shut.

This is not how I planned to tell her, which is to say, there was no plan because I had no idea how to broach the subject. She'll never understand such a fast-moving relationship, especially in light of Biba's involvement. I don't want her to think poorly of Tommy or minimize what he's doing for me. If she thinks he's taking advantage of the situation for his benefit, it'll color her perception of everything.

"Tommy just asked me earlier today, actually," I try to explain. "With Gran going missing, it didn't seem like the right time to tell you."

As if any time would be the right time to tell her I'm getting married.

Mom eyes Tommy as he wheels the cart toward the bedroom while Sante pushes his cart down the guest hallway. "Dani, that's awfully fast. Why the rush?" she asks warily.

"There's no rush, Mama."

It hits me that Tommy said we'd marry immediately but

never explained what that means. I assume in a matter of weeks, but there's no telling with him.

I give her a reassuring smile and take her hand in mine. "We haven't set a date or anything. I don't even have a ring, so don't get all worried. It's more of an understanding about the future, that's all." I don't think she's buying it, but she's wise enough not to push further with Tommy and Sante around. I'm relieved to have a little time to come up with a more convincing explanation.

"Any word on Gran?" I ask when the two guys return with empty carts. The tension in the air shifts to a blanket of worry at the change in subject.

Tommy frowns. "No, but we're working on it. I promise."

I nod and force a thin smile. "I know you are, and we both really appreciate it." I look at Mom, who nods as well.

"Food ready?" Tommy asks in a welcome redirection. "It smells delicious."

Mom and I jump into action, explaining the options. Sante doesn't join us for dinner. That leaves the three of us at the kitchen bar, eating as much as we can while trying to distract ourselves from the herd of elephants in the room. In an unexpected twist of luck, Mom excuses herself for the night as soon as we finish eating. Maybe she's feeling as overwhelmed with life as I am. Whatever the reason, the reprieve from an inquisition is a relief.

Tommy and I put the extra food away and load the dishes in the dishwasher. Mom and I cleaned as we cooked, so the kitchen isn't in bad shape. I'm glad because a full stomach combined with a day of worry is quickly drawing on exhaustion.

"Come have a look at what I brought over," Tommy says, taking my hand to lead me back to the bedroom. "I'm sure I probably missed a few things and may have brought stuff that needs to go back, but it's a start."

"That's very thoughtful of you." I look at the small pile of boxes and am struck by just how little I own. We never had enough room to have much stuff. "What about the boxes on Sante's cart?"

"That was all art stuff. I had him put it in the spare room. I figured we could convert it to a studio."

"You'd really do that? Let me have a whole room for my art supplies?" I'm not sure where I thought they'd go. With his propensity for tidiness, it wouldn't have surprised me if he preferred to rent me a space outside the apartment rather than bring that sort of chaos into his home.

"You don't have to sound so surprised," he chuffs.

"I'm sorry, it's just really generous and caught me off guard."

His dark eyes warm to a sultry mocha as he loops a finger into my jean shorts and pulls me closer. "Nothing generous about it. I want my wife here where I can see her." His hand cups the back of my head, fingers threaded through my hair as he angles my head to the side. "Where I can touch her," he whispers by my ear before grazing his teeth over my lobe. "Taste her."

A battalion of goose bumps stands in formation down my arms. "Oh," I breathe, my brain short-circuiting.

What were we talking about?

"Let's get you unpacked." Tommy gives my backside a pat, then drops to his knees to open the closest box.

"We don't have to do it now," I tell him. Between the exhaustion from before and my newly frazzled brain cells, the last thing I want to do is unpack. "It can wait."

"No, it can't," he says firmly.

"There's no rush, Tommy. I'm not going anywhere."

"It's not about rushing," he says, irritation seeping into his voice. "It's about needing my bedroom to be a certain way before I can go to bed. I can't go to sleep knowing there's a pile of boxes in here." He's talking while emptying the box, not looking at me. He's obviously agitated, but I get the sense he's also embarrassed or worried about my reaction.

"Okay," I offer gently. "It's probably best to get it done now rather than put it off for later." I kneel beside him and start on the next box. After a minute, I pause when I realize he's still staring at me. "What?"

"I knew you were perfect."

Heat warms my cheeks. "I'm far from perfect, Tommy."

"You're perfect for me, little thief, and that's all the perfect that matters." He returns to his task as if he didn't just say the sweetest thing I've ever heard.

I tuck the words away in my memory bank like I would a cherished ticket stub into a keepsake box. Even his nickname for me, which isn't all that applicable, but I sort of love it anyway. That's how I feel about Tommy in general. He has a way of endearing himself without even trying. His methods are unconventional and unintentional, and I think that's precisely why they're so effective. It's impossible not to fall for a man who's so transparently himself while being unerringly devoted to the people around him.

My wandering thoughts are a revelation I didn't see coming.

I'm falling for Tommaso Donati.

Piece by piece, he's unveiled himself to be a man of character and commitment. A man with a decidedly dry sense of humor yet a passion for life. He's seductive and thoughtful and protective and honest to a fault. He's a criminal and a killer. My savior and damnation.

Tommy is too complex to label except for perhaps with one word. A word as simple as it is monumental.

Mine.

Tommy is *mine*.

I'm struck by the resounding sense of rightness that settles over me at the thought. I don't know how it's happened in such a short amount of time, but I can't deny the feeling. I want him to be mine as much as I want to be his. And that's what's going to happen when we're married. We'll be bound together for the rest of our lives.

Are you seriously prepared to make that sort of commitment?

I suppose I'll find out soon enough.

From captive to roommate to husband, all in a matter of days. I'm a little afraid to ask what fate has in store for me next.

"I didn't realize you had so little stuff." Tommy studies the tiny corner of his massive walk-in closet that now houses my entire wardrobe. "And I checked my card. You still haven't ordered anything." If I didn't know Tommy, I might be offended at his comments, but I know he's merely stating the obvious. There's no judgment involved, so no reason to be upset.

No, I don't have much. That's a fact. He's not intending to imply I'm poor or less than.

"I don't need much." I smile at him. "And now that I have all my stuff, I have plenty."

He huffs. "Go get your tablet while I take these boxes out." He goes about his task, removing all evidence of my move. I have no reason to argue because I have no clue what he intends, so I get my computer and sit on the bed reclined against the headboard.

When he returns, he flips on the overhead light, then squats beside the bed. I'm about to ask him what on earth he's doing when he pulls out the long gun case.

"Did you want me to do something in particular with my tablet? Or were you just wanting me to occupy myself while you clean your gun?"

"You're supposed to be shopping," he says while setting up his gear on the bedroom floor. "Where do you like to shop?"

"Resale shops, mostly."

Tommy pauses to shoot me a glare. "You're not helping. When you treat yourself, where do you go?"

I think for a moment, my lips pursing as if that somehow helps my brain trudge along. "I guess I like to window shop at Anthropologie." The stuff's ridiculously expensive, though, so I never buy anything. I leave that part out as I doubt he'd want to hear it.

"Good, that's a start. Pull up the site, and I want to see your cart before you order. It had better be full, or I'm going to hire a personal shopper to do it for you."

I stare blankly at him, not that he notices. He's moved on to his cleaning ritual while my brain glitches. It does that a lot since meeting Tommy Donati.

Guess it's time to shop. I click on everything that looks cute and add to cart. More things that I even want, but his edict seems to have called me out, so I'm apparently going to rise to the challenge. I'm so engrossed I don't notice him approach until he taps the cart icon in the top right corner. My eyes dart to the total, and when I see a string of numbers totaling over thirteen thousand dollars, I suck in a lungful of air that was supposed to be a maniacal peal of laughter but ends up choking me instead. I launch into a coughing fit.

"Jesus, Dani. Try to breathe." He pats my back—not at all helpful but still sweet. Once I'm no longer on the verge of dying, he drops the black credit card in my lap. "Looks good. Check out, and we'll get ready for bed. I'm beat." Then he walks away as though he didn't just authorize me to charge a small fortune to his card. I can't. There's no way. Maybe I'll just take a few items out—some of the high-dollar pieces.

I'm still gaping at him when he stops to peer over his shoulder at me. "And if the number on my card statement doesn't match what I just saw on that screen, we'll pick another store and start from scratch."

Of course, he knew exactly what I was planning to do.

"Tommy! I can't just—"

"You can, and you will."

Bitch, listen to the man and buy the clothes.

I roll my eyes at my inner voice as if anyone asked her opinion.

"Where are you going?" I call after him.

He peers around the corner from the hallway, only meeting my gaze briefly. "I just have to check a few things. I'll be right back." Domineering Tommy from seconds ago is suddenly gone, a shy, almost embarrassed version of himself remaining.

I'm so confused. What is he doing that caused him to retreat into himself like that? There's no way to know, so I don't bother guessing. I use the credit card to complete my purchase and try not to think about how much money I just spent. When I'm done, I tie my hair on the top of my head for a quick rinse in the shower.

His shower allows for privacy, but I can't stop thinking about what happens after. Do I towel off and dress in front of him, or do it hidden behind the shower wall? Will he even be in the bathroom when I get out? I'm swimming in questions and anticipation as I wash my face and body, so absorbed with my curiosity that I don't realize until I turn off the water that Tommy never even waited until I was done.

He leans against the edge of the floating wall, just behind my towel hanging on a hook. His ravenous stare laps at the water dripping down my body. The sight is just as arousing as any touch could ever be. My inner muscles clench in my core while my nipples pebble as if trying to draw the rest of my body closer to him.

"You could have joined me," I say in a sultry tone I hardly recognize.

He shakes his head slowly from side to side. "Told you, not until you're my wife. And if I step foot in there naked, I *will* fuck you against the shower wall."

The only thing keeping me from begging him right now is my own insane arousal. It's sucked all the words from my brain. Absently, I reach for my towel, unable to speak. He takes it in his hands before I can and instructs me to hold out my arms, then proceeds to towel off my entire body—every crease and crevice.

"*Tommy.*" The whispered plea slips from my lips when he slowly swipes the towel along my slit.

A groan is wrenched from deep within him right before he drops to his knees and props one of my legs over his shoulder. He's instantly devouring me. I have to clench his hair to steady myself.

"Yes, Tommy. God, it's so good." Like some kind of hair trigger, I don't have time to say more when a blinding wall of pleasure crashes over me. It feels extra intense being upright. I've never had an orgasm on my feet. It's incredible. I gasp and shudder and shake, doing my best to stay on my feet until Tommy rises and helps to support me.

"D better hurry the fuck up." His words are spoken through teeth clenched so tightly I struggle to understand.

"What does that mean?"

"It means you need to get in bed before I do something I'll regret. *Now.*" He steps aside, his body rigid with restraint.

I put on my pajamas and brush my teeth while he takes his turn in the shower. I'm snuggled under the covers when he joins me, though he doesn't get in bed right away. He checks the alarm panel first. I hadn't noticed it until now. Once the alarm is set, he closes the blinds, stepping back twice to make sure each set hangs at exactly the same height. After that, he opens his nightstand drawer and takes out a gun. I watch with a bit of unease as he unloads and reloads the weapon.

"Should have done this earlier while you were in the shower, but watching you was too tempting."

"It's not a surprise to me that you have guns in the house," I inform him softly.

"It's not that," he says almost to himself. He gets into bed and begins to situate himself, but in the process, his attention is drawn back to the blinds. He sighs heavily and gets up, adjusts one of the blinds, steps back to assess them one last time, then opens the nightstand again. As though he hadn't already checked, he unloads and reloads the gun again.

His lips are pulled into a frown throughout, and his gaze keeps far from mine. There's something about his movement, too. A stiffness that signals agitation. Annoyance. I think, maybe, he's annoyed with himself for being unable to resist the compulsion to check these things.

I've known he suffers from these sorts of obsessive tendencies but haven't seen much sign of them while I've been here. The part that bothers me most is seeing how upsetting it is to him. I can only imagine how vulnerable it feels to allow someone new to witness these challenges.

How very humbling to think he wants me close more than he cares about his pride or discomfort. I remember my years of speech therapy and my reluctance to talk to the other kids at school—those were the hardest years of my life. I've overcome those challenges, for the most part. Tommy is still right there in the trenches. It hurts my heart.

Once he's finally settled under the covers, I scoot closer and wrap an arm and leg over him, snuggling into his side. His entire body relaxes beneath me. So much pent-up tension. I kiss his chest in one more silent reassurance and drift into a deep, dreamless sleep.

24
Tommy

THE THING ABOUT HAVING OBSESSIVE-COMPULSIVE tendencies is I rarely vacillate ... on anything. That includes my emotions—especially anger. Once I'm pissed, I'm *pissed*. It can take days for me to shake the stabbing irritation of whatever upsets me.

Hearing Danika downplaying our relationship to her mother sank me into a foul mood. Irritation and stress amplify my compulsive behaviors, which means running the course of a routine once isn't enough. The cloying need to repeat and recheck tasks I've already completed screams so loudly in my head that I can't focus on anything else. Feeling compelled to give in and allow Danika to see my inability to control myself made my mood infinitely worse.

I didn't want her to see that side of me. The sickness.

Every second I spent on my insidious rituals, I berated myself for ruining my chances of Danika ever wanting to be with me. How could she? I know how ridiculous my compulsions seem to the people around me. I see the looks people give me. Even my family. Just because I keep doing it doesn't mean I don't care about the disapproval. I keep doing it because I *have* to. I don't know how to make myself stop.

The epitome of weakness.

I was certain any progress I might have made with her was being demolished with every second that passed. When I got into bed for the final time, I was furious with myself and knew I'd likely need to get up to run my routine again but swore I would wait until she was asleep first. I expected her to pull away when I joined her in the bed, but to my amazement, she didn't. What's more, she voluntarily curled her body around mine. Every acrid thought I spit at myself was drown into silence by her healing touch, as though the anger simply disappeared.

Danika had me experiencing such a whiplash of emotions I felt like I'd just taken my first steps on land after spending a year at sea. She has to be some sort of goddess from above. There's no other explanation for the power she holds over me. It's not just my obsession for her—she pulls my strings in places I didn't realize strings existed.

A perfect example is my inexplicable desire to wait for sex until we're married. I've never once in my life considered that remotely important. Not until Danika. I feel a strange fear that if I don't make her mine in the proper order, I'll lose her. It doesn't make any sense, but my compulsions rarely do. I have to commit myself to her in an oath of marriage before her body can be mine. It's as simple as that.

Following through is a whole lot easier knowing I won't actually have long to wait. I'm so close to having everything I want that I go to sleep swathed in an unfamiliar sense of hopefulness.

Morning is filled with getting Petra moved to a safe house, which turned out to be a hookup pad used by one of our guys before he recently got married. I've decided to keep that little tidbit to myself. It has all the basic necessities, and he assured me the sheets are clean. Would I trust his assertion if it were me staying there? Probably not, but my standards are stricter than most. I figure Petra will survive.

"Where to now?" Danika asks, noting we're headed away from home.

"Staten Island."

"What's on Staten Island?"

"Not what. Who."

She cocks her head to the side in playful disapproval. "Okay, then. *Who* is on Staten Island?"

"My mother."

"Oh!" She stares straight ahead out the windshield, though I can tell she's not paying attention to a single thing in front of her. What I wouldn't give to hear the clambering thoughts so obviously bouncing around her head.

"Last night, when we were eating, it occurred to me that if we're getting married, you should meet my mom."

"Right," she says distractedly. "And what about your dad?"

"He died almost five years ago, not long before Sante and I went to Sicily."

"I'm so sorry. I didn't realize." She's quiet for a bit before continuing. "When you say Sicily, you mean Italy, right?"

"Yeah, that Sicily." I can't help but grin. She's so damn adorable.

"How long were you there?"

"Four years."

"*Really?* That's so long—oh my gosh, tell me you learned to speak Italian." She says it with such enthusiasm that it's infectious.

My heart thuds in my chest as if trying to show off its strength, preening from the attention.

"Ti direi qualsiasi cosa tu voglia sentire, se questo significa che mi guarderai così per sempre."

I'll tell you anything you want to hear if it means you'll look at me like this forever.

"Oh, Tommy. It's *beautiful*," she breathes.

"Non è niente in confronto a te."

It's nothing compared to you.

Danika sits back in her seat with a happy sigh. "Someday, I'm going to go tour every museum in Italy. I want to see all the art and immerse myself in the culture."

"Il tuo desiderio è un ordine."

Your wish is my command. And I mean it. I'd take her to the airport now if I could, but I know she'd never leave the country with her family in danger.

"What did you say?"

"I said you'd love it there."

"I bet I would," she adds dreamily. We spend the rest of the car ride in comfortable silence, each of us captive to our thoughts. Danika gapes out the side window when we pull into the driveway of a white stucco mansion complete with geometric sections of glass block windows that would look perfectly at home in a 1980s *Miami Vice* episode. "Is this where you grew up?"

"Yup." If she thinks the outside is something, she'll lose it when she sees the inside. Dad had a flair for the dramatic. He strongly believed appearances were everything.

If they think you're a king, that's what you'll be.

I used to hate when he'd say that, but as I've matured, I've come to accept that he wasn't entirely wrong.

I knock on the door, expecting Mom to see it's me through the cameras and unlock the door. Instead, the intercom pops on and off, letting through a few clips of hushed voices. I start to reach for my gun, worried there's a problem inside, when the door flies open. Mom and my sister Terina stand opposite us, wide-eyed.

"Tommy, you're here, and you brought someone." Mom's words reek of hopeful anticipation. It's a bit insulting.

"I did. How about we come inside, and I'll introduce you."

"Oh! Yes, my God, where are my manners?" She shoves Terina aside and steps out of the way.

The grand entry is plenty large for all of us and then some, with a crystal chandelier hanging from the two-story ceiling above and a curving staircase built into an alcove off to the side. The floors are glossy marble, and the white walls and windows make for perpetually bright surroundings. It echoes. I was never a huge fan.

I place my hand on the small of Danika's back and keep her close. "Mom, Terina, this is Danika. We're getting married, so I thought you might like to meet."

All three women stare back at me, and I have no idea why.

"What?" I ask.

"You're getting married?" Mom breathes. I can practically

hear the tears pooling in her eyes. I'm twenty-five, yet she acts like I'd joined the priesthood.

"She's marrying *you*?" Terina blurts, then instantly clamps a hand over her mouth. "Oh my God. I'm so sorry. I didn't mean it."

My lips part to unleash a scathing rebuke when Danika's hand presses flat on my chest in a possessive gesture as she scoots even closer to me. I swear she casts a spell with that hand because she sucks the wind right out of me, anger included.

"We totally understand," she says with a smile. "It's all happened very quickly. I'm so sorry to catch you off guard like this." The thing about Danika is she doesn't just handle the slight with grace. She seems genuinely unruffled by their comments.

Mom plows forward and pulls Danika into a suffocating hug. "Oh, Dani. We're absolutely thrilled you're going to be a part of the family. Is it okay if I call you Dani? You should call me Zuzu. My name's Azzurra, but everyone calls me Zuzu. It's easier."

Danika is sucked from one hug into another as Terina takes her turn. "And I'm Rina. No reason to be formal around here." She takes Danika's hand and grins. "Come sit and tell us all about yourself and how you two met. Ma, why don't you grab that tea from the fridge? Tommy, help her with the glasses."

Terina is three years older than I am. I'm not sure if it's that or the fact that she's the youngest girl, but she's always run the show. When her husband passed away unexpectedly, not long before Dad died, she seemed to get even more bossy. I need things to be a certain way in my life, but Terina tries to control the entire world around her. It's got to be exhausting.

Watching her makes me wonder about Danika and how she'd feel if something happened to me. I'm not sure I like the answer either way. I wouldn't want her heart broken, but it might be worse to think she'd be relieved to be rid of me.

The thought is an insidious virus that takes root in my brain.

I want Danika to want me and not just be resigned to her situation. But how can I make that happen when I don't know how to be anyone other than myself? If I could have changed, I would have done it long ago.

I set the four glasses on the coffee table, then pour the tea while my mother dishes tea of her own. An entirely different kind of tea, that is.

"I was just so surprised because Tommy here has never brought anyone home, and not just girls. He never even brought a friend over his whole childhood."

Danika smiles and nods. "I wasn't social as a kid either. I had a speech delay after losing my hearing in my left ear when I was an infant, and it took a while to overcome some of the resulting challenges."

And she did overcome. All I see when I look at her is radiant perfection.

"That's awful. What happened?" Terina asks.

"I got a CMV infection from my mother at birth. It's one of those viruses that isn't dangerous for adults, but a small percentage of newborns can end up with hearing loss. Mom felt horrible when they confirmed I'd lost hearing, but I'm just so grateful it was only one ear."

Her father abandoned her. Kids likely teased her. She had speech delays and who knows what other difficulties, yet somehow, she's not remotely bitter. That shit could have scarred her, but her positive nature kept her focused on the light instead of wallowing in the dark.

I'm not the greatest at optimism, but at the moment, I can

hardly believe my luck that this incredible creature tumbled into my world. And she's agreed to be mine.

I've got to find a way to make her want me so she never decides to leave.

Not that I would let her go.

Danika is *mine*.

25
Danika

I'M ALL OUT OF SMILES ON THE RIDE HOME. I ENJOYED meeting Tommy's family, but with the return to the city comes the return of reality—Gran is still missing. Tommy says he's working on finding her, but that doesn't ease the relentless worry.

What if she's already beyond help? What if her disappearance has nothing to do with Biba, and she's had a stroke, leaving her incapacitated in an alley somewhere? What if Biba *does* have her, but Tommy's connections aren't enough to get her back?

Biba is a hateful, horrible man. I have no doubt he'd kill my grandmother just to hurt me. I know Tommy thinks he's equally as tough as the Russian Vor, but how could he be when I've seen so much kindness from him? Biba isn't capable of kindness or love. An enemy like that is on another level, and I worry that Tommy can't possibly win against someone so depraved. In a way, it's a good problem to have. I'm glad Tommy isn't like Biba, except it doesn't help get Gran back.

The leaden weight of my fears drains my energy such that even simple conversation on the way home feels exhausting. Thankfully, Tommy isn't the chatty sort, so I spend the time trying to fortify myself for whatever life has in store for me next.

Turns out, it's a complete curveball having nothing to do with Biba or Gran.

An hour after returning home, Tommy has a visitor stop by. A woman visitor. She looks like a cross between a news anchor and a runway model—impeccably dressed with a smile that could end wars. Her chestnut hair is silky smooth in a way my red frizz could never comprehend, and her lean musculature suggests she has a second home in a Pilates studio. Her name is Carmen, and she's friendly. *Very* friendly.

I watch with escalating irritation as she continues to hold Tommy's arm after greeting him with a hug. And a smile. And a kiss on the cheek. And a plethora of compliments.

Tommy motions to where I stand in my yellow muslin sundress like Anne of Green Gables fresh from the garden. "Carmen, this is Danika." Despite repeatedly calling me his wife or fiancée every chance he gets, Tommy is suddenly silent on the matter, and I'm stunned to find myself fighting back my own declaration.

Instead, I smile and reach forward to shake her hand. "It's lovely to meet you, Carmen." Such an alluring name—so sultry without even trying. I hate it.

"The pleasure is all mine." She clasps my hand in a shake, then brings it closer as if to examine me for imperfections. "Your skin is flawless. Whatever you use to moisturize, it's working wonders." As if that isn't awkward enough, she looks at me from top to bottom without any attempt to disguise her perusal. "Yes, Tommy. You've done very well, love. She's absolutely stunning."

Tommy frowns. "I'm not her father. I had nothing to do with her genetics."

Carmen waves him off with an airy laugh. "You know what I mean, silly. You chose well—the same with this place." She does a slow spin to scan the apartment. "I'm so glad I got to stop by and see the progress."

She's been here before, in his home, and recently since he hasn't lived here long.

I don't know who this woman is or why I'm having such a visceral reaction to her, but it's taking everything I have not to stomp my feet to the guest bedroom and lock myself inside.

"It still needs a few more paintings, according to my designer. I enjoy the simplicity."

"You're so right. I appreciate it when a beautiful work of art can be cherished without clutter distracting the eye away. Why have it if you're not going to spotlight it? I think the same goes for fashion. Don't you agree, Danika?" She looks back at me expectantly. "But of course, that depends on whether you want the focus on the dress or the woman wearing it."

"Um, I guess," I say limply, not sure if we're talking hypotheticals or if she just called me out for being plain.

Tommy's phone rings, capturing all our attention. The angular lines of his face sharpen in severity when he sees who's calling. "Yeah?" He pauses, then adds, "Got it," and disconnects.

"Carmen, I hate to send you on your way so soon, but something's come up."

I desperately want to ask if it's Gran, but not in front of the succubus.

Carmen waves him off. "Not at all. I'm on a tight schedule today, anyway."

Bye, Felicia.

"Tomorrow," Tommy says in a firm tone.

Wait, what?

My poor heart can't decide if it's drowning or flying or fretting. What's tomorrow? Was the call about Gran? Why isn't this woman leaving already?

Carmen tosses her head back in a peal of bubbling laughter. "Oh, Tommy. You're pushing your limits, but I can't say no to you. Now, I *really* have to get going." She comes to give me a kiss on each cheek. "Until tomorrow!" she calls over her shoulder on her way out the door.

I take two swift steps forward and slam the door behind her. For a second, Tommy and I stare at each other, equally surprised by my actions.

"Um, I ... I was anxious to know about the call." And send a parting message to the she-demon. "Was it about Gran?"

"It was. We have her location." He starts unbuttoning his cuffs while walking to the bedroom. "I'm getting changed, then DiAngelo and I will go retrieve her."

"Where is she? Is she okay?" I have to hurry to keep up with his long strides.

"She's at a hotel in Brooklyn—no word on her condition." He puts on a black undershirt, then a black long-sleeve shirt on top, completing the SWAT look with black cargo pants and black boots. I watch in silence because the outfit reminds me of the severity of the situation. Tommy is about to raid a hotel room—guns will most certainly be involved, and any number of people could end up dead, including Tommy and Gran.

My chin quivers as I fight back a torrent of fear.

Tommy catches sight of me in a mirror and pauses to come closer, bringing my glassy eyes to his. "I know you haven't really seen this side of me, but trust me when I say I've got this, okay?"

I nod, desperate to believe him.

"Good girl." He presses a kiss to the top of my head, then takes out his phone and sends several short texts. "Hand me your phone."

I open the lock and give it to him, watching as he adds a new contact.

"Sante is on his way over. Should something happen to him, I'm putting DiAngelo's number in your phone as well. I'll be with him. If you can't get ahold of me, he'll know what to do." He hands the phone back, a harsh shadow darkening his eyes to the same severe black as his wardrobe. "If all goes as planned, I shouldn't be long. Remember there's a gun in the nightstand if you need it. Do you know how to use a gun?"

I shake my head.

"I know Sante will be here, but I'd feel a whole lot better knowing you can use a gun. Come on." He takes my hand and leads me back to the bedroom. He gets out the gun from the nightstand and tells me it's a nine-millimeter, whatever that means, and shows me how the safety works. He then demonstrates how to chamber a bullet and hold the gun when I shoot so that I don't hurt myself.

I'm pretty sure in the heat of the moment I wouldn't remember a word of what he's told me, but I keep that to myself. "I'll be fine. Promise." The last thing I want is him worrying about me when he should be focused on his mission. I force a thin smile and throw my arms around his neck. "Thank you, Tommy. And please be safe."

He stills beneath me for a fraction of a second before pulling back and kissing me breathless. "Tomorrow," he says in a raw, raspy tone that reminds me of a ravenous bear eyeing a fresh kill.

I don't have the capacity nor is there time to ask what he means by *tomorrow*. He arms himself with an arsenal of weapons I had no idea were here right under my nose. He even puts on a Kevlar vest. The gear would be sexy as hell if I wasn't so worried he was going to need it. Anxiety thick as tar clots in my stomach by the time Sante shows up and Tommy leaves. All I can do now is wait.

Deciding to distract myself by unpacking paint supplies, I excuse myself to the guest bedroom. I suppose it's my studio, now. All my tubs of paint and other accoutrements were already chaotic—I can only imagine what state they're in after being packed by someone else.

The boxes and canvases are piled in a corner. The room isn't large, but it's plenty of space for what I need. I was used to working in a corner of my old bedroom, so having any dedicated space at all feels opulent. I even have the use of the entire dresser for storage, which can also house the pile of random items we unpacked with my clothes but didn't need to be kept in the primary bedroom. Things like a set of poker chips and cards, an expandable folder filled with important documents, and a bag full of cross-stitching materials from a bygone era when I thought it might be a fun hobby. Those items and a few more sit on the bed along with the disposable phone Sachi got for me. I haven't needed it since Tommy got me a new phone but didn't want to get rid of it in case I needed it again.

I open it, surprised it still has charge, and see no new missed calls or texts. A tiny sliver of me had hoped to see something from Gran even though Tommy's already located her. One little text would have done wonders to lift my spirits.

Sitting in the guest room looking at the phone brings back the memory of Tommy asking about who I was texting. I remember being surprised he knew I'd been texting but never had an opportunity to ask him about it. I swear that I didn't use the phone in his presence—I was too scared he might take it away. So how could he have known?

I look around the room and wonder if Tommy could have been watching me. He installed a lock after that first night—could he have put in a camera as well? It doesn't take but a minute of looking to spot the small device in the flower arrangement. In fact, I'm a little put out with myself for not noticing before, though I was rather distracted with life and death matters. Still.

As a touch of indignation takes hold, I search the bathroom, ready to pitch a serious fit if he installed a camera in there, but I don't find anything. Unless he has something behind a mirror or hiding in a socket, it was just the one.

In here. What about the rest of the house?

Does he watch me when I'm alone? I get his worry at first. He didn't know me at all. But this man has decided he wants to marry me now. He can't be ready to commit himself to a life with me while simultaneously not trusting me in his home.

Our home. He told me this was our home.

Exactly! Our home, and if that's really true, I have just as much of a right to know what's here as he does.

Between my bruised ego after meeting Carmen and the

discovery of the camera, I decide to embark on an exploratory expedition. Unpacking can wait.

I take a quick spin around the living room, but I'm not comfortable snooping in front of Sante, so I wind my way back to the primary bedroom. If I still have the guts to keep looking when I'm done in here, I'll take a peek at Tommy's office, but for now, that feels especially taboo.

I go for the nightstand first because that's usually a place for personal things, right? Journals or old letters. Not that I would read something quite so personal, but you get my drift. Aside from the gun, extra bullets in a box, a ChapStick, and a few odds and ends, there's nothing of interest. I head to the drawers in the primary closet. My things went into the bedroom dresser because it was still empty since the closet has a whole chest of drawers within. That's where Tommy keeps his things.

I open the top drawer. Socks in rolled bundles and a swatch of shiny pink fabric that catches my eye.

My heart lodges in my throat before I even have a chance to see what it is—I've already told myself it's undies left by another woman. Carmen, perhaps?

Pain lances through my chest.

Why does this hurt so bad? How? We've only known one another for a little over a week, yet I feel so betrayed. It must be my emotions already on edge because of Gran. Surely, that's it.

I can feel the slightest tremble of my fingers as I pull the item out from beneath his dark dress socks and realize it's not lingerie at all. Not only that, but it's familiar. It looks just like the pink scrunchie I keep in my purse. What are the odds he has the same pink scrunchie stashed away in his drawer?

I go out to the entry where I left my bag on a table and dig through it, trying to look casual. No scrunchie. The hair tie in Tommy's drawer has to be mine, but why would he have it? And when did he take it? He could have taken just about anything of mine since I got here, but there'd be no reason. It's all here already. But if it happened that very first time we met—the day I ran into him outside the police station—he would have had no idea we'd meet again.

Did he take a piece of me home with him? Why? I can't fathom hanging on to something totally useless to me that a stranger left behind. He saw my address—had he planned to find me?

I'm not sure there's any way to know without asking him, and then I'd have to admit to snooping. I'll have to think it over. I put the hair tie back in his drawer, my rebellious impulse drying up. It's best if I stick to my paints—something much more cathartic and healthy.

Paints that Tommy brought for me to a room he's selflessly surrendered to me. And not just that, I've taken over his space in so many little ways, and he hasn't complained once. I know it has to bother him on some level. I've never seen a pantry in such perfect order. The clothes in his closet are hung in color groups. He's a man of habit who thrives on order, and I've upended all of it.

He's so incredibly different than I expected. He's a little crazy but sweet, too.

Such a complex web of contradictions.

I suddenly feel a surge of inspiration—an impulse of colors and shapes that need to come to life. How better to help me understand my confusing feelings for a confusing man than to paint them?

I go to the stack of canvases to find something I can use and see he's brought one painting I didn't expect to see. My white lilies on black that I painted for Gran. Seeing it winds me a little.

I set it on the dresser, leaning against the mirror, and worry flutters in my chest. I'm not sure I could ever forgive myself if something happened to her because of me. I know Mom and Gran encouraged me to run, but now I'm facing the reality of those consequences. I have to wonder if I shouldn't have gone to the police from the very beginning.

26
Tommy

"How'd you find her?" I'm damn good with a computer. If there'd been any way to tap into cameras or otherwise use online data to find Danika's grandmother, I would have tracked her down myself. There was no trail to be found. I looked. DiAngelo used other methods, and I'm curious enough to ask, even though I know it'll feed his already gargantuan ego.

"That's just what I do—I find people." He keeps his eyes forward as he drives us deeper into Brooklyn.

"You're not a fucking bloodhound, D." He's always so damn vague. I think he likes pretending he's mysterious, but that shit doesn't impress me. I literally don't understand it. All I want is a straight answer.

DiAngelo lets a smirk slip. "Dobrev is Slovakian, and they live in the center of Little Odessa. Slovaks generally run with the Russians, but there's a small group of holdouts. I know a guy. Turns out Dobrev is connected to a few of those holdouts. They had to confirm for themselves that she'd been taken, which was the only reason this took as long as it did. Once they got confirmation, they were able to use their connections to get her location. They were willing to risk giving that info to me but not go as far as rescuing her themselves. They already walk a fine line with Biba."

"I bet. He'll want to root out the leak."

"Yeah, which is why I now owe *them*, and *you* owe *me*. Again."

What I really want to say is don't agree to help if you're going to bitch about it, but I don't because he's right. I already owe him big for the Grisha introduction, and I don't need to add to that debt by being ungrateful.

"You know I'm good for it."

"Yeah, well, let's hope I never need it," he mutters as he parks the car out front of a seedy hotel. We both take in the shoddy exterior—paint flaking off the sign, making it illegible, World War Two–era brick, and windows so corroded they're no longer translucent. "I'm gonna have to fumigate my clothes after this, aren't I?" he asks. It's rhetorical, but I answer anyway.

"Might be better to burn them." I suppress a shiver as the sensation of bugs crawling all over me threatens to derail my composure. "Let's get this over with."

We exit the car and head inside. The one good thing about a

shitty hotel is no one is going to question us despite the obvious gear we're carrying under our clothes. This type of place is strictly don't ask, don't tell.

On the way up to the room, we recruit one of the housekeeping ladies to help us. She doesn't speak much English, but the hundred I hand over helps facilitate communication. We have her knock on the door and announce herself.

A heavily accented male voice from inside calls out for her to go away.

I meet DiAngelo's stare. This is the room.

We have the woman unlock the door with her key card, then allow her to scurry away. The man inside is starting to holler. I wait to hear him closing in before I open the door fully and shoot him square in the chest with a tranquilizer gun. It's not how I normally roll, but we're trying to keep this mess from snowballing into an outright war.

The barrel-chested Russian stares stunned at the dart sticking out of his right pectoral, then pulls it out and tosses it to the floor.

"Thought you said one would be enough," DiAngelo says behind me.

"It should be, but this guy is built like a rhino." I shoot him once more for good measure.

The asshole opens his mouth to roar in anger but ends up doing what looks like a yawn instead as his eyes roll back into his head. He collapses backward like a fallen tree.

"I don't envy the headache he's gonna have," D murmurs.

I nod, then look to the back of the room where an old woman is tied to a chair.

She's staring intently at the man on the ground. "He dead?"

"No, but he's going to wish he was when that headache kicks

in tomorrow." I step over him and take out my knife to start cutting away the zip ties holding her in place.

"You must be the Italian."

"I am *an* Italian," I answer vaguely.

"You're Dani's guy—the one letting her hide out at his place. I don't suspect anyone else would be here rescuing me, though I'm not sure why you would be either."

Dani's guy. Fuck, I like the sound of that. "Yeah, that's me. Now, let's get you out of here." I lead the way but turn back when I realize she's still standing in the same place. "You coming?"

"What's in this for you?" She's demanding for someone in her predicament, but I can't say I don't appreciate her directness.

"You mean why am I here to rescue you?"

"Exactly. What are you getting out of taking this kind of risk?"

"I get Danika," I say simply.

She eyes me as though trying to hear what's going unsaid. She doesn't trust me for a second.

"We really don't have time for this," DiAngelo interjects irritably.

I raise my brows at the woman questioningly. "You'll have plenty of time to sort out your suspicions once we're out of here. We've got Petra in a safe house with room for you. First thing tomorrow, you'll both get to see Danika. Or, you can wait here and keep this guy company until the next shift shows up." I nudge the unconscious Russian with my boot.

The spitfire woman Danika calls Gran grunts and finally starts forward, though she pauses long enough to kick her captor in the junk and mutter something about kidnapping an old lady.

She's got serious balls. I'm glad they didn't kill her.

Danika is going to be over the moon.

And even more importantly, I've fulfilled my end of the bargain. It's time for Danika to fulfill hers and become my wife.

27
Danika

It's exactly 9:57 at night when Tommy finally returns. I know because I've been sitting in the living room staring at the clock for over an hour. Setting up my painting supplies only occupied me for so long. Once the worries grew overwhelming, I couldn't concentrate on anything else. Sante's had the television going, but I haven't paid any attention.

I jump to my feet when the front door opens, then see that Tommy's alone. No Gran.

My emotions are swept high in the sky only to plummet back to earth in the span of seconds like a defunct paper airplane. I press my hand over my mouth, silencing myself. I'm too scared to ask.

Tommy sees my fear and raises his hands reassuringly. "She's safe with your mother." He grimaces. "I should have texted. I'm sorry. We went back to the old apartment to get her things, then took her to the safe house. It was a process. She's not exactly compliant, and we had to be overly cautious in case Biba was watching the apartment."

I suck in a gulp of air like a drowning swimmer reaching the surface, then devolve into a fit of tears. The very worst of my fears revolved around something happening to my family. I've been holding those thoughts at bay because my imagination is too vivid to even entertain the possibilities. I had to block it all out, but now that they're safe, it's like letting water out of a dam that leads to a total structural collapse.

I plop back onto the sofa and ugly cry. Sobbing, sniffling, snotty weeping.

Sante makes a hasty exit as Tommy joins me on the sofa, pulling me onto his lap.

"Fuck, Dani. I said I'm sorry."

"I'm just ... relieved. I was ... so worried," I say between hiccuping breaths.

Tommy holds me close, pressing kisses to my head. "Everything's fine now. I'll take you to see them first thing tomorrow, yeah?"

I nod and try to wipe the torrent of moisture from my face. "Thank you, Tommy," I whisper against his chest. "I don't know what I would have done without you."

His hand rubbing circles on my back stills momentarily. "Me either, little thief," he returns equally as softly. "Have you eaten?"

"No, my stomach was a mess."

"Let's eat, shower, and head to bed. I think we're both exhausted." He gives me one more squeeze, then helps me to my feet.

When we get to the kitchen, he instructs me to sit at the bar, then warms up leftovers for us. Once we're done, we shower together. Tommy undresses me, then insists on washing me from top to bottom with immaculate reverence. Every touch is a benediction. Every caress, an ode. He worships my body, and though he's hard as a rock the entire time, he never makes any of the exchange sexual. And when I'm aroused beyond comprehension and try to take him in my hand to encourage him, he withdraws from my touch.

"Not tonight, Dani," he says in a voice ravaged by desire. "It wouldn't be right."

I don't fully understand since I'm telling him with my touch that it is alright—everyone is safe—enjoying a physical release isn't inappropriate. But that hardly feels like something I should argue about. If he's not comfortable, then I won't push him.

He towels us both dry and minutes later, we're snuggled in bed. He doesn't even check his gun or the blinds a single time. Every ounce of his attention is focused on me, and I've never felt more cherished.

I WAKE CONFUSED. The sun shines into the room, yet Tommy is still here with me. When I lift my head to get a look at him, I see that he's wide awake.

"What's going on?" I ask in a voice husky with sleep.

"Nothing, why?"

"You didn't work out." I scoot closer and curl into his side, my head resting close to his shoulder.

"There's a lot going on today. I thought it would be nice to enjoy the morning with you." He trails a hand down my arm. "Though, I will say that my resolve was wavering. If you didn't wake up in approximately one minute and thirty-five seconds, I was going to have to wake you up. I couldn't lie here any longer."

I grin sleepily. "That's more like my Tommy."

My Tommy?

I'm too groggy for a filter. The words simply slipped out, and I only realize that's how I feel once they're in the air for both of us to hear.

Tommy squeezes me gently. "And on that note, we should get moving."

"Why? We have somewhere to be?"

"I made you a promise, remember? It's time to go see your mom and grandmother."

"Oh! Right." I sit up and rub my eyes, dumbfounded that I could possibly forget something so important. My motivation ignited. I'm dressed and ready to go in record time. Tommy makes us a quick plate of eggs, then we're on our way.

The smile etched into my face is so ingrained that it doesn't even waver when we pull up to an ancient little church sandwiched between two giant buildings. "Is this where they're staying?"

"This is where we're meeting them," he explains.

I realize that's probably much safer than going to their place and possibly leading Biba's men to them. I'm so glad Tommy thinks of that sort of thing. I truly feel safe in his hands.

The blackened stone exterior of the church shows its years of wear, but the inside is magical—even more so with gorgeous bouquets of fresh white flowers all around. Someone must be getting married. I'm struck by the oddity that we would decide to meet them here if there's going to be a ceremony soon, but figure we don't have to stay long. Seeing Mom and Gran at all is a selfish treat. I could have done with a call, but this way, I get to give them hugs, and that is too much to pass up.

As though hearing my thoughts, my two most favorite women on this planet round the corner and come into view. I launch myself at them. We hug and cry in a tangle of limbs and I love yous.

Eventually, we pull away but still clasp hands. None of us is ready to relinquish our hold on one another quite yet. I look them both over joyfully. "You two look lovely—so dressed up today!"

Mom quirks her head and shoots me a funny look. "Of course, we're dressed up. What did you think I'd wear for your wedding?"

My wedding?

I study their twin expressions of confusion, prompting Tommy's words to replay in my head.

I will get your grandmother back and keep the two of them safe, and you will marry me immediately after.

I look over my shoulder at the flowers leading into the chapel, then back at Mom and Gran.

It can't be.

He would have said something, wouldn't he? Sure, he's literal, but immediately could mean anything. If he meant we'd get married the very next day after Gran was returned, he would have specified, wouldn't he?

Not if he thought I might back out.

I slowly revolve to meet Tommy's stoic stare and feel the truth hit me like a fist to the gut.

He meant immediately.

The world spins as I realize Tommy and I are about to get married.

28 Tommy

I SWEEP DANIKA INTO MY ARMS BEFORE SHE CAN TOPPLE over, then glance at the two Dobrev women gaping at me. "Must have been overcome with joy." I clear my throat. "Excuse us for a moment."

Danika isn't unconscious, but she's clearly woozy. Her arms are loosely draped over my shoulders, while her forehead rests against my neck.

"Tommy? Why didn't you tell me?" she asks weakly.

I go to the nearest room—a small family chapel for private worship—and sit on one of the wooden pews. Danika tries to wriggle off my lap, but I refuse to let her go. "Sit still and listen," I order in a firm voice.

The fog behind her eyes miraculously clears, leaving in its stead a pair of emerald daggers.

"Tommaso Donati, we cannot get married today. We don't even have a marriage license."

"Yes, we do," I correct her.

"I never signed one." A finely sculpted auburn brow arches high on her forehead in challenge.

I shrug. "The paper I have says you did."

"But that's not legal!"

"Says who? Who's going to challenge it?" I've drawn a line in the sand, and she knows it. The only person who would have any reason to argue about the validity of our marriage license is one of us, and I'm certainly not saying a word. I stare deep into her wide, innocent eyes as I take a small box from my pocket. "Danika Dobrev, I *will* marry you. There is nothing about this life that I want any part of if it's not with you. You quiet my demons and fill me with hope. Please, don't make me wait a minute longer. Marry me here, today." With every raw, unfiltered word, my emotions bleed into my ragged voice.

I open the black velvet box and take out a diamond ring that couldn't be any more perfect if I'd dreamed it up myself. Danika gasps. It's a tiny reflexive breath I never would have heard if she wasn't so close. I'm so grateful I did because I'm certain her genuine reaction was pure awe. It's understandable. The craftsmanship is exquisite. The large pear-cut diamond is set among the ropes of a woven gold vine with tiny delicate diamonds as leaves. It's whimsical yet elegant and perfectly suited for my divine goddess.

I slide the symbol of my commitment onto her trembling finger.

"It fits perfectly," she breathes, eyes fixed on the diamond.

"That's Carmen for you. She's damn good at what she does, and she knows it, too. Woman is practically a professional racketeer, considering the rates she charges."

Danika turns to meet my eyes. "Carmen? That awful woman who came to the apartment?"

I battle back a smile. "Yes, that *awful* woman. She's a personal shopper, which is why she had to meet you to see your sizes. She helped me find the ring, arranged for the chapel and flowers, and above all, she sourced that—" I direct her attention to a white satin gown hanging by the door behind us.

When Danika sees the long luxury garment bag, she lifts off my lap and practically floats over to the dress. I'm probably more eager to see it than she is because I've had a vision of her in a white gown since the moment I met my Grecian goddess. I told Carmen exactly what I wanted, and from the looks of it, she delivered.

Danika gently extracts the dress from the bag, keeping it on the hanger to step back and admire its beauty. "It's incredible."

"And just like the ring, it should fit you perfectly."

"How? How could she possibly get this done in a day?" She finally looks back at me, eyes full of bewildered awe.

It wasn't exactly done in a day, but she doesn't need to know that.

"You can buy anything for the right amount of money, and if it means calling you mine, I'll spend every dime I have." I didn't come anywhere near doing that, but I would if it came down to it, and I want her to know it. I close the distance between us and cup her face in my hands, bringing my lips to her cheek. "Please, little thief. You've stolen my heart. Put me out of my misery and say you'll be mine." I craft each softly spoken word in the hope that it forms a tether between us, anchoring us to one another.

When she pulls back and I see the tears in her eyes, I know I've succeeded.

"You better not make me regret this, Tommy Donati," she says, laughing through her tears.

I sweep her into a hug, spinning us in a joyful circle like I haven't done since I was a kid. When I set her back down, I bring my lips to hers, sealing the deal with a kiss. Somehow, she tastes even more irresistible now that I know she's about to be mine. The only reason I'm able to pull myself away is the knowledge that every minute we're in here is another minute of delay, and I'm done waiting.

"I'll send in the ladies to help you get ready. You have one hour."

29
Danika

"You've been crying." Those are the first words out of Gran's mouth when she and Mom join me in the small chapel. She scrutinizes me with the eagle eyes of a septuagenarian who can read a room ten times better than she can read a crossword, even with her glasses.

"I have, but in a good way, I think."

Mom and Gran exchange a look. Mom closes the chapel doors, and Gran guides me to sit with her. She takes my hand in both of hers and levels me with a no-nonsense stare.

"Dani, girl. What on God's green earth is going on here?"

"I'm getting married?" It's supposed to be a statement but comes out as a question.

Her thin lips purse until they're just a collection of wrinkles. "Is that what you want?"

I try to come up with the right words to answer her, then decide there are none. "I'm not sure how to answer that, Gran," I admit softly. "None of this was my choice, but that doesn't mean I don't want it. I want my family safe. I want to be with someone who wants me, and if I know one thing at all about Tommy, it's that he's crazy about me. It's just all so fast, and he's Mafia. I never saw that for myself." I look from Gran to Mom, who is in the pew in front of us, and search for answers in their familiar faces.

Gran gives a single affirmative nod. "If I told you that you could walk out that door today and never see him again, what would you do? Because I could make that happen, so answer honestly."

My chest constricts as I look at the double doors and genuinely envision that outcome.

Would I leave? If my family's safety wasn't at stake, and I could leave of my own free will, would I do that and choose to never see Tommy again?

A flood of memories washes over me—the feel of his body wrapped around mine at night, the way he always makes a plate of food for me first, the terror in his eyes when he jumped out of the shower to protect me when DiAngelo broke into the apartment. I can't think of a single time he's been anything other than kind to me, even when he soothed my fears after taping my mouth shut. From that very first night all the way to moments ago when he cradled me protectively, Tommy has gone out of his way to care for me.

You quiet my demons and fill me with hope.

I suddenly realize I'm slowly shaking my head. "No, Gran. I don't want to leave. I'm scared, but not scared enough to walk away."

She grins broadly. "Well, child, that tells you all you need to know."

Mom doesn't look convinced. "They haven't known each other for two weeks, Ma. That's not enough."

Gran waves her off. "Sure, it's fast, but time isn't a great predictor of how well you mesh with someone. Milo and I only knew each other for a month before we got married. How long were you seeing that degenerate Biba before you learned his true character?" Gran knows exactly how long. We all do. But the question makes her point—relationships are always a gamble to some degree.

Mom's frown doesn't waver. She leans forward to hiss at her mother, "And what about his business? What about the danger Mafia brings to our Dani?"

Gran shrugs. "Life is dangerous, Petra. Better she's with a man who knows how to protect her." Gran grins at me while Mom makes a disgruntled scoffing sound. "You know your heart, Danika. The rest will work itself out in time." She scoots closer and gives my cheek a kiss.

"Should have known you two would overrule me. You always do," Mom grumbles with just enough dry humor for us to know she's not actually mad. "I suppose if we're going to do this, we better get started. We've eaten up too much of our time already."

I jump to my feet. "I don't even have my makeup here. What am I supposed to do? I can't get married like *this*."

The chapel doors burst open at that exact moment to reveal Amelie with a man and woman flanking her.

"Did someone say makeup?"

My jaw drops. "Were you waiting outside the doors for me to say that?"

Amelie grins from ear to ear. "Nah, just lucked out. We were running late, and I happened to hear you panicking as I walked up to the door. Epic timing, right?"

I double over in a fit of laughter that spreads to the others, except for the beauty team who look at us all like we might be slightly unhinged. I want to tell them how right they are, but I don't want to scare them off. I *really* need my hair and makeup done. I may be marrying a mobster on short notice using falsified documents under threat of death from my criminal father, but I also have standards. I want to look unforgettable as I walk down that aisle and become Mrs. Danika Donati.

THE DRESS IS MAGNIFICENT. White satin fabric hangs loosely over my body to accentuate my modest curves, including the draped cowl neckline held up with tiny spaghetti straps. It's ethereal and feminine and elegant in its simplicity. I feel like a fairy queen.

And my hair. *Oh my God.* My hair.

It's always been half wild—never quite sure if it wants to be wavy or curly or straight and is usually a touch of all three at any given time. But not today. Today, every strawberry strand has been expertly secured in an artful updo with just the right number of loose tendrils to be casually elegant. Add a light application of makeup to help my green eyes pop, and

I've never felt more beautiful in my entire life. Or more nauseous.

I stand only a few feet from the entrance of the main sanctuary, hands clutching my bouquet for dear life as I try to convince myself not to vomit all over my dream wedding dress.

Am I really going to do it? Am I really going to say I do?

Life is so unpredictable—that is the only true certainty. We can plan all we'd like, but sometimes fate takes the reins. I never could have imagined I'd be in this position two weeks ago. It's been a roller coaster of events that has left me no choice but to hold on tight and rely on my gut to guide me. Right now, I'm holding these flowers so tightly, I'm practically strangling them, and my gut, despite its queasy revolt, insists that my future stands around this corner waiting for me at the church altar.

I inhale a slow, steadying breath, then take the first steps toward this new journey. My gaze is immediately drawn to Tommy standing opposite me at the end of the aisle. His possessive stare explores every inch of me with ravenous intensity as though he's laying claim to the most precious treasure on earth. His gaze makes me feel more adored than any limelight could ever achieve.

Yes, I'm doing the right thing.

One look from him, and I'm cloaked in a reassuring warmth. And with every step I take closer to Tommy, my fears grow a little more distant like roaches running from the light. That is instinct drowning out the insidious voice of doubt. Deep down, I know Tommy is meant for me.

The small church is empty save for the preacher and the six of us—Mom, Gran, me, Tommy, Sante, and Amelie. The beauty crew split as soon as they were done, and I'm not sure of the reasons, but Tommy's family isn't present, aside from

Sante. It's a tiny ceremony, but I don't need it any larger. I always figured Sachi would be at my wedding when the time came, but I'm kind of glad she's not here. Sorting through my feelings has been hard enough. Explaining everything to her would have been exponentially more difficult. I just hope she doesn't disown me when I see her next and tell her all that's happened.

The music playing softly over a speaker system quiets as I finally join my husband-to-be in front of the minister. Tommy takes my hands in his, flipping them over and reverently kissing the inside of each of my wrists.

"You are the most stunning woman to ever walk this earth."

"Thank you," I whisper as my cheeks flush with warmth. "You look incredibly handsome in this suit." The black jacket and matching pants with a white shirt and no tie are simple yet classic and a perfect complement to my dress. I don't know what it is about men in suits, but I could stare at him for days and never get bored.

The minister clears his throat, encouraging us to face him and proceed with the ceremony. "Welcome, everyone, on this very special day when we celebrate the joining of Tommaso Donati and Danika Dobrev in holy matrimony."

"Don't say another fucking word, Preacher."

We all whip around to see two men holding guns at the entrance to the sanctuary where I'd been only moments before. I recognize one as the bald man guarding Biba's office door. He's traded in his stoic indifference for a face full of malicious rage. And his partner is no different. Both look like they're ready to skin us alive.

"Danika, come here," Biba's guard orders.

Tommy eases himself in front of me. "She's not going

anywhere." His voice is devoid of emotion—chilling in the same way an arctic breeze foretells of a coming storm.

"Biba wants his daughter back." The man shrugs. "Bonus for me if I get to shoot you in the process."

"You do that, and you better pray you kill me instantly, or I will make you live to regret it." Tommy manages to paint a horrific picture of carnage using only the hollow tone of his voice. I should be horrified, but I find myself impressed. This isn't Tommy. This is Tommaso, the Mafia assassin. This is why Tommy assured me I could trust him to handle Biba. He's every bit the badass he claimed to be and then some.

The Russian roars, "Danika, get the fuck over here before I kill everyone in this room."

My entire body recoils at the fury in his voice.

"Stay put," Tommy clips back at me through gritted teeth. He means it. He'd rather take a bullet than risk me getting hurt or captured.

I'm humbled by his selflessness and shamed by my cowardice.

These men wouldn't think twice about killing everyone in here. Am I willing to risk that so I can keep hiding in fear? No, there's absolutely no way. I won't let—

I don't get any further when a gunshot explodes with two more following in rapid succession.

My body curves in on itself instinctively. I drop to my knees with my hands over my ears but the gunshot echoes in my brain. Images of blood splattering across greasy concrete flash through my mind as I desperately try to cast them away.

Fear rages like blood through my veins.

I can't look. I don't want to see it. I'll never be able to forget the lifeless eyes.

So much blood.

My eyes are squeezed so tightly shut that it takes a second for me to realize Tommy has left me. He's surged forward toward the men, which means he must not be hurt, but I can hardly make myself look to check. Instead, I scurry to the front pew, where Mom, Gran, and Amelie huddle on the floor. We cling to one another and peek over at the guys standing in the aisle, looking down at what I assume are the two Russians.

"One of you carrying a gun?" Sante calls over to us with a hint of confusion.

Gran lifts a small black handgun in the air. "I am, thank the Lord." She pulls herself to her feet and slips the gun back in her purse.

"Where the fuck did you get a gun?" Sante demands.

"From me," Mom answers as she helps me to my feet.

I hear everyone around me, but I feel removed like a hazy filter has formed between me and the rest of the world.

"Jesus. And where the fuck did *you* get a gun?"

"We got it from a cousin when Dani first told us about Biba coming after her. I brought it with me when I went to the safe house. Ma asked me last night if I still had it, so I gave it to her."

Gran nods sagely. "It's a good thing I did." She leans toward the dead men and makes a spitting gesture.

I keep myself staunchly faced forward toward the altar. I can't look.

I don't want to see.

Amelie wraps an arm around me. "You okay?" she whispers.

I nod, but I'm not okay. So many images that I never wanted to see again are resurfacing.

Sante chuckles. "She damn near shattered this guy's shin."

"Not bad, considering I had to shoot from around the bench.

Besides, I wasn't trying to kill him. I just needed a distraction so you two could do the rest."

Three shots. Or was it two?

And so much laughter. Horrible, heartless laughter.

Gran finally looks back at me and stills. "Oh, sweet Dani. I'm so sorry you had to see that. Come here, sweet girl." She wraps her arms around me, and I finally feel a semblance of stability. I anchor myself in her touch and force out the horrible memories. "They were bad men, Dani. They would have killed all of us."

"I know. Let's just get this over with and get out of here." My voice is almost unrecognizable. So fragile. So empty.

She pulls back and looks searchingly at me, then nods with solemn acceptance.

"Danika?" Tommy's voice calls from behind me, but I can't look. I don't want to see.

I move mechanically to my place at the altar and wait. Footsteps and shuffling noises echo behind me as everyone resituates themselves.

I don't look.

Then Tommy is there beside me. We are two islands with an ocean of unspoken words between us.

"You can come out now," he barks at the altar, prompting the minister to peek around the side of the wooden structure. "We aren't leaving here until we're married, so I suggest you start talking."

The man nods his sweat-covered head and drags himself to his feet.

Tommy and I are married in what has to be the fastest wedding ceremony in history. The sanctuary is silent, the atmosphere is suffocating, and I am a prisoner to my memories, unable to shake free of the horrific devastation.

Tommy can sense the change in me. I know it. I hate to upset him. He doesn't understand, but I can't force out the words. Not now. Not ever.

When he kisses me, his touch is a mix of punishment and pleading.

I try to soothe the ache in the only way I can by kissing him back with every ounce of want and need I feel for this beautiful, complicated man who is now my husband. The numbing promise of his touch becomes my sole focus. I vaguely hear the encouraging cheers from our family nearby, but even that feels removed and fuzzy.

Tommy eventually forces us apart, his demanding gaze scouring my face for understanding.

"I need to get out of here. Please, take me home." It's the best I can manage.

"I can have Sante take you—"

"No." I cut him off quickly. "Please, come home with me." I know this chasm between us will grow exponentially wider if we don't leave together. I can't undo what's happened, but I can try to keep it from getting worse.

Tommy drops his chin in a sign of acquiescence. Ten minutes later, we're finally out of the church and on our way home for the first time as husband and wife.

30

Tommy

SILENCE BY NATURE SHOULD BE SOOTHING. IT IS CALM AND still and quiet. Peaceful.

Yet the silence surrounding Danika and me in the car on the way home is pure agony. Invisible shards of glass press in all around me. I want to scream and end the torment, but what would I say? I don't regret anything I've done. I am exactly the man she thinks I am. There is nothing for me to explain away or apologize for.

All I can do is absorb the stabbing pain and try not to bleed all over the place by lashing out and making a mess. I think I've nearly made it as the elevator doors close around us, but before we can reach the forty-second floor, Danika finally pierces the insufferable veil.

"I'm sorry, Tommy." Her childlike voice is wrought with sorrow that only stokes my anger.

"Don't apologize."

"It had nothing to do with you."

A huff of condescending laughter rolls past my lips. "Sure, whatever."

Every goddamn thing that happened in that church revolved around me—I set up the ceremony, I failed to keep our location adequately protected, I killed a man, and I didn't call off the wedding despite the two corpses bleeding out in the aisle. Whatever element she found particularly upsetting is irrelevant—it's all a reflection of me.

The elevator doors open before she can respond. I hold my hand over the gap to keep the doors from shutting, and Danika leads us to the apartment. Once inside, I set down my keys and go directly to the kitchen to pour a drink, hoping she'll take the hint and let me be. It's not even noon. I have no idea what I'm going to do with myself for the rest of the day, but I'm not doing it sober if I have to stay here.

I down nearly half the scotch I've poured for myself, then turn to see Danika standing in the living room in nothing but her bridal heels. Her satin gown is a shimmering pool of white at her feet. I toss back the rest of my drink and set down the glass before slowly stalking closer to my beautiful wife. The fickle goddess who captured my heart only to rip it to shreds.

I allow my eyes to rove over her porcelain skin mottled with amber freckles as I start a slow circle around her. "After everything that's happened, you still think you're willing to give yourself to me?" Each word is a blade dragged across her delicate skin. This is wrong. My head is in the wrong place to let this unfold now, but I've been craving this moment for weeks—the moment when she'd finally be mine.

"I wouldn't offer if I didn't want to," she insists in a voice that doesn't waver.

Fuck, I want to believe her, but my brain tells me it's impossible. I saw the desolation in her eyes today. Even I'm not that obtuse. There's *nothing* about me a woman like her should want, no matter how hard I try to convince myself otherwise. She's been forced into every second of this relationship—whether hiding from her father to a coerced marriage with me—she never had a choice in any of it. No real alternative, and now she's stuck with me, trying to make the best of it.

Makes me so fucking angry.

A voice in the back of my mind screams at me to walk away, but that primal beast inside me has taken control, and he wants his prize. Death is demanding his favor.

"Get on your knees."

31
Danika

This is a show. Tommy is trying to be cruel and distant. And that's exactly why I need to do this. I decided to strip and offer myself to him because I know he's hurting, and it's all my fault. He's protecting himself. Trying to push me away so my rejection will be meaningless. The only problem is I never meant to reject him. I have to prove my commitment to him, and this is the only way I know how without cutting myself wide open. I don't want to do that. Not today. Not minutes after saying I do. Our wedding day is supposed to be special. I don't want to taint it worse than it already is.

I lower myself to my knees.

"Take out my cock." Tommy's words are carved in ice.

My tongue sweeps across my bottom lip as I peer up at him through my lashes, then unbuckle his belt. When I tug his shirt free, he impatiently rips the shirt open, causing buttons to fly everywhere, so that it doesn't hinder his view of me. I help his pants fall to the floor, then palm the throbbing bulge in his boxer briefs. I rub my hand up and down a couple of times, give him a squeeze, then lower the waistband of his underwear to free him.

I'm about to take his cock into my greedy hand when his hand clasps the hair piled on my head and demands my attention.

"You should have run when you had the chance," he says almost to himself. "Open your mouth."

I do as he says and am surprised to feel moisture start to leak from my core. Even this pitch-black side of him turns me on because, despite it all, I know he'd never hurt me.

"Flatten your tongue." He holds his cock in one hand and my head in the other, guiding himself into my mouth. When I close my lips around him, he gives me a little tug. "Open," he demands in a rasp. The touch of my tongue on the sensitive underside of his shaft has him ragged with need, but he doesn't lose himself. In and out, he drags himself across my tongue over and over. I get the sense it's a test of his control. Like he's teasing himself. Or is it a punishment?

Yes, that's exactly what this is, and I refuse to allow myself to be his weapon.

I look him square in the eyes and suck him all the way to the back of my throat. His composure shatters. He drops his head back with a roar as I take over, gripping his balls in one hand while squeezing the base of his shaft with the other. I lick and suck and twist every masculine inch of him until I feel his balls pull tighter. His shaft swells even thicker, and I know he's seconds from exploding. That's when I pull away.

"*Fuck.*" His violent curse shakes the rafters. "What is it, Danika? Can't stand the thought of my cum on your tongue?" he asks viciously, chest heaving.

I wipe my mouth and shake my head before lying on my back before him. "You said the first time would be inside me. You promised." I know how much this means to him, and I won't let him deny himself.

I spread my bent knees wide to present him with my weeping core. "Please, Tommy," I beg softly. I want him to hear the sincerity in my voice and know that I want this just as much as he does.

With a growl, he kicks off his shoes to free himself from his pants, then aligns his body with mine. He doesn't wait or ask permission. He simply surges inside me.

My entire body seizes from the painful intrusion, and he seems to sense the hurt he's caused because he freezes with his shaft buried deep inside me. His forearm slides behind my neck to cradle my head, his lips pressing a kiss to my forehead.

"I didn't just..." His ragged question fades away as if unable to say the words.

"No, but it's been a while." I'm not a virgin. I would have said something if I were. "I'm okay, now, I think."

Tension eases from his body, and he starts to slowly rock inside me. He keeps our bodies held tightly together and continues to hold my head as though trying to protect me from himself. I know why when slow and steady quickly escalates to hard and fast. Tommy fucks me with rabid desperation, so intense that it doesn't last long. My body is just blossoming with sensation when he stiffens and moans his release, cum jetting inside me.

Relief washes over me. This may not be the ideal start to our marriage, but it could have been so much worse, considering the way things were going.

We lay still for several minutes as he recovers. I expect him to pull away at any second, and I wonder which Tommy I'll see in his eyes, but that doesn't happen.

I arch and moan as he starts to move inside me again, already thick and hungry for more.

"Tommy, we're gonna make a mess," I say distractedly, worrying about his gorgeous rug.

"Don't give a fuck."

After a minute, he pulls back to his knees and grabs a pillow from the sofa. "Lift," he instructs.

I bridge to lift my butt off the ground. He puts the pillow under me, then admires the view of my well-fucked pussy. I imagine it's red and swollen and glistening with our combined juices.

A rumbling sound of masculine pride resonates from deep in his chest.

"This is mine, Danika." His finger enters me, then glides up to swirl around my clit.

I writhe from the pleasure. "Yes, Tommy. I'm yours."

"Say it again," he demands.

"I'm yours."

His touch feels so good that I clamber for more. My hands go to my breasts and tease my nipples while his agile fingers work miracles at my center until I'm panting and shaking and begging to come. That's when he fills me with his cock and fucks me on his knees so that I have an incredible view of his body towering over me, hands clamped on my hips, driving himself into me. The coil of hard-earned muscle, the smattering of masculine hair, the branding touch of his savage stare—everything that is Tommy heightens my pleasure until I'm shattering like a thousand shooting stars across a cloudless night sky.

We come together, squeezing and panting. Worshipping and claiming.

His body lowers to rest over mine, holding me close again. Too soon, he's pulling free of me, helping me to my feet. He treats me gingerly, but he's still not himself. Part of him is still a million miles away.

"We'd better clean up." He takes me to the bathroom and starts the shower. I resecure some of the strands of hair that were pulled loose, then join him in the spray of water. I wonder what he's thinking, but most of all, I worry what he'll say when I tell him I'm not on birth control.

32 Tommy

The beast inside me has withdrawn to his cave, satisfied with his acquisition, but his absence creates an empty void. That's what I deserve for such a hollow victory. Danika gave herself to me, yet I can't stop myself from asking whether she did it to appease me or out of obligation. Either way, she didn't do it out of sheer desire. I wanted her to want me so badly that I let myself pretend that's what was happening, but now the doubts are eating at me, and once a thought like that starts feasting on my conscience, it's as unstoppable as a horde of locusts.

How can I trust my interpretation of the situation when my

compulsion for her warps my perception? How could she possibly know what she truly wants when she's been manipulated at every turn? And worst of all, how can I ever expect to keep her if she never wanted to be with me in the first place?

My turbulent thoughts haunt me as I wash her body clean of my presence.

All afternoon, doubts stare daggers at me while I work in my office.

Anger rakes its scaly talons under my skin as I cook dinner.

Shame clots in my lungs while we watch TV, making my chest burn with every breath.

And throughout it all, Danika smiles as though she's trying to reassure me that everything's fine when I know it's not. More than anything, I hate that I can't figure out the problem. If I can't figure it out, I can't fix it.

We're crawling into bed at the end of the day when I reach the end of my threshold because I know I'm agitated enough that I'll endlessly check my guns, arm the alarm, and ensure every object in the apartment is set at a right angle if I can't get a resolution. My compulsions will own me, and she'll know. As embarrassing as it is to force the issue and ask her why she rejected me, I'd rather do that than let her see me as a slave to myself.

"You couldn't even look at me." The words tumble from my lips as though they'd been pressed against a door, waiting for the handle to turn. It's not how I planned to broach the subject, but at least it's done.

Danika's brows furrow. "You mean earlier ... in the living room?"

"No, at the wedding. After the Russians attacked. You turned your back on me."

The addition of a frown turns her confusion to remorse. "I

turned my back on them. I couldn't bear to see them." She scoots closer in the bed and takes my hand in hers. "I swear, Tommy, it had nothing to do with you."

She lifts her lips to connect with mine, and I kiss her back because fuck do I want to believe her. I considered that it was simply the trauma of seeing two men get shot that had upset her. Of course, I considered that. I'm an overthinker. I've conjured every possible scenario I could come up with over the past ten hours and debated the merits of each. I can't shake the feeling that it's more than that. She was practically catatonic.

But if not me, then what?

"You'd tell me if you were upset with me?" I ask, hating the vulnerability inherent in the question.

"I promise," she says without hesitation. "You're my husband now, Tommy. We're a team."

It doesn't fully erase the residue of my fears, but I can hardly ask more of her. It will have to do for now.

I place a kiss on her forehead and pull her body against mine beneath the covers. "Let's get some sleep." A part of me would love to reassure myself of our connection by slipping my cock deep inside her, but I know she's already going to be sore. I don't want to make it worse.

The cathartic feel of her skin on mine keeps my compulsions at bay enough for me to resist the pull. I want to stay with her more than I need to perform my routine, and I relish that feeling. The peace and contentment that comes when my mind and body are not at war with one another for once. It's enough to ease me into a deep sleep, which leaves me especially disoriented when a piercing cry yanks me awake in the night.

It's Danika. She's having a nightmare again like she did the first night—the night we spent handcuffed together. I pull away so that I can see her better just as she whimpers, her beautiful face scrunching in agony.

"Don't look at me. Please, don't look at me."

For a heartbeat's time, I think she's talking to me but then realize it's the dream. She's talking in her sleep.

"Dani, baby. Wake up. You're having a nightmare." I give her arm a little shake.

Her eyes pop open, meet my wide stare across from her, and she screams—a bloodcurdling, heart-wrenching scream of terror—then scuttles away from me so frantically she falls off the damn bed.

"Jesus, Dani. Are you okay? It's just me, baby."

She slowly rights herself and looks around in confusion. "Oh God. I'm so sorry. I freaked out, didn't I?" She crawls back into bed and takes a deep, harrowing breath.

"Yeah, and that's the second time. What's this about, Dani?" I try to use a soothing voice, though I really want to demand an explanation.

"It's just a bad dream I used to have. I quit having it years ago, but Biba coming after me seems to have brought it back to the surface. I'm really sorry if I scared you."

"What's it about?"

"I can never really remember. I just wake feeling creeped out." She snuggles closer as if signaling she's ready to go back to sleep, but I have one more question I need to ask.

"You said, 'Don't look at me.' That ring any bells?"

Her entire body shivers.

"No idea." Desolation carves the warmth out of her voice. Sweet, innocent Danika is lying to my face, and I have no idea why.

DEATH'S FAVOR

THE FOLLOWING MORNING, I can't outrun my worries, no matter how hard I push myself. My own personal storm clouds hover overhead as I exit the home gym and head to the kitchen. Danika is cheerfully making breakfast, so I try not to be an ass, but the number of unsolvable problems mounting up against me has me feeling irritable.

I know the day is thoroughly doomed, however, when it's not even eight and Renzo's name appears on my phone screen. I knew he'd get word about the wedding when we had to call in a cleanup crew to help with the bodies. I knew he'd be pissy about it even though he already knew I was committed to her, which is why I didn't give him a heads-up. I wasn't asking permission, so why give myself the headache? Except I didn't anticipate a bloodbath at my wedding.

After the day passed and I never heard from him, I figured he was going to give me a break for once. I know it was delusional of me to be so optimistic, but I've already got too much shit on my plate to worry about him. But now he's calling, and it's not even eight in the morning. Renzo never calls this early. Something's up.

"Yeah." I brace for the worst.

"Were you ever planning on calling me, or were you hoping Biba would do you a favor and take me out?"

"The fuck is that supposed to mean?" I demand, my hackles fully raised.

"It means I need to fucking know when we're on the brink of war. You marry his daughter, kill two of his men, and you don't think I need to know about that shit?"

"You telling me no one told you yesterday?"

"No, Tommy. They told me. But it should have been you to fucking tell me. It was *your* wedding, and you're *my* brother. You should have had the balls to pick up the phone." He's beyond pissed, and it's hard not to follow suit. He's attacking me without asking a single fucking question or even trying to give me the benefit of the doubt.

"And the fact that it was my goddamn wedding day, and I had a traumatized bride on my hands, does that mean anything to you?" I shoot back at him.

My pulse pounds in my eardrums, counting off the beats of his silence.

"Look," he says in a more resigned tone, "we could argue about this all day, but it's not the reason I called."

"If you didn't call to bitch me out, then why are we talking?"

A weary exhale crosses the line. "Biba retaliated last night. Explosives went off on Pier 49. Two men are missing, and three were taken to the hospital. Leadership is meeting in ten to plan our response, and I think you need to join us since you're at the center of it."

Fucking Christ.

Every bit of wind deflates from my sails. I knew Biba would be upset, but I didn't think he'd act so quickly, nor did I expect him to escalate things to that degree.

I run my hand through my sweaty hair. "Jesus, yeah. I'll be there in ten."

"Bring Sante. He's a part of this as much as you are."

"Got it."

The line goes dead. I suck in a deep breath to get my bearings. Danika is white as a ghost, standing motionless as she watches me.

"What's happened?" she asks in a tiny voice.

"Biba happened. I've gotta go."

"Please, don't go," she begs, eyes full of worry.

"Don't have time for this, Danika. You remember how to use the gun?"

"Yes." She sounds reluctant, but I'm not sure if it's her memory that's an issue or her fears.

"I'm having a guy come stand guard outside the door. Do not leave the apartment. Do not open the door for him or anyone. I'm going to tell lobby security to turn off access to the forty-second floor via the elevator. I will text you when I'm on my way back, okay?"

She nods with unsteady, jerking movements.

"Give me your lips, little thief. Show me you're listening." I wait for her to rise on her toes and bring her lips to mine, then kiss her back with weeks of pent-up passion. "It's just a meeting with our team. Everything's going to be fine, understand?"

She nods, but her fear saturates the air. There's nothing more I can do, so I head out to face whatever comes next.

A DOZEN of us sit around a small conference table—everyone is leadership aside from Sante and me. The atmosphere is so severe that a single misstep would be equivalent to a drop of blood in a piranha tank. Figuratively speaking. I've taken an oath and am a part of this family as much as any other man sitting at this table, but that won't stop them from verbally ripping me to shreds if they think I deserve it. The fact that I'm here means I'm already on very thin ice.

Stress will only increase the chances of saying the wrong

thing, so I pretend I'm behind my scope preparing to hit a distant target. I clear my mind and slow my breathing.

"As you've probably all heard," Renzo starts once everyone has gathered. "My brother Tommy eloped yesterday with Biba Mikhailov's daughter." His accusatory stare bores deep into my skull. "Two of Biba's men tried to stop him in the process and were killed. Last night, explosives were set off on Pier 49. Two dock workers are missing and presumed dead, and three others were taken to the hospital with extensive injuries. The infrastructure is devastated. It's going to take months to rebuild, if not a year."

"We know it was him?" one of the capos asks.

Renzo nods. "A note was left at the entrance gate. Said I won't stop until I get my daughter."

Fuck, that's pretty definitive.

I shut out the glances I feel prodding me from all directions and keep my eyes on Renzo as he continues.

"We have to end this before it's a full-blown war."

Nods and murmurs of agreement fill the room.

DiAngelo is the first to ask the big question. "What are we prepared to offer? He's going to want remuneration for his daughter."

I want to demand that Danika was never his to sell off, but I know that won't help. All that matters is how Biba sees it, and to him, he's been severely wronged. Even though he's caused untold damages with that explosion, we'll still be expected to pay up.

"Anyone have insight into something Biba's been after? Dock access or a break in port fees?"

"We could always try a simple payoff," another capo suggests.

This is why I'm here, and I can only hope any help I offer will get me back in the good graces of the men sitting around this table. "The whole reason Biba wanted Danika was to marry her off to The Reaper because he's losing his battle against the guy. He wanted to link the organizations and absorb that outfit into his own. Without his daughter, he's fighting a losing battle. What Biba needs now more than anything is a solution to his Reaper problem."

The room processes the information in a blanket of silence.

DiAngelo is the first to speak. "Are you suggesting we pay off The Reaper, or take him out? Those are two very different situations. It's hard to kill a man who's practically a ghost already."

"I've already spent some time thinking about it. Biba's been just as elusive as The Reaper since that guy entered the stage. What if we convince Biba to draw out The Reaper under the guise of a truce. Reaper is bound to show if he knows Biba will be there, and Biba will go if we agree to take out Reaper in exchange for peace."

My brother's blue stare is unrelenting. "The only way either would agree to that sort of thing is if the meeting took place somewhere isolated where security could be assured. How do you propose conducting a hit if we can't get close?"

"I'm suggesting I do it. I don't need to be close."

I see the faintest twitch of his eyes as they narrow. "Elaborate."

"I'll guarantee my accuracy within a thousand meters."

Whistles and chuckles of surprise and disbelief erupt around us.

I never take my eyes from my brother, my stare plainly stating that you don't know anything about me.

His head drops a notch, lips thinning, and maybe it's more

wishful thinking, but I get the sense his nod is more than an acceptance of my plan. Maybe, just maybe, he's starting to realize I'm more than the kid brother who got upset when his toys weren't neatly arranged in straight lines.

"There's only one way to know, and that's to ask," Renzo says. "I'll reach out and see if I can set up a call with him. I suggest everyone keep their eyes open in the meantime and report any concerns." He raps his knuckles on the table, ending the meeting.

I let Sante know that I'm sticking around and wait until the others have left so I can get a word alone with my brother.

"I'd like you to consider letting me be a part of the call with him if he accepts." I infuse confidence in my voice—an essential component in any conversation with Renzo.

"It's a call. No reason for you to be there."

I tell myself not to assume it's a brush-off and try again. "Yes, there is. What if something's said that only I have the context to understand? You said it yourself that I'm the one in the middle of this."

"Exactly, and you've got too much at stake—too many emotions wrapped up in this outcome. I can't risk you saying something that pisses him off."

His words are so infuriating that I struggle to reply. When I do finally speak, my words are clipped and thin. "You really aren't interested in ever giving me a chance, are you? From the minute Dad died and you got to take over his empire, you were only too happy to see me leave. I bet you wish I'd never come back from Sicily."

Renzo grabs my shirt in his fists and brings his face inches from mine. "I never wanted you to leave. Don't you make up fucking stories about me."

"If you want me here so goddamn bad, why pretend I don't exist?" I spit at him angrily. "You've kept me on the sidelines since the minute I got back."

"Only because Dad made me promise—" Renzo stops himself, eyes spitting fire before he shoves me away and turns his back on me.

"Oh, fuck no." I grab his shoulder and spin him back around to face me. "You can't stop there. Tell me what you promised him."

Renzo's jaw flexes, and his lips thin before he loses whatever internal battle he's fighting. "He made me promise to keep you safe."

I physically recoil because it's confirmation of what I've always suspected. My family truly does think I'm broken. That I'm some sort of invalid in need of coddling.

Renzo releases a weary exhale. "Listen, Tommy. You were still a boy when he died. He didn't get to see how different you are now."

I raise my hand to silence him. "I was the same person then as I am now—all the same struggles and all the same abilities. If you two think that makes me incapable, then fuck you."

I walk away. Renzo calls after me, but I ignore him.

I've had enough. Of him. Of the doubts. All of it.

33
Danika

Tommy's text letting me know he's coming home is a welcome embrace that goes cold the second he arrives and I see how upset he is.

"What happened?" I ask while trying to give him the space he obviously craves.

"Renzo is setting up a meeting with Biba. We're going to try to negotiate a truce." He continues past me to the primary suite and goes right for the shower. I follow but am not going to chase him into the shower, so I wait on the bed until he's done. It doesn't take long. Once he's out and toweled off, I try again.

"Is this truce a bad thing?"

"It is when my brother doesn't trust me to be a part of it."

"Did you guys argue?" I ask hesitantly, already sensing the answer.

"You could say that."

I bite at the inside of my cheek, feeling horrible for the conflict I'm causing. "So what are you doing now?"

He's dressed in record time and arming himself with a small arsenal of weapons—even more than normal. Alarm bells blare in my mind as fear sends a cascade of tingles to my fingers and toes.

"I'm not going to just sit on my ass and do nothing."

"What does that mean, Tommy? I don't like it. Please, don't leave."

He levels me with a glare. "Why? Why shouldn't I go?" Each word feels like the pull of a rope suspending a guillotine above me. My answer will determine my sentence, and I have no idea why or what the right words will be.

"Because I'm worried for you."

Wrong. The giant blade crashes down as thoroughly as his eyes shut me out of his thoughts.

I don't understand. Why would me being worried about him upset him so badly? He doesn't give me a chance to ask.

"Stay here," he says before grabbing his keys and walking away.

I stare blankly at the wall, hardly able to believe what's just transpired. What is Tommy planning to do? Would he be foolish enough to confront Biba? God, please, no.

I start to pace the living room. Down and back. Down and back.

I do this for fifteen minutes before I cave and try to call him.

The phone rings and rings. I hang up and try again to the same end.

This isn't like him. He wouldn't not answer my call. I can't imagine he's already in danger, but what else would keep him from answering? He could be on the other line. Or maybe he needs space.

Maybe you're massively overreacting and need to calm down.

Give him time—thirty minutes. If he doesn't call back, then I can worry. Okay, I can live with that. I'll paint. That will hopefully distract me and calm my nerves at the same time.

I go back to the guestroom and look at my current work in progress and get out the colors I'll need to work with, but every few minutes, my eyes are drawn to the canvas of lilies on the dresser. Funeral lilies. Gran says her love of them has nothing to do with the association. I could never separate the two. When I see those lilies, I'm reminded of death and the danger Biba poses to me and my family.

It suddenly occurs to me that I really hate that stupid painting. I hate it with every fiber of my being—enough that I grab it and a bottle of rubbing alcohol and take them to the bathroom. I slowly pour the alcohol at one end of the shower away from the drain so that it pools. I lay the canvas face down in the liquid, sliding it around to make sure the face is covered, little by little pouring the entire bottle until it's saturated. Then I walk away.

I don't go back to painting. My mood will ruin the piece, so I clean up the paints I opened and doodle on my tablet instead. The second my half hour is up, I open my phone and call Tommy again.

Still no answer.

I open the contacts and look at my options. Sante and DiAngelo. I'm more comfortable with Sante, but if I ask him to go looking for Tommy, and he ends up hurt, Amelie will be devastated. I'd hate to be responsible for that. DiAngelo doesn't wear a wedding ring. It's no guarantee he's unattached, but it eases my conscience. Tommy probably wouldn't want me calling anyone, but he can deal with it. That's what happens if you ignore me.

I dial DiAngelo's number, and he answers after a single ring.

"Yeah?"

"DiAngelo?" I ask, just to be sure.

"Yeah, Dani. What do you need?" He doesn't seem upset that I'm bothering him, which is a tiny relief. He's kind of scary.

"I'm worried and not sure what to do. Tommy got back from some meeting with his brother and was really upset. He left, saying he was going to do what he could. I have no idea what that means, and I wouldn't freak out, except I've been trying to call him since he left, and he isn't answering. It's not like him."

"How long's he been gone?" His gravelly voice takes on an edge, and I appreciate that he's taking this seriously.

"A little over thirty minutes ago. I'm worried something's happened. I think someone needs to go look for him."

"Hold on a second," he says, then the line clicks silent. A minute later, he's back. "He didn't answer me either."

"Please, do something. This isn't like him."

"You just try to calm down and stay put, okay?"

"Are you going to find him?" I demand, frustrated that he hasn't actually agreed to go looking.

"Dammit, woman, just give me a minute. Can you do that?"

I'm so damn frustrated that I hang up on him. What is wrong with these ridiculous men that they can't give a straight answer? I'm not going anywhere—Tommy would be furious, and I think his guard from earlier is still in the hall. All I can do is pace. And pace. And pace. I'm five minutes from wearing tracks in the rug when I get a text.

DiAngelo: Let me in.

I look at the front door, then dart in that direction. I look through the peephole to make sure it's him, then debate whether the alarm is on, deciding it doesn't matter. If it's armed and goes off, hopefully that will get Tommy back here, even if on false pretenses.

I let DiAngelo in, then make sure to lock the door behind him.

"Thanks for not breaking in," I say. "Have you heard from him?" It's only been maybe fifteen minutes since we spoke on the phone, but it feels like an eternity.

"No. I called Sante, but he hasn't heard from him either." He walks into the living room and sits on the sofa.

"What are you doing? Aren't you going to look for him?"

"Where exactly should I start?" He directs a hand toward the skyline view of the city out the window. "You considered how fucking huge this city is?"

"I know, but we have to do *something*," I whisper, sensing the onset of tears.

"I am doing something. I'm making sure you're safe, though I didn't realize he already had someone stationed here. He'd haunt my ass for all eternity if I let something happen to you."

"Why—" Emotion constricts my throat, cutting off the words. "Why are you talking about him like he's dead?"

"*Jesus.*" He heaves himself off the sofa with a sigh and pulls me into a giant bear hug. "He's fine, Danika. That kid can take care of himself, right?"

I nod shakily and try to calm myself. When DiAngelo senses

I've regained control, he pulls back to meet my eyes, his hands still firmly but gently holding my upper arms.

"If you're gonna be a part of this world, you're gonna have to get used to this shit." He raises thick brows at me, and I nod, though I'm not sure I ever will.

He huffs irritably like he's reading my thoughts and drops his hands just as Tommy walks in the front door.

"Tommy!" I cry.

He freezes, taking in the sight of me with DiAngelo. Ominous shadows darken his face. "What? I'm gone an hour, and you've already replaced me?"

His unexpected accusation is a slap that pulls a gasp from me.

"Watch your fucking tone, kid," DiAngelo barks. "She called me because she was worried about you. Try checking your phone, for fuck's sake."

"Left it here. That's why I came back. Didn't realize I'd have a search party waiting for me after just a fucking hour." Tommy's glare winds me because I can't imagine what I've done to deserve such ire. "You're just like my brother, aren't you? You think I'm totally incompetent. Guess that's what I get for forcing you to marry me."

DiAngelo surges forward like a dog on a squirrel. Tommy never flinches as the larger man gets in his face.

"It's about time you pull your fucking head out of your ass. Someone worrying about your safety is a show of love, not distrust, and if you're too insecure about your idiosyncrasies to think caring about you is an insult, then that's on you, not her or anyone else. Danika and your brother—they both just want you to be safe because they don't want to lose you. Grow the fuck up." He checks Tommy's shoulder on the way out, slamming the door behind him.

Tommy's words cut me, but more than anything, I'm heartbroken for him. I've seen how he struggles to be what he thinks is normal. I didn't realize that struggle extended to his family, as well. My challenges always felt manageable because my core support system was always there for me. If I felt I had to prove myself to Mom or Gran, I can only imagine how much harder life would have been.

That's what the problem has been all along, and I didn't realize it. He's been worried I'll decide he's unworthy and reject him. He thinks I've been forced into this and am making the best of it but am bound to want out.

If we have any hope of making this work, he has to believe in my feelings for him, and that's not going to happen unless he knows the truth. He's already sacrificed so much for me. It's my turn to give a piece of myself for him.

I walk over and take his large hand in mine. "Come here. I have something I need to show you."

34
Tommy

Fucking DiAngelo. With a few simple words, he's ripped off my skin and exposed every fleshy detail of my insides—all in front of Danika. And the look on her face. Jesus, the pity. I hate it. I want to be furious. I want to rage and deny every word he said, but I can't because what he said struck a chord. I'm afraid he might be right, and I don't want to risk fucking up any more than I already have.

Tail tucked between my legs, I follow Danika to the guest room. I have no idea what this is about. She's set up her workspace, and it looks like she's been painting while I was gone.

When she opens the bathroom door, the acrid scent of rubbing alcohol wafts into the room.

"What on earth have you been doing back here?" I squint my eyes against the smell like that's going to help.

Danika doesn't answer me. She simply continues toward the enclosed shower where she has a canvas lying face down, soaking in what I assume is alcohol. She opens the door and picks up the canvas. It's the painting of the lilies. Or, it was. The paint is clumping and peeling off in chunks, revealing a different image beneath.

"When I was fifteen, I decided to go in secret to meet my father for the first time." Her softly spoken words unsettle me more than any yelling would. Whatever she's about to share, I won't like it.

"I was so curious about him even though Mom told me he was a bad man. A part of me needed to see for myself. I went in secret because she would have been furious if she knew I'd gone. I figured out that he owned some kind of auto repair shop and went there one day when I'd told Mom I was at the movies with friends. It was almost closing time, so there weren't many people around, but a garage bay was still open, so I went in to take a peek. I wasn't certain if I was going to tell him who I was. I figured I'd check him out first, then go from there. I never got that far, though."

Her solemn words take hold of my stomach and squeeze it beneath an angry fist.

"There was a commotion—angry voices coming closer—so I hid behind a car in the far bay. The next thing I knew, the garage door was closing, and a man was pleading for his life. He said he had kids and a wife. His voice was ..." She shakes her head as if trying to rid her mind of the memory. "I've never heard someone plead with such fear in their voice. He kept saying, *please, Biba, no*. It felt surreal, like it couldn't be real. Like I had to be listening to some sort of television broadcast or something. I peered through the window of the car just as the man holding a gun to his head—my father—laughed at the man's fear. I'll never forget that evil laugh so long as I live.

"The gunshot exploded in the air around us. So incredibly loud. I dropped to the floor, hands covering my ears, and when I looked to the side, the man was on the ground. Wide dead eyes stared at me from across the garage, blood pooling all around him from the hole in his forehead. I couldn't move. I was so terrified that I stayed curled in a ball with those eyes staring at me until I was sure the others had left. I snuck out after that and spent the next day painting this."

I can hardly breathe as I watch her scrape away the paint with a flat tool. Underneath the lilies are two images, one from a distance and the other up close—the wide open eyes of a dead man staring eerily out from the canvas. It's superimposed over the main scene, which is Biba standing near a white Mustang holding a man at gunpoint. The details are exceptional.

"At first," Danika continues, "I painted hoping to get it out of my head, but then it evolved into a testament. A way to memorialize what I witnessed. The acrylic lilies I painted on top were a tribute to the man and a way to keep the painting around without anyone suspecting. Over the years, I got so used to them that I hardly thought about the scene underneath. Not actively, anyway. Then on the day we first met ..." She brings her eyes to mine, and they're full of torment. I want to tell her no—that I've heard enough, and she doesn't have to say another word, but that would be wrong. She's sharing this with me for a reason, and I need to listen.

"Yes, I remember outside the police station."

She nods. "Biba had just told me his plans to force me into a marriage, so I went straight to the station to report him. I actually wasn't thinking about the murder. I was too terrified about becoming the property of some killer, but while I sat waiting to talk to someone, I saw a wall of photos displayed to honor officers taken in the line of duty, and I recognized the man who'd been killed. I'll never forget those eyes." A shiver racks her entire body. "I felt like it was a sign. A warning to get out of there, so I ran."

"Right into me," I finish for her.

She nods and sets the painting back in the shower. "Keeping that secret has been unbearable. I've called myself every name in the book, most often a coward because I never stood up for what I witnessed."

"You were a kid, Danika. You can't blame yourself."

"I know, but I'm not now." She shakes her head. "That's not why I'm telling you all this. I'm telling you because I want you to know I did have options. I could have gone to the FBI and asked for witness protection. I would have missed my family, but I could have done it. I considered it even after coming here. I've looked at that painting over and over, and you know what I've come to realize?"

I wait for her answer with bated breath, knowing whatever she says next will change everything. One way or another.

"I realized that I wanted you more than I wanted to hide, and I think that scares me more than anything because I know who you're going up against. Yes, I'm terrified for you, but that's because I'm terrified he'll take you from me, and it would be all my fault."

Her breathing shudders on a suffocated sob that shifts the

earth's rotation until it's aligned on an entirely new axis. That must be what happened because that's the only way to explain how I could suddenly see everything so very differently.

DiAngelo was right. I've been so fucking blind.

"I love you so much, little thief." I say the words that have been dancing in my mind for days because she needs to know now more than ever. "And I will always come back to you." I seal my promise with a kiss, lifting her into my arms, her legs wrapping eagerly around my middle.

"We need to get out of here before we pass out from the fumes," I say, nipping at her bottom lip.

She nods, and I walk us toward the primary bedroom.

"I'm sorry, Dani. I'm so fucking sorry that I've been so self-centered."

"It's not self-centered."

I grimace. "That's sweet of you, but it's not true. My first inclination any time I sense the slightest degree of hesitancy or concern about me is to assume it's a rejection. That I'm being seen as less than and unwanted. Between my issues and being the youngest in the family, I've always been treated like a child. Earlier today, my brother told me that Dad made him promise to keep me safe."

I sit on our bed with Dani straddling my lap and continue to explain why I'm upset. It's the least I can do when she's been so open with me. I owe her that much.

"My brain frequently sees things in black and white. In the past, I was kept on the sidelines because I was too young. If Renzo continued to keep me on the bench, I assumed it must be for the same reasons—he thought I was incapable of protecting myself. I never considered that he could have other reasons like a promise to a dying man. Renzo was closer to Dad than any of us since he was next in line for leadership. He took the loss hard, and I imagine a promise like that would weigh on him."

"Definitely, but also, he could just be scared of losing you," she adds gently. "If losing your dad was hard on him, it could make him extra scared of losing anyone else. We're your family, Tommy. We worry about you because we care."

I grin against her lips, my tongue teasing along the crease. "That's right. We are family." This time, I plunder her mouth, staking my claim. She welcomes me with hungry abandon. I'm hard as steel in an instant, rocking myself up against her center, making us both moan with pleasure.

"Actually, that reminds me," she tries to say, but I cut her off with another kiss. "Tommy," she chides, pulling free. "There's something I need to tell you." She smiles, but it's riddled with uncertainty. "I'm worried you'll get upset, but I've told myself you would have said something if you had a problem with it."

She's rambling nervously. I want to tell her that nothing in this world she could tell me would make me love her any less.

"Dani, baby. Spit it out," I say instead.

She gives a tiny cringe, then whispers, "I'm not on birth control."

35
Danika

I NEEDED TO TELL HIM. IT'S THE RIGHT THING TO DO, BUT God, am I nervous. I have absolutely no idea how Tommy feels about kids. And then to find out after the fact that we were unprotected? He doesn't exactly give off family vibes. This could derail all the good that's come from our conversation—the dropping of barriers and sharing of our pasts. But I had to say something. Glossing over the subject would have been wrong.

I wait for his reaction. A matter of seconds that feels like hours.

His lips twitch. "I know."

"You what?" It's so far from anything I anticipated that I'm confused.

"Remember when I found your birth certificate? I did a deep dive into your whole background, including your medical records. I know you're not on any meds."

"That's not possible. Medical records are private."

His head tilts, and a brow arches as if to say, *Come on, Dani, don't be so naive.*

"You broke into my doctor's computer?" My voice jumps an octave.

Tommy shrugs. "It's a bit more complicated than that, but yeah. I'm good with computers."

"So you knew?"

"Yeah."

"But you came inside me anyway?"

His eyes are warm like hot chocolate on a snowy day. "Yeah, Dani, I did." His whispered words are a prelude to the most romantic kiss I've ever been given, then he pulls away, and the heat in his eyes begins to boil. "And I'm about to do it again."

"It doesn't worry you that I could get pregnant?"

Tommy's gaze drifts reverently over my face. "It scares me shitless, but that child would be an extension of you, and I can't imagine anything more incredible than more of you. Plus, there's no more permanent way to bind myself to you than with a child."

Well, that took a bit of a crazy turn, but I'm not mad about it. It's sweet in a Tommy sort of way.

"Okay," I whisper with a smile.

He stands, setting me on my feet, then lifts my shirt over my head. What follows is a sort of liturgy as Tommy devotedly removes my clothes, showering ardent attention on each newly exposed bit of skin along the way. The press of his lips. The whisper of tender words. He sanctifies my entire body before stripping his own and laying us on the bed.

"This should have been our first time." His words are painted in remorse.

"No, Tommy. Everything has unfolded exactly as it should. I genuinely believe that—from the moment I ran into you to those men interrupting our wedding—that is our story, and it's perfect exactly as it is."

He seizes my lips in a kiss that plunders my heart and promises forever. His body rocks against mine. I spread my legs in welcome, but he stays where he is.

"All that's left is to resolve things with Biba." He gives me an unguarded look deep into his soul. "I promise you I'll take care of it."

"And come back to me—that's the most important part."

A smile tugs at his lips. "Death itself couldn't keep me away." He starts a trail of kisses that extends from my throat down to my slit.

"Did you tell me—" I gasp as his tongue takes a languid, leisurely swipe from my entrance to my clit. "That they call you ... Death back in Sicily?"

"Exactly." He nips my inner thigh. "And you're my Persephone. Together, we'll rule the underworld." And to that end, Tommy starts by ruling my world, giving me a toe-curling orgasm before making love to me, first slow and ardently, then without restraint—forging a bond between us in ways I never could have imagined possible. But that's Tommy. A man beyond comprehension, and best of all. Mine.

"You were right, you know," Tommy tells me after we're sated and sweaty, wrapped contentedly in one another's arms.

"Of course, I was," I muse smugly. "About what?"

He gives my ribs a playful squeeze. "I've been worried you only married me because you had no other option."

I lift my head off his chest and give him a soft smile. "That's why I wanted you to know." I drop a kiss on his chest before resting my head back down. "I had options. Gran even offered to help me escape before the ceremony," I tease.

"Can't believe that woman was carrying a gun on her."

"I can." My smile has a life of its own. "She's a different breed."

Tommy huffs. "You didn't take her up on it, though."

"I'm here, aren't I?" I hug him snugly. "And I'd marry you again if need be."

"I like that idea. I think I'll take you up on it."

"Marry me again?"

"Every year on our anniversary." His words are resolute, and I have no doubt he'll follow through. He's a man of his word.

"I do believe in you, you know," I tell him softly.

He drops a kiss on my head. "That's good because it's important to me."

"You're important to me, so I'll do my best. I don't trust Biba, though. He worries me."

"It's smart to respect an opponent, but he's just a man like any other."

I nod, then broach something I've been mulling over. "I could still do it, you know. I could still report him. It's the right thing to do."

"That's never happening," Tommy quips immediately. "I'll

chain you to my bed before I ever let you testify and risk yourself like that."

I bite back a smile. "Chain me to the bed, huh?" I ask, my voice going husky.

"Oh, little thief, you're playing with fire." In a heartbeat, he rolls us over so that he's on top, his molten stare fusing with mine.

I flash him a wicked grin. "Go on, Death, do your worst."

36
Danika

The gun is heavier than I anticipated. It's also cool to the touch despite the heat on this sunny afternoon. We're in the shade, so that helps. Just two people on a blanket in the middle of a farm with a picnic basket, a box of bullets, and a sniper rifle.

"This has got to be the strangest first date known to man," I muse.

Tommy removes his eye from the scope to peer up at me. "Because of the gun or the fact that we're already married?"

"C, all of the above."

"At least it's memorable."

A giggle tumbles past my lips.

Tommy returns to his task, spinning dials and knobs between looks through the scope. "Alright, I think I'm ready to take some test shots. Time to put on the noise protection." He hands over earplugs and thick black headphones.

I told him I only needed one earplug, but he insisted I use both. Once I'm geared up, I squint at the distance, where I know he's hung a target, but I can only make out a small white blur. The large poster paper is attached to a tree trunk and consists of the silhouette of a man's upper body in black on a white background. It's so freaking far away that I have no clue how he could possibly hit it.

He hands me a pair of binoculars. "Watch."

I focus them on the target, trying to steady my breathing to hold as still as possible. My body tenses in anticipation of the shot, and when the gun goes off, I think he's missed until a hole bursts through the paper a second after the explosion.

"Oh my God. That was amazing." The accuracy. The insane delay. It's one of the coolest things I've ever seen.

Tommy grumbles something, and I have to take off my headgear and ask him to repeat himself. "Didn't even hit the damn thing," he says again, starting a new round of tweaks on the gun.

"Yes, you did! I saw it."

"I hit the paper, but I was aiming for his head."

"Considering how far away we are, I'd say you got damn close."

"Once my sight is properly calibrated, I'll be nearly one hundred percent from this distance." He gives me a wicked glance from the side of his eye.

My jaw hangs wide open. "Are you serious? That's nuts!"

"I am, but she hasn't been properly calibrated since I moved back to the States."

"She?" I ask in a playful tone.

"Yup, the only other woman I'll ever have in my life." He brings his eye back to the scope while I preen like a schoolgirl. "Headgear." The single-word warning tells me he's ready to shoot. I replace my headset and lift the binoculars. This time when the gun goes off, a patch of pale tree trunk is visible behind the new hole right in the middle of the silhouette's head.

Damn, he really is good.

I continue to watch as he performs several more practice shots. Once he's comfortable with his calibrations, he begins to disassemble the weapon.

"Hey, Tommy?"

"Yeah?"

"Have you killed many people?" I'm not sure what possesses me to ask. I probably don't want to know the answer, but I can't hide from it either. We're married. I need to own the choices I've made.

"I suppose that depends on your definition of many. The count isn't all that high, but it doesn't take many to create a reputation, especially as efficient as I am. My targets go down before they ever know what hit them."

And that's what he plans to do to The Reaper. A man he knows nothing about. I'm not crazy about the idea, but I understand the necessity, and I've heard the things Reaper has done.

"Dani, look at me," Tommy orders softly. "You've heard that the attorney general of New York is being prosecuted, right?"

I nod, not sure where he's going with this.

"Companies put deadly chemicals in products. Clergymen abuse children in their congregations. Husbands beat their wives. Scammers steal people's life savings without a second thought. That's life. We're not as civilized as we pretend to be."

I chew the side of my cheek while I ponder what he's said. He's definitely on Gran's team, and maybe they're right. People really are the worst.

But they're also the best.

For every act of violence or hatred, just as many acts are made in the name of hope and charity and love and forgiveness. If it's up to me to decide how I see the world, I choose to focus on the best attributes of humankind. Dwelling on the ugly will only add another soul to the dark side.

I giggle to myself.

"What?" Tommy asks, brow heavily furrowed.

"Just thinking I choose to be on the side of the Jedi, that's all." And Biba is definitely Darth Vader. Does that make Tommy Han Solo? I giggle again.

He shakes his head and laughs. "I have no clue how that relates, but whatever works."

Yeah, he'd make a decent Han. The antihero. He's shown me in so many ways that the difference between good and bad is a broad spectrum, and people are forever sliding from one end to the other. If I had to choose between Tommy and the moral high ground, I'd choose Tommy ten times out of ten.

"THE CALL IS tonight at seven. Can you make it?" Renzo's voice fills the car over the speakers as we're reentering the city. Tommy said he and his brother fought, so I'm curious about what this means.

"You sure about that?" Tommy's words are uncertain, and

his posture behind the steering wheel has gone from casual to rigid.

"Yeah, I'm sure."

"Then I'll be there."

The call ends. I watch Tommy like a hawk. "You have a call tonight?" I ask, hoping he'll open up.

"Guess so. The last time Renzo and I talked ... it wasn't pretty. He didn't want me in on the call with Biba, and it pissed me off. I sort of said some shit that didn't go over well."

"But now he's decided to include you," I surmise.

"Yeah, it looks that way." He's uncomfortable, and I get it. Conflict is icky.

"You might feel better if you talk to him again, you know. Now that you understand a little better where he's coming from." I really hope I'm not overstepping, but I hate to see him so at odds with his family. Especially his brother since they also work together. It's important they find a way to relate to one another.

Tommy tosses me a side-eye. "I'll think about it," he says dryly. "Me going out tonight means you're going to be home alone. I was thinking about that tiny girl with the purple hair—"

"Sachi?"

"Sure. You're close to her, right?"

"Yeah, she's my best friend." Where's he going with this?

"What if you give her a call now and see if she's free? We could pick her up, and she could hang with you at the apartment while I'm gone. That way, you're not alone worrying, and I know you've got someone to keep you company. Female company." The last part is added as a tiny verbal jab.

"You know she's a lesbian, right?" I deadpan.

Tommy looks over at me, face twisted in confusion, and nearly hits the car beside us.

"I'm kidding! Watch the road. I was kidding," I laugh and yell at the same time.

He snarls, but in a grumpy teddy bear kind of way. It makes me want to laugh harder, but I don't want to distract him again, so I choke back a snicker.

An hour later, Sante is at our place to keep watch, and Sachi is on her way over. She was at a friend's orchestral dress rehearsal when we called, so we weren't able to pick her up. I'm kind of glad because that's given me a little time to figure out how I'm going to tell my best friend that I got married since the last time she saw me. I'm not sure if I'm more nervous about Tommy's call with Biba or a pissed-off Sachi. At least I can only really worry about one at a time. And by the end of the day, I'll probably have a whole new checklist of things to worry about.

Huzzah.

37
Tommy

"Where's DiAngelo? I figured he'd be here by now." I take a seat in Renzo's office, surprised to find the room unoccupied aside from the two of us.

"He had somewhere to be. You and I can manage a video chat, even if it's with Biba Mikhailov." He sounds worn down. I realize I haven't asked about his wife recently, and I feel a twinge of guilt. They're expecting their first baby in another month, and I've hardly acknowledged the new addition at all.

"How's Shae feeling? Everything okay with the baby?"

"Yeah, baby's doing great." His entire face softens as though the mere mention of his unborn child erases all the world's troubles. It's fascinating. And I suppose I have a tiny inkling of how that might feel now that I know there's a chance Danika and I could have conceived a child of our own. The anticipation and uncertainty are a thrill unlike any other—one that's also absolutely terrifying.

"That's wonderful," I offer genuinely.

"Yeah, and I think we've got all the baby stuff we could ever possibly need—I know Shae is ready. She is desperate to get the kid out of her already." He chuckles to himself.

"She's due on the eighteenth, right?"

My brother looks at me, a tiny bit of surprise registering. "Yeah, that's exactly right."

"I'm sure you'll do great. God knows you had plenty of experience taking care of kids as the oldest, especially with Dad not around much of the time." I'm trying to apologize in a roundabout way, but Renzo's grimace tells me I've fallen short.

"I hope you understand that the only reason he worried about you was because he loved you. He worried about all of us."

My gaze drops to my hands, and I lean forward to rest my elbows on my knees. "Sometimes worry looks a lot like doubt to me," I state quietly, letting the words flow without overthinking them. "Danika and DiAngelo helped me see that I've been a bit harsh in my judgments lately. I left for Sicily not on the best of terms and never really gave either of us a chance to prove things were different since I got back. I think it was easier to assume the worst than show what I have to offer and find out it's still not enough."

"Fuck, Tommy. You've always been enough. Though, I agree we haven't given ourselves much of a chance to get to know one another now that you're all grown up. It probably helps that I've mellowed out, too. I was a little uptight when I first took over. It was a lot of pressure."

I raise my brows. "A little?" I jab, praying he hears the playfulness in my tone.

He smirks. "Yeah, yeah. I could be a dick, but I felt like I had to prove myself worthy of being the boss. I faced a lot of doubters, you know?"

"Actually, I do know exactly what that feels like."

His lips thin, and he gives me a single nod of acknowledgment. It's such a tiny gesture, but it's filled with so much meaning that my breathing catches. I'm momentarily speechless.

Renzo saves me by steering us back to shallower waters. "When do I get to meet this new bride of yours? I hear you've done well for yourself."

The mention of Danika brings a smile to my lips. "I know she'd love to meet Shae—we should do dinner before the baby arrives, assuming we can get things cleared up with Biba. I know this has put everyone at risk, and I truly am sorry about that."

"Some things are worth the risk. Sounds like your girl is one of those things. I'm glad you found her."

"I appreciate that." Fuck if my voice doesn't almost break. That's my cue. I've waded through as much touchy-feely crap as I can manage. It's time to talk business. "So what's the plan for this call? You get any insight into his frame of mind when you set this up?"

Renzo sighs. "Hell, no. That fucker has no frame of mind except crazy. There's no predicting crazy."

We spend the next ten minutes prepping as best we can for the call then get online and enter the virtual meeting room. A few minutes later, Biba joins us as if we are any ordinary businessmen gathering to discuss mergers and acquisitions. Except in our industry, the outcome of our talk will have life-and-death consequences.

"Biba, it's good of you to join us. We appreciate your generosity." Renzo shows right away why he was the natural choice in leadership when Dad died. Despite his age, he keeps a cool head and knows how to use the right amount of diplomacy.

The best thing I can do to contribute is keep my damn mouth shut because anything I say will probably end the conversation.

"I am curious to hear how you propose to make right such an unforgivable situation." Biba sits at a desk with two thugs standing behind him like sentinels. It's a ridiculous attempt at posturing, considering we're not actually in a room together.

Renzo and I sit together at a small round table in his office somewhat squeezed together to fit in the camera view of his laptop. "I think we can all agree it's been a regrettable series of events. I know the families of the innocent men who lost their lives last night wish things were different." Renzo artfully incorporates a reminder that Biba is not the only one who has suffered.

The Russian frowns with a shrug. "These things happen when you steal a man's daughter. Now she is tainted and useless to me. What could ever compensate for such a loss?"

"We've been considering that—"

"Nyet, not you. I want to hear from him." He points at me. "You're the one who's taken her, no?"

Shit. Don't fuck this up, Tommy.

"I am." I'm hoping simple is best. If I don't say much, I have less of a chance of pissing him off.

"Did your father not teach you it's impolite to steal a man's daughter?" Biba's accented words are clipped and dripping with venom.

"My father died before I started dating, so I suppose he never got the chance," I say honestly, then continue to try to move this conversation in a better direction. "I understand, however, that I've deeply injured you, and I want to make it right."

Biba snickers. "*You?* What could you possibly offer me to make this right?"

"I can kill The Reaper for you."

The old Russian is so still that I start to wonder if the computer signal's been interrupted.

Renzo leans forward. "The Families haven't had any issues with Reaper's crew, but we understand he's been giving you problems. Normally, we wouldn't make trouble with someone like him without cause, but in this case, we're willing to eliminate the threat he poses to you in exchange for a truce."

"How?" he finally asks, his weathered features drawn in skepticism. "The man is a shadow. A phantom."

"We would need to work as a team. Tommy here has trained as a sharpshooter. All we'd need is for you lure Reaper out of hiding—maybe under the guise of a truce. Whatever the angle, as long as you can coax him to appear, we can get him."

Biba stares, his lips pulled into a deep frown as he looks down his nose at us. "And what's to keep you from shooting me instead?"

"Your sons would never let us do such a thing without retribution, and that's exactly what we're trying to avoid. Plus, your organization is much more formidable. With him gone, his limited followers will likely scatter back into the gutters the second he's gone."

I'm curious how much Renzo believes that versus how much is lip service. We need Biba to trust us if we're going to pull this off.

I decide to take a chance and interject. "Besides, this marriage is just as much an alliance as the marriage to Reaper would have been. We have an opportunity to cooperate in a way the Italians and Russians never have in the past. This could usher in a new era of prosperity for us both."

One of Biba's guards leans in and whispers something to him. Biba lifts his chin. "I will not make any agreements without fully considering. And even if I did decide to do this thing with you, it would be on my terms."

"Of course," Renzo says with a nod.

"You will hear from me when I have decided." As soon as Biba's words are out, the connection severs.

Renzo closes the laptop, and we melt back in our chairs.

"That went better than I expected," my brother muses. "I try to mentally plan for the worst when dealing with assholes like him."

"Hey, that's my father-in-law you're talking about." I stare at him out of the corner of my eye, and he stares back until my smile breaks free. He starts to chuckle, and before I know it, we're both nearly in tears.

"Jesus, you're fucked, you know that?" he says once we start to collect ourselves.

"Yeah, it's like trying to make a pet out of a rabid dog."

Renzo sobers, lifting his gaze to mine. "Is she worth it?" he asks quietly. "Tell me she's worth it, Tommy."

"I'd lay down my life for her in a heartbeat."

Renzo nods. "The let's do this right. We have no margin for error."

We spend the next two hours hammering out a plan, and by the time I leave, I feel an unexpected surge of hopefulness because, for the first time in my life, Renzo has handed me the reins. He has put faith in my judgment and given me the gift of his trust. I will not let him down—*if* Biba gives us this opportunity. That part of our fate has yet to be decided.

38 Danika

"But, how?" It's the third time Sachi has asked me the same question, making me laugh because I've told her how I ended up married. I've told her twice, in fact. She's still dumbfounded. "It's only been a week."

"Ten days, technically."

She glares at me, then reaches for my hand and looks at the rings. Again. "I can't wrap my head around it."

"I know, and if roles were reversed, I'd say the same thing."

We're sitting together on the bed of my studio while Sante watches TV in the living room. I wanted privacy for what was bound to be an awkward conversation. Sachi's handled it well, but I can tell she's worried about me.

"Sach, I know it seems crazy, but I really do care about him. And I swear I'd tell you if I was being coerced or in danger."

"What if you can't? What if he's love bombing you and six weeks from now he becomes a monster but you're scared to leave by then?" She's dead serious, and I love her for it.

"Then we should probably have a code phrase—something I could say that only you would know was a cry for help."

Her eyes light up. "Like what? It'd have to be something we'd never say ordinarily."

It only takes me a second before I have the perfect idea. "I'll tell you that I've decided to take up Crossfit." There is no way in a million years I'd ever, *ever* voluntarily say those words and mean them. As I've noted before, I'm an artist, not an athlete.

Sachi nods approvingly. "Perfect. I'll know immediately that you need my help, that, or you've been abducted by aliens."

I purse my lips. "And if that's the case, I'm not sure there's much you can do."

She narrows her eyes. "Don't underestimate the powers of a BFF."

We both giggle, and I wrap my arms around my bestie.

"Thank you, Sach. Love you bunches."

"Love you, babes." She pulls back, her eyes cutting toward the living room. "Sooo ... the hottie in the living room?"

"Married."

"Cool." She nods. "You hungry? I'm starved."

I grin and lead her out to the kitchen. We sit at the bar and munch on some snacks until Tommy comes home. I lean around Sachi to give him a huge grin and wave. When I look back at my friend, she's staring at me, a soft smile lighting her eyes.

"You really do adore him, don't you?" she whispers.

"Yeah, I kinda do."

Tommy comes directly to the bar and presses a kiss to my cheek, then gives my best friend a smile. "You must be Sachi. It's good to meet you officially." He extends a hand, and she shakes it.

"Hurt my best friend, and I'll kill you." The words tumble from her lips in one quick breath without a smidgen of humor. Not even a trace.

I laugh nervously. "That's Sach—did I tell you she minored in performing arts in school?"

Sachi grins broadly, and we all laugh together. When I get down from the bar chair, I pretend not to notice her glare daggers one last time at Tommy. I know he wouldn't hurt her, but I'm not so certain about Sach. It might be good for him to know she's team Dani all the way.

"It's getting late. We could give you a ride home. I'm not crazy about you walking." I'm probably being paranoid, but lately, I've got good reason.

Tommy stands behind me and wraps his strong arms around me. "Sante's heading out. He could give you a ride."

We all look at Sante who's stretching after getting up from a loungefest on the couch.

"Yeah, I want to hear about the meeting, but you can call me later."

Sachi shrugs. "Works for me."

We say our goodbyes, and the two of them head out.

"So what happened? What did Biba say?" I ask eagerly the second we're alone. I'm desperate to end the torment of having a psychopath after me and my family.

"He's going to think about it."

"For how long?"

Tommy stares back at me with a blank face.

"Ugh, that's so annoying. Doesn't he realize how many lives he's toying with?"

"I'm sure he does, and if he delays a minute longer than necessary, I'm sure that's exactly why. Fucking with people is his favorite pastime."

I groan. "He should really take up golf or something." I sit at the bar again while Tommy rummages in the fridge.

"How did things go with Sachi? Between her and your gran, my balls are in serious jeopardy."

"Stay on your best behavior, and you have nothing to worry about," I tease him.

He arches a single brow at me, then takes a large bite out of an apple. My brain glitches for a second.

What did he ask me? Oh, yeah!

"Things were good with Sach. It was great to just hang out like normal for a bit."

"You'll have normal again, soon, little thief. I promise." His words are spoken with such sincerity that my throat tightens.

I nod to give myself a moment. "I know." And I do. I'm confident Tommy will get rid of this awful Reaper character, and Biba can go back to ruling his corner of the jungle and forget I ever existed. Again.

So we wait.

And we wait.

And we wait some more.

We don't leave the apartment, and we jump to attention every time Tommy's phone chimes.

My new clothes arrive. I have a small panic attack at the

enormous mound of packages, then put on a fashion show that ends in both of us naked.

Two endlessly long days pass before we finally get word.

Biba has agreed to the plan, and the meeting is in three hours.

Chaos erupts.

Tommy paces while going from one phone call to the next. Every clipped word has me more on edge than the next. Keeping myself from asking questions has never been such a challenge. I want to know what's happening, but he's on an impossibly short timeline. From what I can gather, they've been given the time and location of the meeting, and now they have to figure out how Tommy can position himself safely for the shot. I pray he can get this done safely.

What a wild fall from grace that I considered myself to be so law-abiding a mere two weeks ago, and now I'm desperately hoping my husband will come back alive from his mission to kill a man. I'm so worried about him that I have to look out the window at the city below to keep myself from throwing up.

Ten minutes of calls, fifteen minutes to gear up, and Tommy is ready to go.

This could be it. This could be the last time I ever see him alive. His work is dangerous on any given day, but this is exponentially worse, and I'm terrified.

I throw my arms around him and squeeze. "I love you, Tommy Donati," I force past the storm of emotions clogging my throat. I'd been feeling those three words dancing in the back of my mind for days and can't let him go without making sure he knows. "Please, come back to me."

Tommy kisses me with such intensity that it feels as though

he's trying to pack a lifetime of devotion into his goodbye. Tears pour down my cheeks.

"I love you more than you could ever comprehend, little thief. You're my everything." He gives me one last kiss on my forehead, and then he's gone, leaving me to battle my fears in a war zone of silence.

He has two men outside the apartment rather than one. I kind of wish they were in here with me so that I'd have someone to distract me. Instead, I pace and check my phone every few minutes to see if by some merciful miracle time has leaped ahead of itself. All I achieve is a slow descent into madness because with each minute that passes, every minute thereafter stretches that much longer. As if time itself is reluctant to arrive at that dreaded hour when Biba and Reaper are scheduled to meet.

I manage to survive until the half-hour mark—a mere thirty minutes left—when my phone rings. It's Gran. I was instructed not to tell a soul what was happening, so I've kept myself from calling anyone because I could never hide my current level of distress. But the time has almost arrived, and I could desperately use this distraction, so I decide to answer.

"Hey, Gran. How's it going?" I figure best not to devolve into tears before I even say hello. They'd panic.

"Hey, sweet girl. It's me and your mom. I've got you on speaker," she says in the most Gran way ever.

My eyes well with tears. "Hey, you two." The words fade as my throat seizes shut, but in a strange twist of events, they don't seem to notice.

"Listen, we called because we got word that something's going on. We were worried and wanted to check on you and Tommy."

"What do you mean, something's going on?" Adrenaline dries up my tears and focuses my mind with an eerie precision.

"My cousin called to check on us. He said there's some big meeting about to happen with Biba and some other guy. He wanted to make sure we weren't in trouble again. You know anything about that?"

"This is your Slovak cousin? The cousin who got you the gun and isn't part of Biba's crew?"

"Of course he's not. None of my family runs with that lunatic. Sorry, Petra," she adds the last part for my mother's sake.

"It's fine, you're right," Mom mutters.

I'm not paying one bit of attention because I'm stuck on wondering how on earth Gran's cousin found out about the meeting. Did Biba intentionally leak the info? No that doesn't make any sense. Why would he put himself in danger like that? Regardless of how the information got out, there's a solid chance The Reaper could have gotten wind that Biba plans to double cross him. If that's the case, he might not show up, or ... he might want to make a statement and take down the shooter before the meeting takes place.

Oh, God.

"Did your cousin know where this meeting was taking place?" I demand.

"What? No, I don't know. He didn't say. Dani, what's going on?"

"I'll explain later, I have to go." I hang up and dial Tommy's number. No answer. I didn't really expect him to answer, so I try not to read into it. He's got more important things to focus on than his phone. I dictate a text telling him everything I've just learned and send it. There's nothing more I can do except pray that he and his men have the situation covered.

39 Tommy

I said a thousand meters was my sweet spot. Biba's chosen a meeting site where the closest I can get is twelve hundred. It's still doable, but I'm not thrilled. While the distance isn't ideal, the location is otherwise superb. The exterior walls of the abandoned factory where I've set my perch extend up about four feet past the roof, giving me plenty of cover to hide behind. The meeting will take place outside at the back end of a parking lot. I have my gear situated and calculations made to adjust for the coastal breeze. I'm set up and ready, which was the plan—I wanted to get here as early as possible—but that means a hell of a long wait.

Every few minutes I run through a series of checks to help settle my brain. Now that we're getting closer to meeting time, I keep my eyes trained on the ground below. There's no obstructions. Trees along the building's exterior help give me cover, though they don't actually impede my shot. I'm feeling relatively confident about the operation until my phone starts to vibrate. Last minute information is rarely good.

I turn to grab my phone from my bag and discover I'm not alone. The man across from me looks just as surprised as I am as he draws a gun from a thigh holster. He's carrying a rifle case in his other hand which tells me this man likely works for The Reaper. He's planning a takedown the same as Biba.

I roll to the side away from my rifle and pull a throwing blade from my combat vest, flinging it at the guy the second he's back in view. He drops the gun case and recoils from the blade now lodged in his shoulder.

"*Motherfucker.*" He yanks the blade out with a curse. He's tough, I'll give him that, and he looks the part. He's probably ten years older than me, tattoos all the way up his neck, and a black glare sharp enough to cut my throat if he could.

The moment it takes him to pull out the knife gives me just enough time to tackle him before he can raise his gun again. I've got a gun on me as well, but I'd rather not alert the entire world we're up here. I can still pull this off if I can just get this asshole subdued.

The guy is skilled. We grapple for what feels like ages. I take several good hits, including a headbutt to my nose that sends blood gushing everywhere and hurts like a sonofabitch, but adrenaline does wonders for that sort of thing. The pain is there yet hardly registers. What does register is that time is ticking by, and if I miss this opportunity, I may not get another one.

Skill is helpful, but this guy isn't motivated the way I am. I've got a wife to protect.

I manage to roll us to the brick exterior wall bordering the roof and gain the leverage to slam his head against it hard enough to stun him. It's the opening I need to gain the upper hand, and in a few quick movements, I've got him on his stomach with his hands behind his back.

"Don't have time for this shit," I grumble as I pull out the zip ties I keep in one of my vest pockets and secure his hands and feet. His resistance is feeble. He's going to have a bitch of a headache tonight. Judging by the ache radiating from my nose, I may not be much better off, but if I accomplish my mission, it'll all be worth it.

Once I've taped his mouth and am confident he's been neutralized, I head back to my gun and check my site just as a black Cadillac appears. I can't see in the tinted windows, nor does anyone exit until a second vehicle arrives. Biba and his two sentinels exit the first car, all wearing suits and looking like the fucking Goodfellas. The two men who exit a Range Rover are much more casually dressed but have their backs to me, preventing me from making an ID. If Reaper has a scar on his neck, I can't see it from this angle.

They slowly approach one another. Biba waves his hand toward one of the two men opposite him. I swear to Christ, he might as well be holding a sign saying shoot this guy.

Time to get this over with.

I take aim in time with my inhale, then pull the trigger in the instant before I exhale. A heartbeat later, Biba is flat on the crumbling asphalt, blood pooling beneath him. His dumbass thugs stare at him in shock. Reaper and his man aren't the least bit surprised, likely assuming their guy did his job. They pull out guns and take care of the two remaining Russians before those two idiots know what hit them.

I take one last second to revel in a job well done before packing up.

When Renzo suggested we double cross Biba after our video call, I was shocked. I'd considered it myself, but I never thought my brother would be on board with something so potentially dangerous. Renzo acknowledged that Biba would never let Danika be—or any of us, for that matter. He was willing to chance further escalation with the Russians to free us from Biba. And what's more, he put all his trust in me to make it happen. I will forever be grateful to Renzo for what he's done here.

As I walk toward the bound man, he fights against his bindings and spits unintelligible words behind the tape on his mouth. Reaper knows he's up here, so I'm confident his crew will find him ... eventually.

"Tell your boss I said you're welcome." And with that, I walk away.

40
Danika

I'M GOING TO KILL YOUR FATHER.

When Tommy said those words to me a few days ago, he was concerned I'd have some sentimental tie to the man and reject the idea. The only thing I was worried about was the danger to Tommy. And when Gran told me there was a leak about the meeting, I was terrified Biba knew it was a double cross and had something planned in retaliation.

Lucky for us, that wasn't the case. Tommy's plan worked perfectly.

Biba Mikhailov is dead.

No matter how many times I say the words in my head, it

still doesn't seem real. I'm not naive enough to think all traces of danger are gone. Biba has sons. Loyalists. And there's always a degree of threat that comes with being part of the Moretti Family. Our lives will always be woven with danger, but one of the most vile, cancerous threats has been extinguished. I have been over the moon since Tommy came home two days ago and told me the news.

It was also two days ago that I learned my call to him probably saved his life. Not in the way I would have expected, but I'm not complaining. It took me a hot minute to calm down when I first saw him covered in blood. Once he explained about his nose and the other guy's stab wound, I was able to celebrate his return. The whole family is celebrating now that it's somewhat safe. Zuzu is hosting a get-together for her family, and it means I get to meet Renzo and his wife. I'm looking forward to the evening, but we have a quick stop to make on the way. One that's long overdue.

"I'm still not thrilled about this," Tommy grumbles as we walk toward the place where we first met.

"I know, and I appreciate you supporting me anyway."

Tommy grunts.

The man waiting for us outside the police station doesn't smile when we approach. Tommy doesn't either. It's odd since Tommy said meeting with Detective Malone was his only prerequisite to this happening. I figured they were friends, but that doesn't appear to be the case.

"Malone."

"Donati."

They nod heads at each other like boxers squaring off in a ring. It's a little ridiculous, so I choose to ignore them.

"Hi there, I'm Danika." I smile warmly as I offer my hand.

He accepts with a dimpled grin in return and holy hotness is he a cutie.

"I understand congratulations are in order," Malone says. "Though, I'm not sure what a ray of pure sunshine is doing with this surly bastard." He motions toward my husband, making me laugh.

Tommy, on the other hand, isn't remotely amused. I can feel the chill of his glare wafting over my shoulder.

"Love works in mysterious ways."

"Ain't that the truth," Malone murmurs. "Tommy said you've got something you wanted to show me?"

"Yeah, um. It's this." I hand over the canvas I've been carrying and feel an intangible weight lift from my shoulders in the process.

Malone's entire demeanor transforms in a heartbeat. "That's Biba Mikhailov," he says in a low, guarded tone.

"Yeah, and I know this isn't a lot of good now that he's dead, but I wanted the family to have closure, if they needed it. I was too scared to say anything before," I admit with no small amount of embarrassment.

"You were there."

I nod. "And a while back, I was in the station and saw the victim's photo on the wall of honor, three over from the left. I had no idea who he'd been until I saw the photo."

Malone dips his chin and lowers the painting. "Thank you for this. I'm sure his family and all of us at the force are grateful."

Tommy decides it's his turn to interject himself. "Don't even think about asking for a statement. The painting is all you're getting from her, and you can count yourself lucky you're getting that much."

Malone smirks. "Come on, Donati. The guy's dead now. He's not gonna care." He's giving Tommy a hard time, though I don't think my husband is seeing the humor.

"He might not, but those prick sons of his might."

Malone sobers. "I hear their outfit's total chaos right now with the two of them fighting over control. Still can't believe Reaper took him out. The whole department's pretty worried about that character."

"Probably should be," Tommy agrees in an eerily cool tone.

I've been told word on the street is Reaper set up the hit on Biba, and the Italians have been more than happy to let that narrative continue. Makes me wonder how Reaper feels about the situation, though I'm content to never have an answer. We're hoping the power vacuum will keep Reaper and the Russians fighting among themselves and leave us be, which brings us back to quieter times and family dinners.

"Well, we better get going," I cut in. "We have a dinner to get to, but it was a pleasure meeting you, Detective."

Malone's grin is back and better than ever. When we shake hands, I notice he's not wearing a ring and wonder what the story is there. I imagine he's got to have a full-blown fan club of women chasing him.

"It's been a very unexpected pleasure. You ever need anything, you feel free to get in touch."

I toss a glance at my glowering husband and smile. "I wouldn't hold my breath if I were you."

We both laugh. Tommy snarls. We laugh even harder.

"You make it too easy. You know that, right?" I ask Tommy once we're back in the car.

"Make what too easy?"

"Ruffling your feathers."

He grumbles something about *gonna ruffle his internal organs* as he pulls away from the curb. I shake my head because I know he's only kidding. I'm pretty sure. I mean, he wouldn't, right? Nah.

"Dinner at the Donati's was awesome," I tell Mom and Gran the following day. Now that Biba is gone, we're helping them move back home.

"Who was there? He's got a brother and two sisters, right?" Mom asks while zipping up her suitcase.

"Yeah, his brother and wife were there along with his sister. The other sister is married with two kids and lives out of state, so she couldn't make it."

"That's too bad."

"The smaller group worked better for me, and we had so much fun, except for when I made his mom cry." I bite back a smile, knowing I've baited my mom.

"Danika, what did you do?" she demands with wide eyes.

"I gave her a portrait I drew of Tommy. She was super grateful—all good tears."

She smacks her hand over her heart. "Oh, thank God. Not that I was worried, but a good first impression with new family is important."

"Eh," Gran says, joining us. "If they can't get along with our sweet Dani, they can take a long walk off a short pier."

I raise my chin haughtily at my mother. "So there."

"There you two go again, always ganging up on me," she

grumbles playfully. "Tell me about the others. How were the brother and sister?"

"Well, I thought Tommy's brother Renzo was a lot more like him than he realizes, but I'd never tell him that. Renzo's wife, Shae, is due to have a baby in a couple of weeks—not that you could tell. She's some sort of martial arts expert and barely has a bump."

"Martial arts? That's interesting." Gran's eyes light up.

"I didn't get the whole story, but from what I can gather, she was part of the Irish Byrne family." I raise my eyebrows meaningfully.

Mom frowns. "Huh, I didn't realize they cross-mojinated like that. Italians and Irish. Now you. These are strange times."

"Shae was hilarious, and together with Tommy's sister Rina and his mom, we laughed so much my stomach hurt. I can't wait for you guys to meet."

Gran beams. "Me too! It's been just the three of us for way too long. I miss big family gatherings."

"I get the sense there's quite an extended family—lots of little kids, too." I agree with Gran that it sounds fun, though the reality of it might be more overwhelming than I'd like. I'm still not a fan of crowds.

Tommy peers around the bedroom doorway. "You ladies going to wrap it up, or are we all moving in here permanently?"

Gran salutes. "Yes, sir. Ready for duty, sir."

I struggle so hard not to laugh that I snort, sending Mom and Gran into their own fits of laughter. Gran starts crying that she's wet herself, and we all laugh even more. Even Tommy cracks a grin.

A half hour later, we pack up the car with their suitcases and head back to their apartment in Brooklyn. As much as I love spending time with them, I'm excited to wrap up the move because I've got a surprise waiting for Tommy at home. He's either going to love it or hate it, and I have no idea which one it'll be.

41
Danika

Me: You know how you aren't a fan of art?

I am positively giddy as I wait for his response.

Tommy: Yeah?

Me: I think I found something that might change your mind.

I can practically see him cringing while reading my text. The dots come and go twice before his reply shows up.

Tommy: What's that?

Me: Come and see.

I set the phone on the dresser of my studio and stand in the middle of the room. Tommy had the guest bed taken over to Mom and Gran's place yesterday, so the room is now officially my studio. I've laid out a heavy-duty drop cloth to cover all the carpet, though my supplies are all still stacked in a corner of the room. I'll get it sorted one of these days, but at the moment, I've got a much more enjoyable project in mind.

I'm standing in the middle of the room when Tommy rounds the corner. A fire ignites in his eyes the second he sees that I'm not wearing any clothes.

"What do we have here?" He stalks closer.

"I got some new paints I thought you might like to try." I point my toes toward the set of edible finger paints off to the side. "I got some brushes out for you, in case you prefer not to use your fingers." After living with him for the past few weeks, I've noticed he washes his hands the second he gets anything on them. It seems to be more of a texture thing than germ-based, but I haven't had the opportunity to ask him about it. I figure there's no rush.

His hungry gaze surveys my body as he circles me like a king touring his lands. "I see you've been digging in my things, as well."

He's spotted the scrunchie. I used the pink hair tie to secure my red waves in a messy bun on my head. I thought it'd be a fun touch.

"I hate to correct you, but I believe that was mine. And if we're going to talk about hidden items, you're welcome to explain the camera in that flower arrangement on the dresser." My heart thrums with excitement.

Tommy stands behind me close enough that his clothes graze

my sensitive skin. The teasing touch sends a wave of need crashing over me. Goose bumps blossom like spring flowers all down my arms and legs.

"You're being rather belligerent, Mrs. Donati," he says in a rakish purr close to my ear.

"I suppose that's what you get for marrying the woman who broke into your house." I'm fighting a grin, feeling wickedly clever, when his fingers unexpectedly snake around to pinch my nipples. Not too hard—the puckered flesh sings with a perfect mix of pleasure and pain that has me clenching my inner muscles in the need for more.

"Close your eyes," he tells me in a husky whisper.

My lids clamp shut so fast I almost lose my balance. I strain to hear what he's doing, and before long, he's back at my side, telling me to sit. He's placed the old wooden chair I use when I paint behind me. I feel it's cool, hard seat against the back of my legs and lower myself to sit.

"Now, hands behind your back."

Here I thought I was running this show, but I was clearly mistaken. Tommy has taken the reins. Ice-cold steel circles my wrists, and I grin at the memory of our night cuffed together.

"Oh, Dani. You are a vision." His voice circles to my front. "Open your eyes."

Tommy stands in front of me. He's removed his shirt and stands in jeans hung low on his hips. My mouth goes dry as the Sahara.

"Spread your legs, little thief. No hiding yourself from me."

I don't know what it is about opening myself to him like that, but it makes me feel like a queen. Like I possess the key to heaven and am gifting my husband with its glory. I know. It sounds dramatic and maybe a little egomaniacal, but that's what happens when Tommy's worshipping gaze sets me high on his altar.

He picks up the red jar of paint and a brush. Every inch of my skin tingles with the need to be his chosen canvas. He starts at the base of my neck and paints a line down the middle of my chest all the way to the top of my slit. I wonder if he'll stray to my breasts next, but he doesn't. He uses the same red to paint lines from my knees up to the apex of my thighs. Blue paint makes arced lines, tracing my ribs, then lines down my arms.

Every few strokes, he stands back and admires his work.

"You may be onto something. I had no idea art could be so ... titillating."

He drags the brush along the underside of my breast and slowly snakes from one side to the other before circling just outside my nipple, then repeating with the other breast. When he swaps out brushes to use a new color, I'm desperate to know where he'll paint next. My nipples are practically singing for his attention.

Thankfully, their chorus does not go unheard. He coats the new brush with yellow paint, then flicks my nipples in short, rapid strokes with the coarse bristles, igniting tiny fireworks of pleasure shooting from my chest to my core. By the time both peaks are bright yellow, I'm writhing with need.

"Tommy, I can't take much more," I admit breathlessly.

"You can. You just don't want to. My wife has a greedy little pussy, doesn't she?"

I nod, desperate for him to touch me and relieve the relentless ache.

"Greedy but also generous for offering herself as tribute. I suppose my little thief has earned a reward." He sets down the brush and jar of paint, then gets on his knees before me, almost immediately hoisting my body forward to the edge of the chair until my butt is perched on the edge of the seat.

"Mmm ... glistening and so perfectly fuckable." He begins to feast, covering my entire slit with his mouth and sending my eyes rolling into the back of my head.

"*Yes*, Tommy. So good."

When my body starts to normalize the sensation, his fingers find my painted nipples, plucking and twisting until I swear my body will combust.

"That's right, beautiful. Come on my face so you're nice and wet and ready to ride my cock because I'm going to fuck you into next week." He doubles down his efforts and sends me careening over the edge into an abyss of pleasure.

Tommy uncuffs me and scoops me into his arms. He takes me to the guest bathroom, where he starts the water running. I'm still half sex drunk when he begins to wash the paint from my body, which does wonders to wake me up in all sorts of ways. I lather my hands with soap and take my turn rubbing him down. Up and down, and up and down. I make sure his rock-hard cock is very, very clean.

"Hands on the wall," he orders coarsely, ending my playtime.

I give him a shy smile and do as he says. Tommy tugs on my hips to angle my butt out, and when I feel the head of his cock tease at my entrance, I lean even farther.

A resounding smack slices through the air as his palm connects with my right butt cheek. I yip at the unexpected sting and peer over my shoulder at him.

"So greedy. I'll give you my cock when I'm ready." His domineering words, honeyed with the promise of pleasure, send a wave of arousal dripping from my center.

Maybe that's exactly what he intended because a heartbeat later, he's easing himself inside me one thick inch at a time until I'm deliciously stretched to capacity. With my insides already sensitive and swollen from my orgasm, every minuscule movement of his feels incredible.

Tommy's fingers dig into my hips as he increases his pace. I can't help but meet him halfway, pushing back in the hunt for more—more pleasure, more friction, more Tommy.

He doesn't object.

In a matter of minutes, he's roaring his release. He pulls my body back against his as the sensations ebb, but he keeps his knees bent so that he can stay inside me as long as possible.

"This gave me an idea," Tommy says, leisurely stroking my arm.

"About what?"

"Art I might like for the apartment."

"Oh yeah?" I'm intrigued but too foggy with endorphins to connect the dots on my own.

"How would you feel about me commissioning someone to paint you? Not on you, but paint *you*. Naked."

I turn in his arms and smile up at him. "You're willing to let someone stare at my naked body for hours to paint me?"

"Ideally, I'd rather not share you like that, but I can deal with it, so long as it's a straight woman or a gay man."

"If you're game, I think it would be incredible." Not only would it be an honor, but I love that he's exploring ways to enjoy something so important to me.

"*You're* incredible, and I can't imagine a painting I'd love more than one of you."

"Love you, Tommy." The words are barely loud enough to hear over the spray of water. I'm so overcome with adoration and gratitude for this amazing man.

"Love you most, little thief."

EPILOGUE
Tommy

"Sorry to interrupt, but I need to put in our next order for groceries. Danika, do you have any requests?" I stare at my phone as I wait for her instructions. Sachi is over, and the two have been sitting on the couch talking for the last hour. I have no idea how they continue to come up with things to say, but they manage.

"No food requests. I need deodorant, though. It's—"

"I'll just take a photo and send it to them. That's easier."

Sachi's brow wrinkles in confusion. "What do you mean send a picture? Don't you have to find it yourself and add it to the cart?"

"Not when you pay for full service," I tell her.

Danika gives her friend a thin smile. "Tommy employs a service that cleans, shops, and even cooks for us—they're kind of like estate managers. It's pretty amazing."

"Oh man. That sounds like a sweet gig—way better than Instacart. I wonder if they're hiring."

I can't help but chuckle. Sachi's mind is a mystery to me, but she's entertaining. I'll give her that. "No other additions? You haven't ever asked for any female products," I point out somewhat awkwardly. I know women don't always have periods in perfect cycles, but she hasn't had one since we met. I figure she's due.

"I brought some stuff with me, and since all the stress from the past month threw off my cycle, I haven't needed any."

"Stress can do that?" I ask, genuinely curious.

Sachi's brows rise. "Yeah, but so can having unprotected sex." She gives her friend a knowing look.

Danika looks from her friend to me and back. "Surely not."

"How long's it been?" asks Sachi.

Dani pauses to think. "My last period started ... I guess six weeks ago?"

Sachi gapes at Dani. "You're two weeks late and never thought to check?"

I'm watching the conversation unfold like it's on television because it feels surreal. I knew there was a chance she could get pregnant, but not necessarily probable. Only thirty percent of women get pregnant in the first month of trying. I looked it up.

"I had a lot on my mind." Dani shrugs impishly. "You don't really think..."

"I think you should find out for sure. That's what I think," Sachi says in no uncertain terms.

"I'll go," I blurt. Both women look at me wide-eyed. "You two stay here." The words are an afterthought. I'm halfway to the door before I know what I'm doing. My wife might be pregnant, and I need to know for sure. Now.

I'm not gone ten minutes before I sweep back into the apartment with a plastic sack full of tests.

"Did you buy *all* of them?" Sachi asks incredulously.

"Two of each. I wasn't sure which was best." And I don't want to fuck this up. I've never felt so damn on edge in my life.

Dani stands and takes the bag from me. "Well, no time like the present, I guess." She starts to walk away, but I snag her arm and spin her back around for a kiss—deep and enduring, just like my love for her.

"Whatever the result, I love you, and everything is going to be wonderful," I tell her in a rush, and I truly believe it because as long as we have one another, that's all that matters.

Relief softens her features. "Thank you, Tommy."

I watch anxiously as she walks away, leaving Sachi and me to stare blankly at one another.

"Well, I did not see this coming today," she says with a smirk.

"That makes two of us." Thinking about kids theoretically is totally different from knowing one is on the way. The reality of it hits me like a Mack truck. The disorder. The chaos. The poop.

I could be a father soon.

The overwhelming surge of fear eases with the mental image of Danika round with my child. I'm not doing this alone. She'll be by my side, helping me adjust to a new normal. Suddenly, I'm overcome with a ferocious protectiveness that I didn't know was possible. We haven't even confirmed if she's pregnant, yet I can say with confidence that I would sell my soul for that baby.

What is taking her so long?

She hasn't been gone five minutes, but it feels like an eternity. Finally, she returns from the bathroom, wide green eyes locking onto mine. She nods.

"*Holy shit*," Sachi breathes. "You're going to have a baby?"

Dani nods again. Our bodies have united to create a child that is now growing inside her.

Unadulterated joy spreads a wide grin across my face.

"We're gonna have a baby," I say in awe.

An anxiously optimistic smile teases my wife's lips. "I'm pregnant."

I surge forward and sweep her into a spinning hug. She squeals with delight, and Sachi dances around us with her arms waving in the air.

Once we settle into the news, I realize I shouldn't have been so surprised. Even my sperm were desperate to claim Dani. I'm committed down to my DNA, and that's a fact.

"Are you going to tell your mom and gran right away or wait?" Sachi asks.

Dani grins. "I could never keep a secret like that from them. They'd sniff it out of me the second I walk in the room." The girls both giggle as my phone starts to ring. It's my brother.

"Yeah?"

"Shae's water just broke. We're headed to the hospital. Need you to let the others know." Every word is spoken with clipped military efficiency. Renzo has slipped into emergency management mode, which tells me, he's freaking the fuck out.

"You want me to do that and not DiAngelo?"

"Called you first. You got this? The Russians will happily use an excuse like this to catch us off guard."

Well, I'll be damned. He's leaving me in charge. "Yeah, I got you covered. Good luck, man."

"Gotta go."

Both Dani and Sachi stare at me expectantly.

"Everything okay?" Dani asks.

"I think so. Looks like today is baby day all around—Shae's gone into labor."

"That's so exciting, but Renzo sure sounded serious. There's nothing wrong, is there?"

"No, he just wants us to be on high alert for anything the Russians might try while he's unavailable." The oldest of Biba's sons recently seized control, and from what we can tell, the youngest has been exiled from the organization. No one knows what he might do. There's concern he could try to blame us for his loss of status since we were the catalyst to his father's death. They can't prove it was us who pulled the trigger, but they likely suspect. The oldest won't care since he's now in power, but the youngest could be a problem.

"I'm going to go make some calls in my office. Holler if you need me."

They both wave. I dial DiAngelo and head for the back hallway. The phone picks up, but no one answers.

"D, you there?" I ask into the phone.

No answer. Nothing audible, at least. I can hear muffled sounds in the background and am instantly on high alert. I put the phone on speaker, turn the volume all the way up, and raise the phone to my ear. I strain to make out whatever clues I can as to what might be going on when D's voice registers in the background.

"Hands behind your back, and they better stay there. You hear me?"

I stop dead in my tracks. What the fuck is going on? Did the Russians come after him?

I listen even harder, trying to determine whether I need to get my gun or if he's got the situation under control. Silence, then a quiet whimper.

"You can do it—I know you can," DiAngelo says in a low murmur. "Fuck, yeah. Take me in all the way. I want to feel my cock against the back of your throat."

I pull the phone away from me and stare at it as though it's suddenly covered in shit.

What in the ever-loving fuck? That prick really must hate me to answer the phone and make me listen to his bullshit. I'm about to disconnect when I realize that asshole is supposed to be on protection duty for my sister. If he left Terina alone while he's off getting his dick sucked, I'll bury that motherfucker.

"*Jesus*, Ree, your face was made to be fucked." DiAngelo's words snag in my ears.

Ree? He couldn't mean ... surely, not. There's no way.

"Tell me you want it. I want to hear the words."

"Please, D," she begs. "Please come on my tits." Her voice is huskier than normal, but there's no mistaking it. That's my fucking sister.

I'm so stunned that the disgust I should be feeling has no room to surface. How is this happening? Terina and DiAngelo argue anytime they're around one another. He's ten years older than her. Hell, that's his best friend's little sister. Does Renzo know?

No, there's absolutely no fucking way.

But man, do I want a front-row seat when he does find out because, for once, it won't be me looking down the barrel of his anger.

Terina starts to moan, and I lose my shit.

"*Jesus fucking Christ, stop before I vomit!*" I scream into the phone.

Muttered curses follow before someone fumbles with the phone.

"Tommy?" D asks breathlessly.

"Yeah, fuckwad. Don't think that's what Renzo meant when he said take care of my sister."

A single curse is his only answer.

"*Fuck.*"

You got that right.

BONUS EPILOGUE
Danika

One year later

I PEEK AROUND THE CORNER INTO THE PROMENADE hallway, where my mom dances with my baby boy in her arms, and marvel at how amazing life can be.

"He behaving?" Tommy's warm hand comes to rest on my lower back when he joins me, peering over my shoulder. The second we finished with the receiving line, I slipped away to check on my baby. I can hardly stand being away from him.

"Yup, you know how he loves dancing." Anytime I have

trouble getting my little man to stop crying, dancing never fails. He loves to move.

"Can you believe we created him one year ago today?" Tommy asks, his voice tender.

"I can hardly believe we've been married a whole year. Time needs to slow down."

Ares Miro Donati was born three and a half months ago, which means he got to join us today at our first annual anniversary wedding. This time around, we went all-out. I didn't think I'd want or need a big wedding, but I have to admit that today has been perfect. All of our family and friends, an incredible gown, cake, and even a DJ—everything a little girl's dreams are made of.

"Thank you, Tommy. Today has been incredible." I look up at him, love shining in my eyes. "I hope you know, though, that we really don't have to do this every year."

"Maybe not a big wedding, but so long as I'm breathing, I will promise myself to you every single year on this day." My amazing husband manages to melt my heart time and again.

"Okay, baby."

He cups the back of my neck with his strong hand and brings my lips to his. I literally don't think it's possible to be happier than I am at this moment. I grin up at him when he pulls away, then take another look at my mom and infant son.

"Come on," Tommy says. "Let's go check on him. I know you're dying to see him."

My grin gets even bigger. He knows me so well.

"How's my boy?" I ask Mom once I'm close enough.

"Who's that?" Mom coos to Ares, angling him toward me. When he sees me, he beams his adorable toothless baby grin.

I will never, ever tire of seeing my boy smile.

"Hey, chunky monkey." I give him a big smooch on the cheek. "You guys doing okay out here?" I ask Mom, who generously volunteered for babysitting duty. She's kept to the back of the ballroom or the promenade where the music isn't so loud. She and Gran have both been such an enormous help with Ares. They even agreed to let us help them move out of Brooklyn so they could be closer to us.

"He's amazing, as always," she answers, still cooing at him.

"You were beautiful, sweet girl." Gran joins us from the bathroom. I should have known she wouldn't be far.

"Thanks, Gran. And thank you for not shooting anyone."

She grins wickedly. "There's still time!"

"Jesus," Tommy mutters playfully.

We all laugh, but just in case, I lean in and ask, "You didn't bring a gun today, right?"

She gives me a look that says, *come on, why would I do such a thing?* It's riddled with sarcasm.

I smack my hand over my forehead because there are no words.

"Hey, you two," Sachi calls from the ballroom entrance. "The wedding coordinator is looking for you. It's time to do the garter and bouquet toss."

One of the best parts about our do-over wedding was getting to have Sachi as my maid of honor. She picked a flowy deep lavender dress that suited her perfectly, and since I didn't care about wedding colors, that made the choice easy. Tens of thousands of dollars' worth of the most jaw-dropping purple and white floral arrangements covered the church and now adorn the ballroom tables.

I give Ares one more kiss, then take Tommy's hand and head back into the ballroom. The crowd circling the dance floor parts for us, revealing a chair placed in the center of the floor. Getting his cue from the wedding coordinator, the DJ announces the start of the garter toss. The room erupts in cheers.

I will note, in case you're wondering, that Carmen did not plan the wedding. Tommy offered to hire her, but I was as big as a house when we started planning and not remotely up for hanging out with Miss Congeniality. Hard pass.

The atmosphere is electric—music pulsing, and the crowd dancing in place all around us. Tommy helps arrange my gown so I can sit, then drops to a knee across from me. I grin like a maniac.

"Okay, now I'm a little worried," Tommy says with narrowed eyes. "What do you have waiting for me under here?"

"You know me too well."

"Oh, baby. I'm just getting started." He glides his hand up my leg, raising my gown in the process until he reveals the pink satin scrunchie circling my lower thigh. I had to do a little doctoring of the elastic so that it wasn't too tight. I'm so glad I did when I see the masculine pride lighting his eyes.

Tommy leans in, his stare holding me captive while he slides the scrunchie down my leg with his teeth. The crowd cheers. My husband stands, waves the pink satin between his fingers, then pockets the token with a shake of his head, refusing to give it up.

I toss my head back and laugh from deep in my belly. I can't blame him. I'm partial to the memento as well. "My turn!" I stand and take the small tossing bouquet from Sachi. The gaggle of available ladies swarm together across from me while the DJ blasts Beyonce's "All the Single Ladies."

I turn my back to them and perform a slow-motion practice toss, peering playfully over my shoulder in the process. Once the crowd is thoroughly primed, I let the bouquet fly. The crowd goes wild. When I look to see who's landed the prize, I realize I've thrown the darn thing way off to the side, right into the hands of my wide-eyed mother, who has apparently handed off the baby to Gran and come to watch.

Giddy delight has me rolling in laughter. "Looks like you're next, Mama!"

She shakes her head and points at me like I did it on purpose. I raise my hands, pleading my innocence. While I've prodded her in the past about dating, seeing her with Ares has made me realize she's blissfully happy with her life exactly as it is.

I cross the floor and give my mom a smothering hug. "Love you bunches, Mom."

"Love you, too, Dani girl." She pulls back and smiles, emotion pooling in her eyes. "You did good, baby. He's a keeper."

We both glance over to where Tommy is talking with a group of guys—well, Tommy is standing with a group of guys who are talking. He's mostly silent but smiling. That's my Tommy.

"Yeah, he's pretty great. It's a good thing, too, because we're sort of in it for life now." I hold up my ring finger playfully.

Mom smiles and gives a slight one-shoulder shrug. "You ever want out, though, you just let us know," she says offhandedly like some kind of female Al Capone impersonator.

And I thought Tommy's family was gangster.

I toss her a wink. "I'll keep that in mind."

"Good, now let's go find our baby. I left him with Gran."

"Our baby?" I tease.

She stares me down like I just lied about doing my homework. "Yes, *our* baby."

I suppose that's why a surprise pregnancy never really bothered me. When you're surrounded by unconditional love and support, life comes with a built-in safety net. Love breeds courage, and my Ares will have enough love to make him a king.

Thank you so much for reading *Death's Favor*! *The Moretti Men* is a series of interconnected standalone novels—there are two directions you can go from here:

1. *Devil's Thirst* (*The Moretti Men*, book 1)
2. *Forever Lies* (*The Five Families*, book 1)
*Read more about each option below.

Missed the first *Moretti Men* novel?
Devil's Thirst (*The Moretti Men* #1)
Amelie falls hard for a new neighbor with a secret identity ... and a deadly obsession to claim her.

Want to see where it all began?
Forever Lies (*The Five Families* #1)

When Alessia gets stuck in an elevator, she's trapped with Luca, the hottest man she's ever seen. But she can tell something dark hides beneath his charming facade—especially once he decides he's not letting her go...

Stay in touch!!!

Make sure to join my newsletter and be the first to hear about new releases, sales, and other exciting book news! Head to www.jillramsower.com or scan the code below.

ACKNOWLEDGMENTS

Life seriously got in the way of my writing this go-around, which meant there were a few more inconsistencies in my initial draft than normal. I want to give a heartfelt thank you to my beta readers who did an amazing job catching my errors and helping this story shine to its brightest potential.

Trish, Megan, and Jen—you did an amazing job!!! Thank you for all your feedback and careful attention to detail. [And for being flexible when I forget to tell you my schedule and throw a book at you last second. 😬]

To my readers, thank you from the bottom of my heart for your patience. Seven months between releases is a long time to wait, and I am deeply grateful for your continued support. I promise I'm taking measures to lighten my workload and give me more time to write. 🩶

I'm a bit of a control freak at times, and I need to learn to let go. I can't do it all on my own. For that reason alone, it'll be good to write Terina's story next because she's got control issues as well. We can walk that path together, and I know DiAngelo is going to make the journey unforgettable.

ABOUT THE AUTHOR

Jill Ramsower is a life-long Texan—born in Houston, raised in Austin, and currently residing in West Texas. She attended Baylor University and subsequently Baylor Law School to obtain her BA and JD degrees. She spent the next fourteen years practicing law and raising her three children until one fateful day, she strayed from the well-trod path she had been walking and sat down to write a book. An addict with a pen, she set to writing like a woman possessed and discovered that telling stories is her passion in life.

Social Media & Website

Release Day Alerts, Sneak Peak, and Newsletter

To be the first to know about upcoming releases, please join Jill's Newsletter. (No spam or frequent pointless emails.)

Official Website: www.jillramsower.com
Jill's Facebook Page: www.facebook.com/jillramsowerauthor
Reader Group: Jill's Ravenous Readers
Follow Jill on Instagram: @jillramsowerauthor
Follow Jill on TikTok: @JillRamsowerauthor

www.ingramcontent.com/pod-product-compliance
Lightning Source LLC
Chambersburg PA
CBHW020749200825
31398CB00011B/611